The Nordiaho Files:

Voyage to Nordiaho

SUMMER RYLAND

This is a work of fiction. Names, characters, places, and incidents either are the product of the author's imagination or are used fictitiously. Any resemblance to actual persons, living or dead, events, or locales is entirely coincidental.

All rights reserved. No part of this book may be reproduced or used in any manner without written permission of the copyright owner except for the use of quotations in a book review.

Contact the author at: summerryland03@gmail.com

Book and cover design: Jack McNeil
Cover Image: Evelyn Kowalczyk

ISBN: 978-1-7334601-2-5

Table of Contents

	Prologue	4
1	The Beginning, Kind Of	8
2	Destiny? Or Just Crazy?..	24
3	Never Say Never!	38
4	Chip-Os, Gummy Bears and Sour Gummy Frogs?........	53
5	The First True Battle	66
6	The SCLs Ruin Absolutely EVERYTHING!	83
7	I Have A Big, Huge, GIGANTIC Problem!..................	90
8	The Problem Becomes The Solution	109
9	Katie, Trapped!..	168
10	The Seventh, Blood	186
11	Escapes And A Complication.................................	224
12	Some Of The Most Fun Two Days Of My Life!	247
13	The Final Battle, For Now.....................................	316
14	Freedom for N.!	348
	Epilogue: This Spells T-R-O-U-B-L-E!	357
	Acknowledgments	359
	About The Author	361

Prologue

The night was dark. The moon had hidden its face behind thick grey clouds. Dense fog pushed between the trees and through the bushes. It was the perfect night for those whose deeds are best done in secret. Following orders from high in the government, kidnappers, and if need be, assassins, crept towards the large manor house on the bluff, voices low, all lights off, feet encased in special shoes designed to make their walking silent. Their targets: one important diplomatic figure and his two children, who were becoming great threats to Their Order.

Inside the manor house, one of the children, a boy almost fourteen and a half, sat straight up in his bed. He had heard the click of a door opening downstairs. The tiny red light blinking on his bedside table alerted him that it was not his father or his sister who had just entered the house, because he knew that they would have disabled the alarms first. He slipped out of his bed, on feet as quiet as a cat's. He quickly pulled on some clothes, in black, grabbed the bulging backpack that was always at his bedside, and grabbed his X-94 three-barrel shot gun off of the wall above his bed. He slipped out of his room and crept to his sister's room next door.

He entered it. Stepping around the booby trap triggers that he knew the placing of by heart, he made it to her bed. He shook her. "Wake up! We have to go! It's happening!"

She sat up groggily. She was sixteen and a half. "What's happening?"

"They're here." He whispered.

That was enough to wake her up. She slipped out of her bed, turning off the booby traps by flipping a switch on the underside of her bedside table. She dashed to her closet, pulled on some black clothing, grabbed her identical and equally bulging backpack from next to her bed and slung it over one shoulder; then she grabbed her nunchucks off of her bedside table and slipped a few throwing-star-like steel disks into her waistband.

"We have to go wake Father." She whispered.

He peered around the doorjamb. "They're already coming up the stairs; there's no time. Sound the alarm, and hopefully that will wake him up and he'll be able to escape. We have to go now."

The girl slapped the red button on the wall near her bed causing a wailing siren to scream through the house. Then she and her brother slipped through a secret door at the back of her closet which led to a secret staircase that descended to a tunnel that ended at the gardener's shed. They exited the tunnel and took off running. It seemed the fog was lifting, which was bad for the two of them. They were almost at the woods when they were spotted.

Shouts and shots echoed through the forest as they ducked into the trees. They ran and ran and ran. Once they were deep enough into the forest, the girl used her special ability to call some animals to their aid. Two winged horses came galloping up, and the two teenagers vaulted up onto their backs. The horses leapt for the skies, flying higher and higher until they were obscured by the thick clouds, ensuring their safety from the men below.

They flew to some other woods, far away from the

manor house. There the teenagers made themselves a fort to live in, where they would be safe for the time being.

A year and a half later...

The air was still. Not a breath of wind sung through the musical crystals hanging like leaves from the crystal trees. The sun was directly overhead, shining down on two teenagers hiding in the bushes- a boy, almost sixteen, and a girl, barely eighteen. Something big was about to happen, they could both feel it in their bones. Suddenly light shone in the nearby clearing. Blue, gold, silver, and purple, the light was brilliant and dazzling, swirling in an almost cyclone-like formation, until it dissipated, leaving three dazed-looking humans in its place.

An adventure was about to begin.

CHAPTER 1

The Beginning, Kind of

It was just a normal day on campus. The sun shone warmly, streaming through the college's windows, making all of us athletic students yearn for lunchtime. I never would have thought that this day was anything other than another ordinary day at college. But I was wrong. Hi. My name is John, Jonathan Matthew Philipps to be exact, but my friends just call me John. You'll meet my friends, Katie and Sarah, in a minute. I go to college in Texas, and I'm majoring in Ecology and Theater. Sometimes I get the feeling that Katie likes me, but then, I'm not the best at reading things like that. At least I think so. I've always known I was tall, and my Dad says I'm buff and good looking. Not to mention, my Mom used to say, "With that thick blonde hair and those bright blue eyes you'll turn a lot of heads." Katie and Sarah are my "neighbors" at college, they share a room next door to mine, and that's how I met them. Thankfully we got assigned as neighbors; otherwise the whole adventure might never have happened. Anyway, enough about us, since you'll learn more about all of us later on. Let me start my story.

We three got transported off to some magical land, galaxies away, and got drafted into saving their world along with a few other locals. And by locals…I mean aliens.

We got transported about two (earth-time) hours ago. I'll start from the beginning for two reasons. One, the beginning is always the best place to start, and two, I don't know what the end, or possibly even the middle, looks like yet. So, the beginning seems like the best option.

* * * * * *

The bell rang long and loud, resounding across the

entire campus. The bell's purpose was to tell everyone within hearing distance that they now had anywhere from an hour and a half to two hours for lunch and free time, depending on how late classes had run. They usually ran a little late, so it was almost always an hour and a half. Lunch was when the first strange thing happened.

Katie, Sarah, and I headed over to the pizza parlor across the street from the campus. Katie (peppy, smart, and caring) is majoring in Marine Biology and is taking several Native American culture classes, and she also retains languages well, so she's learning several (She's almost fluent in seven by now.). Sarah (gentle, sweet, and shy) is majoring in Archeology and Ancient Civilizations.

The parlor was packed, but we managed to find a table in the middle of the room. It was pretty noisy, but we were so hungry we didn't care. The parlor has white walls with a huge Italian flag on every wall. The tables are round with red and white checkered tablecloths and oil lamps in the middle. The entire room smells like pizza, and the kitchen is open so you can watch them spin the dough. Soft Italian music plays over the speakers, from popular numbers to operas and everything in between. We ordered the College Special. The chefs rotate the pizza for the College Special every day, and college students get it for free since our college sponsors the pizza parlor. Today the College Special was pepperoni and cheese.

Several minutes later our waiter brought our pizza, piping hot and steaming, straight from the brick oven. What struck me as odd was that it wasn't a pepperoni and cheese pizza but an olive and mushroom pizza. What was even weirder was that when I told the waiter we had the wrong pizza he looked at me and said, "You ordered the college special, did you not?"

"Yes." I responded.

"And it is pepperoni and cheese today, is it not?" He said, staring at me like I was, let's say, touched.

"Yes, we did. . .," I trailed off.

"Well then, this is a pepperoni and cheese pizza. Enjoy!" He said it like he was talking to a five-year-old (don't you just hate it when adults do that?), and walked off.

We accepted the change in toppings and prepared to dig in. Now, Katie is obsessed with photography and loves her camera app, so she insisted we let her take some silly photos of us about to bite into our pizza. We agreed, as long as she made it snappy and then let us eat, 'cause we were starving.

Once Katie was satisfied with her photos, we happily ate some pizza.

Now, I know what you're thinking; *'Nothing strange has happened yet! When does the action start?'* Well, don't worry; I'm getting there.

I was the first to take a bite, followed by Katie, then Sarah. The pizza tasted odd, like glitter, air, and cloud vapor. I know that sounds weird but trust me; it did. The room suddenly erupted in a bright blue flash of light. When the light subsided, we looked at each other and realized we were all glowing and sparkling! What was weird was that no one in the entire pizza parlor seemed to notice! (Not to mention, we were *glowing* and *sparkling!*) All of a sudden, I disappeared. I was blinded temporarily, and then I shot into a somewhat cramped, glowing, revolving tunnel.

At first, I thought the tunnel was growing larger, it did become much roomier, but then I realized that I was growing smaller. Now I realized this when Katie shot into the tunnel; I came up to her knees! Which, obviously, scared the living daylights out of her. The same thing happened to Sarah, except now Katie came up to her knees. I only came up to Sarah's ankles.

Eventually, we stopped shrinking once we reached our, um, I guess *appropriate sizes*: Sarah the shortest, myself the tallest, and Katie in the middle of the height spectrum. We were all temporarily blinded again, and then we were shot out of the tunnel into an absolutely gigantic clearing in the middle of a wood. We all stood up slowly, feeling dazed and dizzy. When the dizziness subsided, we took in our surroundings.

We were in a vast, expansive clearing surrounded on all sides by dense woods. The trees were rather tall, yet they were unlike any trees I had ever seen. They had some of the normal characteristics of trees, like branches, leaves, and a trunk, yet some of the leaves were colors other than green, and some of them weren't even *leaves* at all. They were more like crystals. The grass seemed normal. It was green, lush, soft, and regular looking. The sky was blue, to our relief. I don't think we could have coped with a *pink* sky or a *yellow* sky. The sky had small, white, fluffy clouds mixed, strangely, with some pinkish ones. However, the pink ones weren't so obvious; they didn't stand out *too* much, so it wasn't that disconcerting.

We were still sort of taking it all in when we looked more closely at the bushes and shrubs that were low to the ground on our right. We noticed two figures watching us from in the bushes.

"Who's there?" Katie hollered, staring somewhat nervously into the bushes.

"No one," answered a soft female voice with a slight Caribbean-sounding accent.

"Well, if it's 'no one' then *no one* should be answering, correct?" I countered.

A fit of boyish giggles erupted from the bushes, followed by a prompt shushing noise. Cautiously the two figures emerged from the bushes, glancing nervously in all directions as they walked. There was one girl and one boy. The girl had dark green eyes, olive skin, and long, dark black hair that fell almost to her hips and swished as she walked. The boy had brown hair that fell to his shoulders, darker olive skin, and black eyes.

The girl introduced herself as Priti and her brother

as Tecumseh Lordsworth. (Everyone called her brother 'Tim' instead of Tecumseh because it was shorter and easier to pronounce.) We introduced ourselves, and then Priti and Tim led us deeper into the woods. We stopped about one hundred paces in, and then Priti announced that it was safe to talk. We immediately started peppering them with questions faster than the bullets popping out from a rapid-fire machine gun.

"Where are we?" Sarah asked.

"Are you humans?" Katie questioned.

"Why are we here?" I added.

"Why did we shrink?" Sarah inquired.

"What is going on?" Katie exclaimed.

"One at a time." Priti smiled brightly, all former traces of shyness having dissipated from her disposition.

"Where are you? You are on Nordiaho, a planet in a galaxy approximately thirty-four and a half light years from the outermost edge of the Milky Way."

"Are we humans?" Tim cut in. "Well, not technically, but it's not like we're aliens either. The only real difference between us and humans is that when you live in Nordiaho, you get a superpower that fits with your personality. You'll all probably get one sooner or later. Just to assure you, this is what we really look like. It's not like we are hiding what we really look like so as not to freak you out. We can't do that."

"Why are you here?" Priti added. "Frankly, I have no idea. I myself was just wondering that. I know that somehow, we transported you here. Why Tim and I transported you here is beyond me. I assume you're here for some special reason. I'm sure we'll find out just exactly what that is soon enough. Why did you shrink? I know that it's partially because Nordiaho is a lot smaller planet than Earth is, and also because it's easier to transport small items through space than big ones, but other than that I really don't know."

"What is going on?" Tim smirked. "That's not obvious? Well, you've all obviously been transported by us to Nordiaho. Why, none of us know, and I'm sure you can take it from there."

"Tecumseh Sollema Lordsworth! You ought to know better! No humans have come to Nordiaho for hundreds of years and here you are sassing them!" Priti scolded.

"Sorry." Tim blushed slightly, as if embarrassed to have been called out like that.

"One more quick question… are we going to be a team or something? Or are we just here to sightsee a little? 'Cause I'd kind of like to know," I asked.

"Yes, you are," said a soft voice.

"Who's there?" Priti called out anxiously, looking all among the surrounding trees.

"I am sorry to have frightened you. My name is Eleanor," said the voice again. A woman stepped out from behind the trees. She was dressed in a flowing blue dress and had on a dark blue cloak. Everything about her was blue. Her hair, her skin, her eyes, her clothes, everything. She looked like a hologram. But then again, I wasn't quite sure, she could have just been a blue alien. "Your mission briefings are arriving, hang on," she said, and then she vanished.

"What does she mean, 'Our mission briefings'?" Tim asked. "Are we gonna be spies?!"

"Well, you could say that; yes." Eleanor reappeared. "Now, let me brief you for your mission. Nordiaho is in great danger. The Supreme Court Leaders are very, VERY evil. They plan to conquer the entire planet of Nordiaho and rule it. But they are also planning a 'side exploit' that is far more sinister than their plan of ruling Nordiaho. They have created a formula, a powder to be exact, that steals powers. When it is blown over another being, that being's power is stolen and transferred to the person who blew it. The SCLs plan is to blow it over every being in Nordiaho. If they should succeed, they will become the most powerful beings in the galaxy! Plus, with their powers taken away, there would be no one in the universe who could stand up to the SCLs. They would be capable of doing, taking, making, or creating anything. And, it is not only Nordiaho that is in danger. Should they succeed, they would be able to travel in between planets, so that every planet in the universe with life on it would be in peril. The SCLs would be able to rule over all of them, creating the largest and most evil empire ever. Your mission is to prevent this from happening. Steal their formula and all notes pertaining to it. If possible, terminate the SCLs. That last part is not required, but Nordiaho and Earth's safety would fare far better if they were terminated. Your mission will not be an easy one, of that I must warn you. I cannot tell a lie. The leaders have very strong powers, and they will not hesitate to injure or kill you and anyone else who opposes them.

You must be on your guard at all times, never let it drop, and learn to master your powers well. Do you accept?" She asked as she finished her monologue.

We looked at each other and decided that, for the moment, yes, we did.

"Excellent, follow me. I must show you something that has been in my family for generations," she said. She led us through the forest, deeper and deeper in. She floated slightly over the ground as she led us. I don't know if that meant she could fly, if she was a hologram, or what.

We arrived at a ginormous boulder, actually more of a small mountain. Eleanor led us around to the far side of the mountain. She stopped and looked each one of us in the eyes. Her gaze was hypnotic, and it was hard for me to look away. On closer inspection, it looked like she was made of outer space, instead of being a hologram. She was, as I said, all blue, and I could see "stars" scattered all over her that kept moving and shifting into different patterns and shapes. She's gorgeous. I reached out to touch her arm when she wasn't looking, and my hand went right through her, and it tingled when I brought it out of her arm. I was filled with a jolt of energy, and I heard the most amazing music I've ever heard singing through my head for the fleetest of moments, and then it was gone.

"What I am about to show you, you must tell no one about. If you do, I must warn you, there are extreme consequences. Do you swaratak to keep this a secret?" She questioned us sternly.

"Swaratak? What's that supposed to mean?" Sarah asked.

"Oh, ha, right, silly me," Eleanor laughed, "It means, in English, 'swear' or 'promise'. Sorry. I momentarily forgot some of you are Earthlings." She finished.

"Oh, well in that case, "yes, I sweara... oh rats! How do you say it again?" I asked, now laughing myself.

"I do too." Katie said, raising her right hand.

"I do as well." Sarah swore.

"Why did you raise your right hand?" Tim asked, perplexed.

"You know, saluting, scout's honor, etc.," Katie answered. Then, seeing the confused looks on Tim's, Priti's, and Eleanor's faces, she went a little deeper. "It simply shows that I am telling the truth, the whole truth, and nothing but the truth when I promise," she added.

"Oh, well, in that case, we do too!" Priti exclaimed excitedly, as she and Tim held up their right hands.

"Good, good." Eleanor smiled. She reached up and grabbed a small rock jutting out of the mountain. She pulled it out and revealed a keyhole in the rock face. She reached into her cape and pulled out an ivory key.

"This key opens any secret door on Nordiaho. I entrust it in your care Priti. Do not lose it." As she spoke, she put the key in the lock and turned it. She handed Priti the key and then pushed on the rock face below the keyhole. To our great surprise, the place she pushed on swung away and turned into a door. We stepped through the doorway.

Beyond the doorway we entered a large room. The ceiling was extremely high; I'd put it at around forty-five feet. It appeared that an already existing cave had been transformed into a secret fortress. The room was *quite* large. There were ten recessed sleeping bunks on one wall. On another wall was a kitchen and a door, which Eleanor said housed the facilities. There was a large table in the center covered in maps and photos of places and people. There were no windows or skylights, but in the center of the room there was a large hanging thing that looked like a huge wagon wheel covered with light bulbs, so there was plenty of light. The walls, though gray, weren't depressing. Instead, they seemed cheery. I'm sure that was thanks to large paintings of landscapes in brilliant colors that were hanging on them.

"Now, down to business," Eleanor said, "For your mission you will, of course, need gear. There is a golden skull key hidden behind the painting of McMatherhill Sound. Once I leave, please retrieve it. The key will reveal a hidden door. Behind the door, which can only be revealed by that key, you will find everything you should need for your mission. There should also be three brief but informative history books on Nordiaho for you three Earthlings. The minute you put on the outfits behind the door you will be a full-fledged part of the mission. So, if you have changed your mind and wish to decline, do not so much as *touch* the outfits. If you should need help, simply yell, 'Freedom for N,' and I will answer. Eleanor out." With that last statement, Eleanor vanished.

"Wow, um, so much for a normal, simple day huh?"

Katie sputtered.

"Mmmm hmmm. Yeah," I muttered, "Hey, Priti, which painting is of McMatherhill sound?" I asked.

"That one over there, right by the door." She said, pointing.

I ran over and peered behind the painting. I spotted the key and reached back to get it. My fingers closed around it and I pulled it out.

"Y'all still in?" I asked, adrenaline surging through my body, as I could hardly contain my excitement.

Katie, Sarah, Priti and Tim didn't seem as excited as I was, but they all nodded. Unable to control myself anymore, I leapt in the air and did a front tuck, and as I did, a door appeared. We all ran towards it. I inserted the key in the lock, turned it, and opened the door.

CHAPTER 2

Destiny?
Or Just Crazy?

We all gasped. Behind the door was an astonishing array of high-tech gadgets and gear. There was everything from ion blasters (which apparently exist on Nordiaho), to grappling hooks, to infra-red goggles, to, well, that room had almost everything! Amidst lots of "Ooohs" and "Aahs" we put on our gear. Surprisingly, there were five of every gadget, gizmo and garment.

Our outfits consisted first of a close-fitting black, oh gee, I guess a leotard with legs, but I'll just call it a super suit. Then we each had some extremely light weight but efficient bulletproof armor. I thought it was like Kevlar, but Priti said it was made with a very strong metal called 'niogenin' (pronounced: knee-oh-gee-nin) that only existed on Nordiaho. (Hence the light weight.) We each had a utility belt that clipped to the armor and draped over our chest from our right shoulder to our left hip and then went up the back to our right shoulder. It had multiple pockets for 'Athapanouan throwing whorls' (Chinese throwing stars), vials of poison, spools of micro-filament wire, 'sparkler guns' (Tasers), mini recording devices, bugs, micro cameras, and other things. There was a low-slung holster for our right leg that held a rapid-fire pistol and one for our left leg that held an ion blaster. There was a belt with compartments for magazine cartridges, lasers, and a flashlight. There were also two knife sheaths, one for a large heavy-duty knife and the other for a 'Pickby's utility knife' (Which was somewhat like a Swiss Army Knife but even more high-tech.). There were also two multi-tools in their respective sheaths. Then there was head gear like infra-red goggles. We also had other things, like more guns, a rifle, more knives, and other stuff, that we didn't put on because we had no more space to put them.

    We each had a special watch that, besides telling

the time, contained a hidden laser and secret codes that hacked computers. The watch also had tools to be used when opening locks and the like; it also contained a built-in camera, an audio recorder, and more. We also had a 'pianthio holo displayer.' Basically, it could project any image up to 75 feet away so that the image would look real, smell real, and even feel real! Talk about fooling the bad guys! Included was an 'eraser spray' with which, when you sprayed it over a room, all evidence of your being there vanished. Both real and digital footprints, smell or anything else vanished, and even something you had lost would be teleported back to you! We also had boot rockets, expandable jet packs and speed boats, etc., etc. You get the picture.

The suits were designed in a way to enhance our physical capabilities as well. For example, we could run faster, jump higher and farther, swim faster, withstand more pressure under water, fall from greater heights, etc. These suits are so cool!

Once we were all suited up Katie insisted, we take some group shots and *a ton* of selfies. We (Sarah and I) sighed, but agreed. She whipped out her phone to take the photos.

"What in Gotteronimies name is that?!" Priti asked.

"This? It's a cell phone. Cell stands for cellular. Don't you have them here?" Sarah explained, somewhat amused and somewhat perplexed.

"No! No, we don't. That is, the public doesn't. The SCLs might, but I'm not sure," Tim responded.

"Hmm," Katie said.

After all of that we set out. I gotta admit, it felt pretty neat to walk out, all five of us in a row, dressed and equipped from head to toe in coolness.

"Wait a minute guys!" Sarah exclaimed, stopping us only seven feet from the door. "If we're going to be a team, then we need a name."

"Good point, Sarah! Anyone got any ideas?" Katie mused.

"Well, there are five of us, so, um, let's think of adjectives that are both bold and start with 'F'," Tim suggested.

"Oooh, good thinking bro. Alliteration and all that jazz. I like it!" Priti smiled. "I've got some words for it too. Ya ready? Fine, Fancy, Fiery, Fantastic, Fearsome, Fierce, Fantabulous…," Priti started spouting off adjectives.

"No. No. I dunno. Maybe. Maybe. Eh…," I said about the adjectives she proposed.

"Hey! What about fearless?" Katie put on the 'table'.

"Yeah! That's a good one," I said.

"Sure."

"Yeah."

"Good thinking!" everyone else replied.

And so, with that, the Fearless Five was born.

* * * * * *

Which meant that no less than two hours later we were all running for our lives. I mean, heck! I'd thought, well, I'd *known* that I was pretty fast from being in the Olympics and all, but running on adrenaline, and, okay, fear, I am like flippin' crazy *fast*. If only I could do that in races. I'd win every time!

I was also screaming. Not like, shrieking, high-pitched, girly screaming, (Thank goodness!) more of a suppressed, half controlled 'aaaaaaaaaahhhhhh'. Tim, on the other hand, was screaming in a very high-pitched falsetto, like a girl. Which was, honestly, quite funny if you ask me. Priti was screaming softly; Katie was screaming as well, although she sounded like she was letting off war-whoops; and Sarah was screaming like I was.

The men behind us were screaming as well, although they were screaming more like war whoops than terrified screams. Each war whoop was followed by a maniacal chuckle.

Finally, we made it to our 'parked' Alpha Class-X Stalker Shuttle (a "present" from Eleanor) in a clearing near the city. We all jumped in and lifted off just as the so-called 'Truth Troopers' reached the edge of the clearing.

Our shuttle is a rare variety. Its name includes the word 'Stalker' because it has a capability that hardly any other shuttles on Nordiaho do. It has Stealth Mode, which is the unique ability to change the conformation of its outer body into a shape, color, and, uh, density, I guess, that make it invisible to almost all detecting radars. The shuttle is also coated with a special paint capable of absorbing any radar beams that hit it, instead of bouncing back the radar beams like most ships do and alerting the SCLs to our presence.

The shuttle has a body formation that is kind of a cross between a helicopter and an airplane. It has no wings, rudders, or propellers, however. Instead, it is propelled by a high powered, first class, generation Y-1000 hyperthrust engine. Inside is open floor space in the middle, with two seats up front for the pilot and the co-pilot, and a row of seats along one wall. The engine is in the back and looks like a square made of four cylinders that are connected to each other.

It clocks out at a top regular speed of four hundred gilometras (miles) an hour. Not to mention the fact that it can go up to point 3 past light speed in emergencies. Now, back to the story.

"Phew, that was close!" Priti remarked as she put the shuttle into stealth mode.

"Yeah, it was! How are you feeling, *Miss* Tim?" I joshed teasingly.

"Hey! It's not my fault I was cursed with a girly scream," Tim protested.

"Sure, right, yeah," Priti smirked, and Katie and Sarah giggled.

"So, did we get *anything* at all during that mishap?" I asked. "I hope we got *something*, because we nearly died, so hopefully we got something to make that worth it."

"Well," Katie mused, dumping the contents of her satchel onto the shuttle's floor. "We got four test tubes of the serum, three whole notebooks full of notes on the serum, and two maps on secret entrances, exits, rooms, and passages of the SCLs lair. That's it," She sighed sadly.

"The maps are great; those'll help us navigate the SCLs' lair. It's good that we got the notes and the serum, but I'll bet they have more; a *lot* more," Priti said somewhat dejectedly.

We all sighed.

"On another note, does anyone know what their powers are yet?" Tim asked.

"No," I muttered.

"Nope," Sarah frowned.

"Maybe...," Katie whispered.

"Yes," Tim said. "Of course."

"Yep," Priti said. "You think you know what your power is Katie?" she asked excitedly.

"Well, I think so. I mean, I'm not sure, but I think so," Katie murmured shyly.

"What is it? What is it?!" Sarah asked giddily.

"I think I can move things with my mind."

"Really?! Try it!" I said.

"Here goes," Katie said, turning to face the shuttle's windshield. Only then did we notice the missile streaking towards the shuttle.

Katie closed her eyes and raised her hands. With astonishing speed, she moved her hands in varying directions. All of a sudden the missile changed its course, streaked towards the SCLs' lair, and exploded right above it.

"WOO-HOO!" We all cheered, causing Katie to curtsy and then blush, smiling wider than I had ever seen her.

We continued flying over the lair, doing a little recon, not to mention resting up after that first mission. Tim and Priti then decided to take us on a small tour via air of Nordiaho's capital city, Quilaxium (pronounced: quill-axe-ee-um). We heartily agreed and so we were off.

Several tour stops later we were flying over a small park in the middle of the city, relaxing and enjoying the view, when, suddenly, the shuttle was shot down!

Spiraling out of control, the shuttle fell down out of the sky. We jumped into the middle of the shuttle, held on tight to each other and…

Sorry to interrupt, but remember how I said that we were in the middle of this adventure, but I'd start from the beginning? Well, this is where we actually are. This is what's happening now. So, since I can't narrate anymore quite yet, I'll take a minute to describe all of us. I'll start with Priti.

Priti is tall and slender. I'd put her at 6', with large, almond shaped dark green eyes. She has beautiful olive skin and long, very wavy, thick black hair that falls almost to her hips. Her voice is soft and she enunciates her words perfectly, with the slightest Caribbean-sounding accent. She has a very sweet personality: well-rounded, smart, kind, and generous. She has an air of grace around her and is very optimistic. She loves wearing dresses, and she wears her hair loose, except in desperate times when she puts it up in a ponytail. (You know the situation is dire when you see Priti with a ponytail.)

Tim is tall and muscular. I'd put him at 6' 2", with black eyes. He has brown hair to his shoulders and the same olive skin tone as his sister, only darker. His voice is loud and deep, and he loves using slang and speaking with a drawl, much to his sister's exasperation. He is a goof ball when you get to know him. At first he seems a little rough around the edges, tough and such, but, once you spend time around him and become his friend, he's really nice. He's an excellent sharpshooter and can handle any weapon from a Samurai-type sword to a blaster or a bow and arrow with almost impossible ease. He, like his sister, is very athletic; he rides horses, hikes, swims, wrestles (unlike his sister), and shoots.

Katie is also tall and slender. She's roughly the same height as Priti, maybe 1/2" taller, with deep, dark brown eyes and black eyelashes. She has thick, wavy, shiny, crow black hair to the middle of her back, which she constantly wears loose or in a fishtail braid. She has dark, reddish-brown skin, and her voice sounds like a river, rushing smoothly over polished rocks. Not to mention she has a gorgeous accent. She is a Shoshone Native American, and she loves her heritage. She makes her own dresses for traditional ceremonies and has lots of traditional tools and weapons.

Sarah is shorter than both Katie and I are. She's maybe around 5' 8". She is also slender, although not as slender as Katie and Priti. She has somewhat small, golden brown eyes, brown eyelashes, and chocolate brown hair that falls a little past her shoulders in thick ringlets. Her skin is pale, and her voice sounds like she is always singing. She excels at gymnastics and has the muscles to prove it. She is an incredibly capable athlete and loves sports. She also loves reading.

As for me, I am quite tall, 6' 4" and 3/4" to be exact, and, uh, buff. As I mentioned earlier, I have thick blond hair and dark blue eyes. My skin is rather tanned, and my voice is "strong and deep", to quote my Dad. My ancestors were hard-working pioneers who persevered out West when it was still "wild", and I am proud of it. Like Sarah, I excel at gymnastics, as well as at most sports. I am rather strong and very fast. I collect arrowheads and coins as well. I also *love* to ride horses. There, that's all of us. Now, back to the present. Well, actually, not really. I took a few minutes doing the character stuff and all, so the story I tell will be a few minutes behind what is actually happening. Oh well, past tense is easier.

The shuttle continued to spiral downwards. We clutched each other nervously, making a tight circle in the middle of the shuttle's floor. I looked around at the ring of faces and wondered if my facial expression matched theirs: scared, uncertain and worried.

Suddenly, there was a 'whump' as we crash-landed. We waited in breathless anxiety. Two minutes passed, then five, eight, and then, on the nose of ten minutes, the doors of the shuttle were flung open. Whoops and yells came from outside the doors. Priti ventured cautiously towards the doorway. (We had slid to the back of the shuttle during the crash so we couldn't see out.) Peeking out, she gasped, and then ran back to our circle.

"It's them!" she exclaimed. "What should we do?!"

"First, let's stay calm. We'll think better calm, and they probably want us to freak out. So, let's not give them the satisfaction of our being scared. Second, let's try to use our powers. Priti, Tim, what are yours?" I said, faking confidence.

"I can talk to animals and I can summon them from anywhere for them to help me," Priti answered, smiling despite the situation.

"I can command water and teleport *ANYTHING*. Well, basically anything anyways," Tim said. "Do you and Sarah have any idea what yours are yet?" he added. Sarah and I looked at each other and sighed, shaking our heads. We still had no idea what our powers were. It was really disappointing.

We felt the shuttle start moving forwards, as if it were being towed, which it probably was. We glanced at each other nervously. We traveled in silence for at least fifteen minutes until the shuttle jolted to a stop.

We all looked at each other again.

"Should we call Eleanor?" I whispered.

Everyone nodded, brightening a little.

"Here goes. Freedom for N.!" I yelled.

In the thirty seconds following my shout, three things happened. One, Eleanor said, "Yes?". Two, several men peeked into the shuttle. And, three, one of them fired some sort of gun… at me.

"*JOHN!*" Katie screamed.

There was nothing I could do. The bullet was almost home. It hit, and I passed out.

CHAPTER 3

Never Say Never!

I don't really remember anything much after that. I remember Katie screaming, me falling, Katie kicking some serious "Truth Trooper" butt, Priti checking my vitals, troopers passing out, then Katie getting knocked out beside me. The shuttle doors slamming shut, then opening. The feeling of being dragged out, plopped on a cold, hard floor, something sliding, metal clanging on metal, and a key turning in a large lock. Then I slipped back into unconsciousness. Honestly, I'm surprised I remembered this much, since I was unconscious for most of it.

I woke up later, groggily opening one eye. Priti, Tim and Sarah were huddling on a metal slab of a bench/

bed. Katie was lying beside me, out cold. I rolled over to get a better look at her. She was smiling slightly, her hands still in fists, with a bruise over her left eye. I grinned. Suddenly, her eyes flickered open and she looked up.

Seeing me, she yelled, "Who are you?! I'll beat you to a pulp!"

"Katie, it's me, John." I said calmly.

"John! You're alive!" Katie said, leaping up to hug me.

"Uh, guys, sorry to interrupt, but we are in a bit of a situation here," Tim said.

Then a man came up to the bars. "Ah, good, you're all up. Now, as you know, we don't hold with anyone opposing us," the man said, smiling evilly. "So, tomorrow, you will all be publicly executed at noon. Oh, and you will *never* escape from here!" he said, walking away.

I frowned. "Never say never." I yelled after him, disgusted. "C'mon y'all; there has to be some way to get out!" I said determinedly.

Everyone hopped up and we started examining the room, inch by inch.

* * * * * *

"ARGH! I don't believe this!" I yelled, in utter frustration. "The walls are a foot thick, and the bars, made of impenetrable Nordiahoan metal casperonium, are set four feet up and four feet down into the cement and are only two inches apart! How do we get out of here?" I added rhetorically.

The cell we were in was the most secure place I had ever seen! The floor was rough-hewn but tightly fitted stone, the walls were made of cement, and the only window was a small slit up by the very roof! It all looked like it hadn't been cleaned in ages. Dingy, dirty, filthy, smelly, the whole thing gave one the creeps. In exasperation I stepped back and raised my arm to punch the cement wall.

"No! John! Don't! That'll really hurt!" Sarah said nervously.

Her warning was too late however, for my fist had already slammed into the wall.

"John! Are you okay?" Priti asked me anxiously.

"Surprisingly, I'm fine," I said. I turned towards where I'd punched, hoping that, maybe, just maybe, the fact that it hadn't hurt meant something. Nothing had happened though, so I guess it didn't mean anything. I sighed.

Katie smiled sadly, then slid over to make room for me on the bench. She patted the spot next to her and I walked over and sat down. Sighing, I laid my head against the wall.

"He was right; we'll never get out of here," I said, sinking deeper and deeper into gloom.

"Yes, we will!" Katie said, leaping up and dragging me with her. "You said so yourself, remember? Now, never say never. We have powers! We haven't tried those yet. C'mon!" she said, swinging me in a circle, laughing. Then, strolling defiantly towards the bars, she raised her hands. "I… I can't… It's not working! It's too strong." she said, exhaustedly.

"Let me try," Priti said, stepping forward. "Animals, animals, from the North to the South, the East to the West. Come, Unite, Help me in this quest!" Priti chanted.

The room was suddenly filled with chirps and squeaks, growls and roars, echoing off the walls and bouncing off the floor. Katie, Sarah and I looked at each other amazed. We'd never experienced something like this before, ever! To us "earthlings" this was a new, crazy thing! In the midst of our amazement, I couldn't help but think, "As long as they can't talk; as long as they can't talk.…"

Priti frowned, concentrating. "It's hard to hear through these walls but…," she paused, straining. "They say they would love to help, but…they can't get in without revealing things that are not to be revealed at this time." Priti plopped down on the floor, rather annoyed.

"Mine won't work in this situation, no water." Tim frowned.

"I wish I had powers." I said. Walking forwards, I shook the bars. Instead of just rattling, the entire wall of bars, concrete and all, sheared off the room. I looked around, astonished. The entire wall was in my hands, and it was as exerting as if I were holding a feather!

"*WHOA!*" Katie exclaimed as I leaned the wall up against a (still-standing) wall. Katie leapt up, ran over, and felt one of my arms. "Dude! You are like flippin' crazy, fantastically strong!" she added, amazed.

"That is so cool!" Priti interrupted. "Glad you found

your power, but we have to go before they realize what happened!"

"That is an excellent point," I admitted.

We bolted out, streaking around the corner, only to find a locked door, two feet thick, solid niogenin. (Niogenin=Nordiaho's strongest metal, even stronger than casperonium!)

"Allow me," I said confidently, rolling up my sleeves. I reared back and *punched*. My fist arced through the air, heading towards what I hoped was the door's sweet spot.

IMPACT! The door popped off the hinges and fell to the floor. The impact shattered the windows and shook the walls and floor.

"Woohoo, John!" Sarah quietly cheered.

"Thank you," I said, bowing.

We ran out the door into the bright sunshine. We were a mere twenty paces from the building when we heard sirens echoing across the compound.

"Draaaaaaat!" I muttered.

"Run faster!" Katie yelled.

I picked up my speed. I felt this odd sensation inside my body: as if my heart was racing double, triple, even quadruple time; as if my cells were regenerating faster than the speed of light. I felt like I was so full of energy all of a sudden that I was going to burst from the sheerness of the power flowing through my veins. And then, all of a sudden, I shot off, moving faster, faster, ever faster, streaking across and off the compound faster than a streak of greased lightning. I was so exhilarated by the sheer speed at which I was traveling, that I didn't really notice what was going on until I broke the sound barrier. The shock wave from doing so bowled me over. I sat up and shook my head to clear it. I looked around, shocked. I remembered from one of my college classes that in order to break the sound barrier you had to reach speeds of over 770 *miles per hour*, which meant I had just *run* at a speed higher than that! I also had no idea where I was, so I stood up and ran back the way from where I had come.

I reappeared in front of the others, panting slightly, but barely registering my slight fatigue through my sheer joy.

"Whoa! Dude! What the heck?" Tim asked.

"No way!" Priti crowed. "Double power! Sweeeet!"

I grinned. Then I had an idea. I picked up a wooden platform and a length of rope that coincidentally happened to be lying on the ground right next to us in one of the compound's many outlying refuse heaps. I poked a hole on either edge of the top of the wood with my finger, then I threaded the rope through and tied each end, creating a sled. "Hop on." I said. "Quick! And hold on tight!"

Everyone obediently jumped on and positioned themselves, gripping onto the rope and each other. I grabbed the rope in one hand and took a deep breath. Then I ran, heading for the hideout in the meadow.
In less than ten minutes we had covered the forty miles to the meadow (I ran a lot more slowly that time, since I had passengers and didn't know if they could handle going faster than the speed of sound.), and I breezed into the hideout. Smiling happily, we collapsed giddily, laughing, on the stone floor.

"Guys... surprise, surprise! Guess what I got?" Katie said, smirking in triumph.

"What?" we all asked in unison.

"I got...drumroll please...all the serum in the compound!" Katie exclaimed, all in one breath.

"Wow!" "How did you do that?" "That's awesome!" "You're awesome!" We all exclaimed at the same time, the last one from me. I didn't mention it earlier, but I kind of like Katie, too. As long as she can't read minds, we'll be good! Ha-ha.

"I kind of just called it with my mind and it followed me all the way here! I didn't know I could do that! This power is amazing! I wonder what else I can do…," Katie trailed off excitedly.

"Good job agents!" Eleanor appeared out of nowhere right in front of us; we jumped. "You performed quite outstandingly under the circumstances. Headquarters and I are all very proud of you! For your two excursions you have each earned two gold stars. Each gold star magnifies your powers a little bit."

"Thanks!" we all chorused as ten shimmering golden stars floated across the room and two attached themselves to the front right breast-pockets of each of our super suits.

"Hey guys," Tim said with a mischievous smirk. "Shall we test out our powers now that they're even more…um… powerful?"

Sarah sighed dejectedly. "I still don't have mine,

but I'll come watch."

"Don't worry! You'll get them soon. I'm sure of it!" Priti reassured kindly.

"As a matter of fact," Katie mused, staring off into space with her eyes half closed, "You'll get them in our next time of peril. I'm sure of it." She grinned as she opened her eyes.

"So, you can predict things, move things with your mind, and summon things with your mind! What else can you do? Read minds? Or, ooh! Control people's minds? Or can you…"

"EH-HEM!" Tim interrupted Priti impatiently. "Test powers, *remember*?"

"Right, right. Um, we should probably go outside," I said, shooting a slightly wary glance at my arms and legs.

Priti grabbed a speedometer, a stopwatch, some orange cones, and some targets.

"We have to be by a body of water, otherwise mine won't work," Tim said.

"Ok, anything else?" Priti asked. We all looked at each other and shook our heads.

"Nope," I said.

"Let's go then!" Tim said, flinging open the door dramatically and gesturing towards the clearing.

"There's a river on the East side of the clearing. Let's GOOOOOOOOOOO!" He yelled, his voice getting quieter and quieter as he ran down the clearing towards the river.

We laughed. "We're coming; we're coming!" Priti shouted after him, still laughing.

* * * * * *

Outside in the clearing we lined up, ready to try out our powers, strengths, and abilities.

Priti stepped up first and called out her chant. "Animals, animals, from the North to the South, the East to the West, Unite! Come and help me in this quest!" she said, her voice ringing out across the meadow, clear and crisp as a bell.

We waited. Soon, growls, howls, chirps, and squeaks resounded from the dense forest surrounding the edges of the meadow. Priti walked from the edge where we were lined up on and ran into the middle of the clearing. She raised her arms and let out a shrill whistle. Suddenly a beautiful, fiery red pegasus with a long mane and tail walked out of the trees. Following it was an Albino Tiger, a Snow Leopard, a Cheetah, other great cats, horses, unicorns, centaurs, minotaurs, griffins, many other mythical and strange (strange as in not from Earth that is) creatures, et-cetera, et-cetera. Beautiful, colorful birds burst from the treetops and landed on Priti's arms, shoulders, and the ground all around her. From another side of the woods came bears, wolves, foxes, other wild dogs and canines, more horses, deer, a few alicorns, et-cetera; you get the idea.

Priti sat down, leaning her head against a sleek and strong black panther's shoulder, running her hands through an alicorn's thick, luxurious mane, talking animatedly with a bird, fondly stroking a young fawn and other animals. Then the pegasus, who had been lying down, stood, pawed the ground, and began talking with Priti. Priti stared at her for a minute, mouth agape in a rather un-Priti-like fashion, before replying. The pegasus nodded, turned towards the rest of us, and dipped her head slightly. I caught a glimpse of her eyes, a glimpse I'll never forget, that's for sure. There was such a fire, and a light, and such perfection and goodness in her eyes that I couldn't quite make eye contact. I had to look away.

Priti walked over to us, moving as if she were in a trance.

"Priti! Are you all right? What did she say?" Tim asked, anxiously. "Something good I hope," he added as an afterthought, catching her arm and holding on to her, steadying her, a look of deep concern on his face.

"I'm fine," Priti said, snapping upright and standing ramrod straight. "She said that now that I have the stars, well, you know how the animals excel at things that humans don't? Things like running, climbing, swimming, smelling, jumping, et-cetera? Well, whenever an animal chooses, all they have to do is say so, and I will 'inherit' the 'powers' they have! As in, for example, a dolphin's amazing swimming and echolocation, as well as their excellent hearing underwater. Well, I have the 'powers' for 24 hours, and I can activate and deactivate them whenever and basically wherever! Isn't that neat? Watch!" At that, Priti turned to one of the tigers. The tiger said something and "smiled" at her. Priti beamed. "Activate!" she yelled excitedly.

A flash of blinding light enveloped Priti for a moment, and then it dissipated slowly as Priti stepped out of its center. She held up her hands, flexed them quickly, and sharp, shiny claws flicked out. She flicked them again and the claws flicked back in. She grinned wider than a kid in the world's largest candy store. Then she opened her mouth and roared. The roar shook the ground and toppled the rest of us, and even some of the animals, flat to the still trembling ground.

"Whoa! Super-sonic roar. Sweet! I had no idea you guys had powers too!" Priti exclaimed, laughing, enjoying herself immensely.

The pegasus turned to her and said something; she frowned slightly.

"What now? What's wrong?" Tim asked, shocked to see his sister's mood change so rapidly.

"She said that in order to uphold Nordiaho's laws of power equality — well, the ones that refer to us, they don't count for you humans and several other groups of people — I can only use the animal's power if they or another one of the same animals is within a three hundred foot circle of me." She sighed slightly. "Oh well, it's still cool!" She smiled, returning to her normal, peppy, optimistic self once again.

"Is it my turn?" Katie asked excitedly, hopping from foot to foot.

"Sure!" Priti replied. "Thank you, animals, for your aid; now fly, run, gallop, and saunter back to your homes. I await the next time we shall meet!" Priti said, as she and the pegasus exchanged formal bows.

Katie skipped up to the center of the clearing. "Hey guys, I'm going to look at my Nordiaho History book while y'all go," Sarah said, sitting under a tree.

I walked over and sat down next to her. She looked up at me, an expression of gratitude on her face. I reached across and squeezed her hand.

She poked her finger against my arm and smiled up at me. "Man, your power made you both taller and, um, broader." We laughed. "Do you want to read our History Books while we wait, or rather, while you wait?" she asked hopefully.

"Sure." I said, smiling down at the tiny figure next to me. (Well, tiny compared to me anyways. Sarah's like 5' 8"; I'm 6' 4".) I pulled mine out of my pocket and cracked the cover.

CHAPTER 4

Chip-o's, Gummy Bears, and Sour Gummy Frogs?

The first chapter was called "The First Human Discovers Nordiaho." Intrigued, Sarah and I looked at each other and then went back to reading. Here's a paragraph from the chapter:

"A young man named James Loralough purchased Chip-o's, Gummy Bears, and Sour Gummy Frogs from a vending machine. He tried them all at once and was transported to Nordiaho, becoming the first human ever, not only to discover a portal to Nordiaho, but also to learn about Nordiaho. Nordiahoan scientists tested the theory and found out that it actually worked! If you are trying to get back to Nordiaho after accidentally getting beamed back to Earth, simply use the formula."

"Whoa! That's both nuts and super, super cool all at the same time!" Sarah said, aghast.

"What is?" Tim hollered.

"It's hard to explain. You guys have to read your History Books; they're insane!" Sarah yelled back.

Suddenly, the trees around the clearing shook and the otherwise silent air was filled with a low "whup-whup-whup" sound.

"RUN!" Sarah yelled, jumping up from underneath the tree.

"Hold on to me!" I said, trying to pinpoint and identify the source of the noise.

She grabbed my arm and we took off. I dashed towards the center of the clearing and then streaked past the others in an attempt to get Sarah out of the clearing, fearing her lack of powers would make her the most vulnerable and in danger.

"John! STOP!" Katie yelled.

I stopped and looked around. That was when I saw the men standing around the edges of the clearing, guns drawn. In the fleet seconds in which I paused, the "whup-ing" noise got louder, and we looked upwards as four, uh, planes, I guess, rose up above the trees. They were sleek and gleaming silver, and they somewhat resembled velociraptors, but larger, with slightly turned down wings.

"Drat!" I muttered.

We backed into a protective circle in the center of the clearing, Sarah on the inside, and the rest of us around her. Katie, with her hands raised, stood poised to leap into battle. Priti, I noticed, had begun silently muttering her chant underneath her breath. Tim's eyes had begun to glow a blueish color and he stood at the ready, waiting eagerly to use his newly enhanced powers. As for me, I stood, muscles (which have quite grown since I received my stars) tensed, straining the sleeves and seams of my super suit, ready to rush the others to safety.

Bullets rang out over our heads. We instinctively hit the deck…er… forest floor. They countered by shooting low to the ground, so *we* countered *them* by jumping up into the air. When we came back down to the ground, Sarah was no longer in our tightly packed cluster. We looked around nervously, unsure as to what just happened. A shrill whistle from above caused us to look up. Sarah was hanging by one hand from a glowing magenta bar suspended in mid-air. She then swung herself up so that she was standing on the bar. Stretching, her hand seemed to touch something that wasn't there, and another bar, cobalt blue this time, appeared.

"WHOA!" Priti said, hopping up and down. She and Tim looked at each other. "That power has only been seen in Nordiahoans, or on Nordiaho, *four times!*" Priti exclaimed excitedly. "It usually also includes invisibility; see if you can turn invisible!" she followed up.

"Um… okay," Sarah said, somewhat shyly. She took a deep breath… and disappeared. We watched as more and more bars appeared, going higher and higher into the sky. Then the bars changed direction and formed a pathway above the treetops.

The men around the edge of the clearing looked at each other. "Rare powers first!", one of them shouted, and they took off running towards the bars. Priti winked at us, and as the men ran for the bars, we slipped quietly to the now unguarded edge of the clearing. Laughing, we watched the men jumping at the bars, as their hands passed through them as if the bars weren't even there.

We ran silently through the forest, undisturbed.

* * * * * *

We met back up with Sarah by a big waterfall in the Western part of the forest. Perched on the ledge of the ridiculously high cliff from which the water fell, we watched the water fall in cascading curtains of shimmering droplets.

Sarah climbed down a ladder of bars and stood next to us, exhilarated. "Katie you were right! I did get my powers at the next time of peril! Now we all have powers!" she exclaimed joyously, breathlessly.

We all grinned. I looked around at everyone. Sarah and Katie were jumping around, hugging each other and talking animatedly. Priti and Tim were sitting together on the edge of the cliff, her head on his shoulder, talking softly to each other. I smiled, knowing that for now we were safe, and we were all together. Even though the three of us "Earthlings" had only known Priti and Tim for a day, we already were fast friends. I guess that goes to show you what getting shot at can do to you! I sat down, swinging my legs over the abyss, watching the sun dip below the horizon, changing the color of the sky from blue to pink to gold.

Sarah and Katie plopped down next to me, grinning as if they might burst.

"Can you believe it? We got out of that battle completely unscathed! That was AMAZING!" Sarah exclaimed, talking more energetically than I've ever heard her, the shyest of the bunch, talk in my life.

"That was super neat! And, even better, you finally got your power, and it's a really cool one too!" Katie said, hugging Sarah.

We sighed contentedly and reclined for what felt like hours in the shade cast by three huge pines behind the waterfall. Finally, Tim broke the calm silence with a gigantic yawn. "Guys, I think we should…yawn… head in…yawn…for the…yawn…night," he finally managed to get out through his yawns.

"Good idea," Katie said, fighting back yawns of her own.

"What say we come back here for a picnic or something tomorrow?" I suggested. "It's so peaceful and calm."

"Ditto," Priti said, hoisting herself to her feet.

We headed back to the hideout, then bunked down for the night.

* * * * * *

The next day, we headed to the waterfall for a dinner picnic. Yeah, yeah, I know — way to shirk our duty to save the world, yada-yada-yada — but we are allowed to have a picnic, ya know. We had just finished and were packing up the basket when we heard a low rumbling noise in the distance.

"On no; not again!" I groaned, stashing the basket in the branches of a tall oak and furtively glancing around the surrounding forest.

"Guys, wait! We're by water!" Tim said. "I still haven't been able to test my power. Before I could only shoot thin jets of water. I wonder what I can do now, with the stars!"

Priti groaned, "Fine, we can stay, but only if we leave if we have to."

"*Alllll riiiiight!*" Tim yelled, throwing his fist into

the air in triumph.

We backed into a circle, and the "Bad Guys" (Who, by the way, call themselves "Truth Troopers", ha-ha-ha, right, 'cause they're all about the *truth*!) had just emerged from the trees, when out of the forest walked a tall man in a long cloak. Priti gasped and then took a defiant step forwards as the man pulled off the cloak's hood and flashed us a sinister smile.

"Good day children...," he said tauntingly, in a voice practically dripping with sarcasm and evil intentions. "I should hope you are enjoying Nordiaho."

"*Lord Johansson,*" Priti said coldly, pausing and spitting on the ground. "You have no business here. I am sure you are well aware that you are trespassing on my father's property?"

Katie, Sarah, and I all looked at each other surprised, as this was a new and intriguing update.

"Ah, young one, I assure you *we* are not trespassing. When your father was put in jail, with no one to claim the land, we repossessed this fine, expansive piece of land until he is released; *if* he is, that is." Lord Johansson smirked.

"Two things," Tim said, jumping into the

conversation. "One: you are not allowed to jail someone without a fair trial, and you did not give our father a trial. You simply threw him, a royal personage no less, into jail with NO trial! And Two: my sister and I own the rightful title to this land, <u>*not you!*</u>" he spat out.

"Well, hmmmm, I wonder what to do about that…," Lord Johansson trailed off, turning around.

Suddenly he whipped around. His hands glowed blue, and Tim went flying up over the edge of the waterfall's cliff.

"*TIM!*" Priti screamed. "You monster!" she then screamed at Lord Johansson.

Lord Johansson just laughed, but then a whooshing noise sounded from below. Lord Johansson stepped up to the edge of the cliff and suddenly was shot backwards by a wave of blue. Tim then flew upwards on a pillar of water.

Lord Johansson screamed in rage as Tim landed next to us and formed a protective tunnel of water around us. He raised his hand and trailed it along the roof of water, beaming like a kid who just got a bike for his birthday.

"Tim! You're okay!" Priti exclaimed. "Obviously

your power's strength rose!"

Suddenly a cacophony of shots rang out around us. The water tunnel/shield served its purpose well (Thank goodness!). Whenever a bullet hit it, the bullet slowed down and then fell harmlessly to the ground inside the tunnel. Tim would then pick up the bullet, place it in the palm of his hand, and stick his hand out the tunnel's wall. After that he would take aim and shoot a tiny, fast stream of water from his palm behind the bullet, and the bullet would pop out like it was being shot from a gun. Lord Johansson's men panicked, turned, and fled into the forest.

"Men! Stand your ground! Just where do you think you're GOING?!" Lord Johansson shouted after them. After about a minute of hollering after the men and receiving no success, Lord Johansson threw his hands in the air in disgust. He stomped off to the edge of the trees. Spinning around, he pointed a finger at us. "Mark my words; you haven't seen the last of me! I will be back! This is not over!"

"Yee-Haw!" I yelled, leaping into the air in celebration. Of course, I forgot about the water tunnel, so I got myself thoroughly soaked from the waist-up in the process.

"We did it!" Priti yelled.

* * * * * *

We hiked down to the base of the cliff, which was thankfully SCL free, and gazed up at the waterfall.

"Hey guys," Tim said with a mischievous grin. "Uh…" He moved his hands suddenly and splashed me in the face with water.

"Hey!" I said, laughing, wiping the water out of my eyes.

He chuckled and then he turned and splashed Priti.

Katie, unbeknownst to Tim, snuck up behind him, and with a warwhoop, jumped on him and shoved him into the pool at the waterfall's base.

"Ooooooh!" Priti laughed. Well, she laughed until Tim redirected the whole waterfall onto her head. "TIMMY!" Priti spluttered, pretending to be all mad.

"Hey guys," Sarah whispered tentatively. "Come look at this."

"What is it?" Katie asked.

"Honestly, I'm not quite sure. I... I think it's a, um, a door?" she ventured shyly.

"A door? Where?" Tim questioned, popping up from underwater.

"Well, right here! Behind the waterfall," she pointed. "I noticed it when Tim moved the whole waterfall. Look!"

"Well I'll be a goobleia's uncle!" Tim exclaimed. "It is a door!"

"What's a goobleia?" I whispered.

"It's got big, round ears, and a long tail, and it's small, and it is a very mischievous and clever little creature. They're usually brown. They're very cute, but they're little troublemakers all right." She laughed. "A lot like Tim, really."

"Oh, we call those monkeys on Earth." I said, while Priti continued to laugh softly. "Let's go look behind the door."

We all stepped up to the door. For a bit we simply stared at the knob. I'm sure each of us was thinking about what might be behind the door. In my case, I speculated that the entire enemy army was hiding behind the door, lying in wait to capture any unfortunate being who happened to turn the knob.

Sarah slowly turned the knob and then pushed the door open. To our surprise, there was no one there. It was a room, or rather a cave. Roughly cut gray walls, black conference-type table in the middle, surrounded by ugly, dark, muddy brown chairs. The only "color" in the room was an almost dead little weed poking out of a crack in the wall. The whole room had an evil, almost ominous and foreboding atmosphere.

"Guys let's leave. This place is giving me the creeps," Priti muttered.

"I agree," Sarah seconded.

We all filed out and, after taking a vote, decided to head back to the hideout and bunk for the night. (It was getting on 8 P.M. after all.)

CHAPTER 5

The First True Battle

The next two days passed completely uneventfully. We spent the time in an almost blissfully peaceful state, getting to know each other better, exploring a little, and practicing with both our gadgets and our powers. Unfortunately, none of us thought for a moment about *why* these two days were so quiet. As it turned out the "lords" were strengthening their forces. But I'll get to that in a minute. I'm sure some of you may want to know what we learned about each other during those two days, so let me delve into some backstories.

Priti and Tim are the children of the palace's stable manager, Chicoyah, and one of the court members, Sharon. They grew up lacking nothing, in a humongous house on an extremely large plot of land, a small part of which (the part with the waterfall) we explored. But one day their mother, Sharon, was captured by the SCLs and Priti and Tim turned their lessons on fencing, gymnastics, marksmanship, and Do Sheng Wo (The Nordiahoan's version of karate), into a way to defend themselves should they ever need to. They soon got so good at it that they appeared on the SCLs' radar. Tim became one of the best marksmen and master of any weapon imaginable that Nordiaho had ever seen, while Priti became extremely skilled at unarmed combat and using her brain to get the two out of almost any situation. (And let me tell you, Tim was almost *always* getting the two of them into situations!) Then, one night, their father was captured by the SCLs and they barely made it out of their house alive, escaping by the skin of their teeth with only their survival packs. They have no idea where their mother is, and all they know about their father's whereabouts is that he is in one of Nordiaho's most secure prisons. They had been living on their own, sometimes with their aunt and uncle, but most of the time in the forest, making runs on their house, which was now a barracks for some of the SCLs soldiers, to get coins and such, for a year and a half by the time we showed up.

Katie and Sarah grew up together, side-by-side neighbors, in the same little Texas country town I grew up in, New Bern. Katie's family have a horse ranch, 200 acres, by Chaibol creek, and Sarah's family live "right next door", on their 250-acre cattle ranch. They went to school together, trained in gymnastics together, and taught each other to perform daring circus acts in the old barn. (Where, apparently, they rigged up a trapeze and everything, and we should all go down there someday and try it out…) By the time they each had turned 16 they knew practically everything about the other and were as close as two peas in a pod. Their story isn't as dramatic as Priti's and Tim's (sorry to disappoint any guys reading this), but they are the best of friends, through thick and thin, etc. etc. They said they remembered climbing a tree one time, near the border of Katie's land, and seeing a boy, tanned, tall, and shirtless, (ha-ha, great), riding a bucking bronco, completely bareback in the next pasture over, on their other neighbors land, the neighbor whom they knew completely nothing about. Yes, to confirm it for all you brilliant people out there, that was me, a dare devilish, horse-loving 15 year old, showing off for a few of his cousins from out of town, who (dare I say it), *had never even seen a horse.* (I know; what a crime!).

As for me, I grew up on a 500 acre cattle and horse ranch (mostly a horse ranch) on the other side of the creek from Katie's family's ranch. By the time I turned 14 I was already 6' 2" and pretty much the tallest freshman, possibly even high schooler, at school. I barely ever spent time indoors except for when I was at school, eating, or sleeping. I spent the rest of my time breaking in rough stock, doing hard work, learning how to fight well from my older brother, Kid, or practicing shooting under the expert eye of my other older brother, Jimmy, (Who's the best with any gun on this side of the Mississippi, although he's better with pistols n' six-shooters than rifles; second best shot going to Kid.), with just about any gun I could get my hands on. (Which out there where I lived, was quite a large number of guns.) I also spent time lifting "weights" (50-100 pound bags of cattle feed or horse feed), scouring the creek bed for arrowheads to add to my collection, or competing in shooting competitions with other guys from school. If I had to choose, I'd say I felt happiest either riding my horse or shooting, or doing both at the same time. I remember, one day I was riding a bucking bronco, bareback and shirtless, and after I had stayed on for about 30 seconds, I heard cheering add to the cheers which my cousins were yelling, and I looked around, surprised. I looked towards a tree just in time to see a pink cowboy boot pull up into the leaves. I dismounted and released Dead Ringer (my bronc) out of the pasture and pulled my shirt on, 'cause I knew no guys wore pink cowboy boots so I was kind of praying that whatever girl was up there hadn't seen me without a shirt. I slunk towards the tree and then stealthily climbed up it, only to find a note pinned to the tree with a horseshoe nail and to see two figures running through the woods. The note said: Great ride cowboy! I would recommend you wear a shirt next time you've got a female audience though. :) Maybe we'll see you around school Lone Rider. ~ Your Neighbors, Sarah and Katie.

Let me tell you, I don't think I'd ever blushed so hard as that day when I read that note. So yeah. Another thing. Ever since I was four years old I, like most boys, wanted superpowers. And I tried everything I could think of to get them. I stood in front of microwaves, went out and swam in the creek where the full moon lit up the water, tried to get spiders to bite me, etc. I stayed like that until I was almost 13 and my parents finally decided I might just kill myself trying to find superpowers, so they, determined not to let me fill a vat with toxic waste (a detailed plan for which they had discovered in my science notebook instead of the anatomy of a worm), told me that if I gave this up they would get me a horse for my birthday. And not just any horse either. A beautiful Quarter Horse that was already trained for cutting, roping, poles and barrels! So, yeah, there went my superpower fantasies down the drain. And now I actually have superpowers. How ironic; five years after I gave that all up, I get them.

Anyway, back to testing the gadgets. We practiced making accurate projections of ourselves with our pianthio holo displayers, and we practiced throwing knives and shooting (Just for fun; none of us really needed practice for *that*.), and we practiced many other things, but let me tell you about the battle!

On the third day we had plans to visit the old

Chandravilla Castle Grounds and then work out a strategy to free Tim's and Priti's father (once we found him, anyway). Let me just say that those plans of ours were dashed — smashed to pieces underneath the booted heels of the marching feet of a thousand enemy soldiers. Completely!

We were awakened from a peaceful sleep at about 5:00 A.M. We could hear men yelling outside. Silently we slipped on our suits and snuck out the door of the hideout. Fortunately, the hideout was about 250 paces back from the clearing and, hidden by trees as it was, I do not think they ever found it.

"Show yourselves, oh-so-called *Defenders of Nordiaho, Guardians of Justice, and Keepers of the Peace*," a man yelled mockingly from the clearing.

"Who calls us that?" I muttered to Sarah.

"I dunno; the public I guess," She whispered back.

We took 90 seconds to hold a quick "conference" on our battle strategy and then, when we had come up with a plan, we slipped up to the edge of the clearing. The sun had just begun to rise when Tim boldly stepped out from behind the trees where we were hiding.

"Are you unarmed?" a man asked.

"Yep," Tim smirked.

"Are you alone?" the man further questioned.

"For now…," Tim said slyly.

"Then stand still."

"As you wiiiish," Tim muttered sarcastically.

The men opened fire, but a millisecond before Tim was mowed down by hundreds of bullets, he drew water out of the river and threw it in front of himself. That created a protective shield and a sort of "smoke screen." When the water dissipated the soldiers looked around, and, to their great annoyance, Tim was gone! All that was left was a muddy puddle and a bunch of lead slugs scattered on the ground.

Tim had darted back into the forest, and we put into play an excellent trick we had found that we could do with Sarah's power. First, Sarah turned herself invisible, and then, by touching us each in turn, she turned us invisible as well. After that, she leaped in the air and grabbed a bar. We had figured out that if she started out invisible, the bars would also be invisible. Well, unless you were also invisible; then you too could see them. Because Sarah had touched us, we could also climb the bars once she created them. (We couldn't create them but we could climb them, or walk on the horizontal ones.)

We started up the bars and then, when we had reached a suitable height, Sarah started walking forwards. She created a floating bridge all the way out until we were over the ranks of soldiers. Priti whistled a shrill whistle, and birds of all sizes appeared, from great Bald Eagles to tiny Hummingbirds, even Gryphons (yes, I know, they're not technically *birds*, but whatever). I looked around and noticed that in all the forest surrounding the clearing hid great cats, wolves, bears, and other fierce animals, even some of the mythical ones.

We waited. Once the sun rose higher than the lone redwood (a.k.a. around 9 a.m., a long time to wait, but hey, all part of the plan) Tim and I war whooped at the top of our lungs, the animals in the forest charged, Sarah turned all of us visible, and the birds opened… um… fire. Katie upset their war machines and orderly ranks with her mind; Priti ordered the animals; Tim "made it pour" on only the bad guys; Sarah turned the bigger animals invisible; and I whooshed up and down, carrying big boulders up with me and sending them plummeting down on the soldiers.

The battle wavered back and forth between who was winning and who was losing. It also raged for hours. After quite some time of winning, all of a sudden, the tide turned and we started losing. Tim had to wait for the river to fill up again; Katie was getting a headache; and I was getting tired after operating at an average speed of 150 miles an hour for several hours on end.

The soldiers were fighting back quite valiantly to be honest. They had quite powerful technology at their disposal — tech such as hand grenades, high-powered, long-range stun guns, gatling guns, and electronic targeting sniper rifles. Unfortunately, they were excellent fighters, obviously well-trained, and very good snipers. We, however, had discovered a weakness in their forces, a weak link. They were actually partly scared of us and of what we could do. They hoped we only had normal powers, but they really had no idea. (Katie read their minds; that's why I know all that, in case you were wondering.)

"Oh, my goodNESS!" Priti suddenly yelled, deafening me in my left ear. "How could I forget? I can harness the powers of animals!"

A peregrine falcon near us looked at her, nodded, said something, and then once again Priti was engulfed in light. Priti smiled, thanked the falcon, and leapt up into the air. She flew higher and higher and then dove towards the ground. She gained more and more speed (Peregrine falcons can reach diving speeds of up to over 200 miles per hour you know) and then, when she was right over the ranks of soldiers, she flapped her "wings", sending out a sound wave which practically bowled the men over. (The animals have superpowers of a sort as well, so she gets those too.)

The peregrine falcons joined in as well, and on the ground the lions let out supersonic, ground-shaking roars. Eventually the animals and Priti created such an assault of noise and sonic waves that some of the men were on their knees begging for mercy.

The tide had, finally, once again started to shift in our favor. More animals had come to help us, and Katie had gotten a sufficient break. Plus, the streams had refilled, so Tim could continue, and I ran in and out among the soldiers at top speed, causing chaos and much confusion.

We took out troop after troop, battalion after battalion. How did we take them out you may be asking? Well, I'll tell you. Once they realized the full extent of our powers and we caused them to suffer many…um…casualties and injuries, most of them pretty much just panicked and ran away, and the ones who stayed realized that without their strength in numbers they were done for, so they left too. Finally, only Lord Johansson's troops were left. I am beginning to eye Lord Johansson as a formidable enemy at this point in our adventures. By now, we were all on the ground, possibly a little battle weary (We'd been fighting all day and it was nearing nighttime), and itching to win.

Priti had now also acquired the powers of a groundhog, and, using that to our advantage, we staged what we hoped would be our last needed move. She turned invisible (thanks to Sarah) and carefully tunneled underneath the men in an inwardly shrinking spiral. Then she popped up, crawled out, came back to us, and re-appeared. She switched to falcon powers, wrapped her arms around my waist, and shot up into the sky. She flew to the center of the soldiers' group and dropped me. Fortunately, super-strength gives one the power to resist hard landings (it strengthens your bones and muscles), and I landed in the center of the men. I landed with such force that it shook the ground, causing the remaining walls around the tunnels that Priti had dug to collapse. Then I used my super speed to dash away right as the earth opened up underneath the men. With a yell, they all dropped fifteen feet down. All of a sudden, the men disappeared.

"What happened?" Sarah asked.

"Oh gee, Timmy, do you think that was what I think it was?" Priti asked, nervously.

"I thought that was a myth," Tim mused. "And please stop calling me Timmy," he added, pretending to gag.

"Sorry. And I guess it's not a myth," Priti sighed.

"What is?!" I raised my voice.

"Oh!" Priti kind of jumped. "Sorry. There is a 'myth' about a portal to worlds that are safe but uninhabited, worlds where evil men are sent to live out their days. I never believed they existed, but this proves me wrong. Something else that proved the myth was that those men were obviously truly evil; they weren't just regular townsmen under the SCLs mind control, like some we've met. That means these men must have been the SCLs cream of the crop. Only the truly evil men are their cream of the crop," She explained.

"Pssssst," somebody said.

"Who's there?" I called out.

"Over here."

"Over where?"

"Over by the tree at the Northern end's stream."

"That sounds like a girl," Katie said, "And how many streams are there around this clearing?"

"A lot," Tim said vaguely. "And not just any girl!" he exclaimed, looking at Priti excitedly.

"MOM!" Priti yelled and tore off running towards the Northern end of the clearing.

Tim looked at us, politely excused himself, and then ran off after Priti, whooping all the way. Katie, Sarah, and I looked at each other and burst out laughing. We followed slowly behind Tim, and, when we arrived, Priti and Tim were furiously untying their mother from a tree.

"Did they hold you captive Mom?" Tim asked energetically as he coiled up the ropes. "Why did they have you here?"

"Yes, they held me captive. And they planned to use me as a ransom for your surrender, but, Lord Johansson, who was supposed to be officiating the ransom, ran off to who knows where." She smiled wanly, sarcastically. "Now, who are these young people?" she asked, gesturing toward us standing behind Priti and Tim.

"Mom, meet Katie, Sarah, and John. They're our new friends; they're helping us free Nordiaho!" Priti exclaimed, bouncing on her toes excitedly.

"Mmmmm. Lovely," their mom said. I could feel her studying the three of us, determining whether or not we were good influences for her children. I could feel the intense heat and strength of her gaze, and I could tell she would be both a tough nut to crack and a hard person to impress.

"What are your superpowers?" she asked us impassively.

"Moving things with my mind and other related abilities," Katie said.

"Superstrength and superspeed," I said.

"I'm not sure what you'd call mine," Sarah started

shyly. "Basically, I can turn invisible and do this." She leapt up into the air and did a quick demonstration.

"Hmmm. You know there is a reason behind every power, or so the old lore goes. It will be interesting to discover the reason behind each of yours. Perhaps you are part of the Great Prophecy from long ago," their mom responded.

We sat on the ground in front of her, Tim and Priti flanking her on either side. We started to trade stories, and I could tell that she was watching me very closely. There was something in this woman's attitude and composure that made you want to sit up ramrod straight in her presence. I don't know why, but her gaze seemed to linger on me the most. I could feel her eyes boring into me, as if she were trying to read my mind. It sent chills up and down my spine, I'll tell you.

After a while Priti yawned. "Let's go back to the hideout."

"Priti, it's only seven o'clock! You sound like it's midnight!" Tim chuckled.

"Tim, we were woken up at five A.M. remember? So, we've been battling *all day!*" Priti said.

"I agree with Priti," I said, fighting an incoming

yawn. "I'm bushed."

I surveyed the group of extremely exhausted friends around me. Katie was sleepily starting to doze off in a tree she had climbed into during our conversations; Sarah had made herself a bed of bars; Tim was sitting on the ground talking animatedly to his mother; and Priti, on their mother's other side, had simply passed out from fatigue. I found myself a spot of springy grass and lay down. Stretching out my aching limbs, I exhaled contentedly. The woods were quiet, and the only light came from the moon and stars. It was all so peaceful and comfortable, I decided to close my eyes for just a minute.

"Only a minute," I thought. *"...Only a minute?"*

CHAPTER 6

The SCLs Ruin Absolutely EVERYTHING!

You know how, later on in life, you'll look back on decisions you made, and you'll realize how dumb they really were and wish for a do-over? Well, I found myself doing that about six hours after closing my eyes. (Six by my guesstimations any how).

"Why?" you ask?

(Pardon the yelling but,) I'LL TELL YA WHY!

I had closed my eyes, and I was so tired, that I fell into a deep sleep. In the middle of the night we must have been ambushed. I have no idea what *exactly* happened, but, then again, like I said, I *was* fast asleep. I never heard anything though. I guarantee that if Priti, Tim, Katie, Sarah, or P&T's mom had yelled, I would have woken up. So, I'm hoping that they escaped.

I was sleeping rather soundly when my entire body started shaking. A tingling feeling crept up my spine, as if someone ran cold fingers up my whole back. A blinding light suddenly hit my eyelids. Blinking I groggily opened my eyes…and nearly died of a heart attack.

To my (rather annoying) surprise, I was back in the flippin' pizza parlor. It appeared, however, that even though over a week had passed on Nordiaho, hardly any time at all had passed on Earth. The waiter was still making his way back to the kitchen. The couple at the next table still hadn't eaten their pizza, and the song playing over the speakers was hardly any farther in than when we left. I was taking all this in when suddenly it hit me, hard. Smacked me in the face like someone had just hit me with a three-foot catfish. I was here on Earth; they were there on Nordiaho. I had no simple way to get back to them, and, worst of all, if a week had taken place there while a few seconds passed here…how long had I been gone? How much time had passed on Nordiaho while I'd been sitting here like a complete idiot? Had anything happened in my unfortunate absence? Had my friends been captured? Or tortured? Or even been TERMINATED? (Curse my overreactive imagination!)

I leapt up from my seat, wove my way through the tables, and dashed out the pizza parlor's door. I ran all the way to my dorm room. To my dismay I seemed not to have my powers on Earth, so the run took a little bit longer than I would have liked. I stopped at my dorm room door, panting, and thought hard.

"My Nordiaho History Book!" I yelled, hit by a sudden flash of inspiration.

"*Is it still in my pocket?*" I thought, hoped. I dug in the depths of my pocket, my fingers groping around desperately. My fingers bumped something hard. I felt around, establishing the fact that it was, indeed, a book. (Although a *very* small one.) My hand closed around it and I pulled it out, slowly, carefully, nervously.

I looked down at the cover only to find out that the book, which had not grown along with me, was far too small for me to read the title. Muttering under my breath, I slipped into my dorm room to grab a magnifying glass. With my magnifying glass in hand, I squinted through it and read the title. *"YES!"*

I shouted, so loudly that I startled a passing college student, who looked at me oddly before hurrying away from my doorway.

I opened the book *very carefully* and flipped to the right page and read what it said. "A young man named James Loralough purchased Chip-o's, Gummy Bears, and Sour Gummy Frogs at a vending machine. He tried them all at once and was transported to Nordiaho."

"Hmmm," I muttered. "It would appear that I have to find a vending machine."

I did a mental calculation, racking my brain to see if I could remember where every vending machine on the campus was. Satisfied with the results I took off running. I got five steps, turned around, ran back, entered my dorm room again, and snagged a five dollar bill off of my dresser. Then I ran, this time for real.

Our campus is quite expansive. It sits on roughly four-hundred acres (everything is bigger in Texas), has *at least* forty-five buildings, ten dormitories, and five eating areas. It has two libraries, not to mention two football fields, four baseball diamonds, two basketball courts, two volleyball courts, four tennis courts, a riding stable, and three riding arenas.

I found a vending machine with a bag of Chip-o's in the Davy Crockett Study Hall. Then I had to trek across the whole campus (thank goodness for my good friend, Buck, who gave me a ride over) to the James Butler Hickock auditorium to find a package of Sour Gummy Frogs. And, of course, there were no Gummy Bears in either of those machines.

Which, as my luck would have it, meant that there were none in *any* of the other vending machines. I went *everywhere,* looked in *every* vending machine - the one in the Annie Oakley dorm wing, the one in the Buffalo Bill dorm wing, the one in the William Cody auditorium, not to mention the ones outside the Alamo, Guadalupe, and Rio Grande cafeterias. Plus, the ones inside each basketball court, and the ones inside the two indoor swimming pool houses… (I looked a lot of other places, but I'm sure by now you get the idea.)

I checked *every vending machine on the campus.* Each one was the same: *NO GUMMY BEARS!* Then, I remembered, Katie *loved* Gummy Bears! Maybe she had some in her and Sarah's dorm room.

After reminding myself that I was only going into Katie and Sarah's room for a matter of National, no, Galactic, no, *Universal* security, I headed over to our dorm wing. We sleep in the Shoshone dorm wing, which really makes Katie happy, since, you know, she is a Shoshone. I headed to their dorm room's door, turned the knob, and slipped inside.

I looked around and spotted several small bags of gummy bears on her bureau. (I will not be describing their room, thank you very much.) I grabbed an open bag and pulled out two gummy bears. I then yanked the bag of Chip-o's and the package of Sour Gummy Frogs out of my pocket.

I got out one Chip-o, one Sour Gummy Frog, and added to the two one Gummy Bear out of my hand. I held the Chip-o still, put the Sour Gummy Frog on it, and put the Gummy Bear on top. I held the stack together with two fingers and then popped it into my mouth.

I started to shake, and then glow, and then I vanished.

The transportation started out fine. I was temporarily blinded, and shot into a somewhat cramped, glowing, revolving tunnel. Completely normal. After a while, when I should have started shrinking, I didn't. I figured that this was because I hadn't been "professionally transported" so I over-looked it.

When I reached the end of the now *EXTREMELY CRAMPED* tunnel I was temporarily blinded again. I shot out into what I thought was the same clearing as before. I landed really *HARD!* It hurt! But, once again, I figured this was only because I had technically "forced" my way into a portal.

I opened my eyes. I was lying on my back in a clearing. It didn't look like the first clearing from before. There weren't any real trees, only bushy type things, and it was <u>*much*</u> smaller.

I stood up, looked around, and gasped. I laid back down as fast as I could. Something was wrong. Something was *very* wrong. Something was very, very, *very, very, very, very, VERY, VERY WRONG!!!*

I.

HAD.

NOT.

SHRUNK!

CHAPTER 7

I Have A Big, Huge (Literally), GIGANTIC Problem!

What in the world?! Why hadn't I shrunk? Was it because of how I transported myself? Or was this done by the SCLs to ruin our mission? Or by the good guys to save it? ARGH!

Whatever the answer was, for now, it was without a doubt a BIG problem. (Literally) I had no idea just *how* tall I was. I could tell by standing up next to the lone redwood (I *was* in the same first clearing) that I wasn't *too* tall. After all, the redwood was only sixty-ish feet tall and I only was about two-thirds its height. So, I could at least guesstimate that I was around thirty or forty feet tall. I also had felt a surge of energy when I had landed, so I figured I had my powers back.

I had to find the others! Maybe they could help me. Or at least add their ideas to what was going on. And what to do… I stood up and looked around. I knew I was risking being seen, but I did it anyway. I looked everywhere, turning around in a circle and scanning the surrounding terrain. I didn't see them anywhere.

With a sigh I sat down again and leaned my back up against the lone redwood. Then I realized I could be seen sitting up, so I lay down on my stomach. (After checking the ground of course!) I sighed again and wondered where they were.

"Oh my GOSH!" I heard someone scream down near my foot.

I held perfectly still, barely daring to breathe. I was worried that if I moved, I might squash someone. I realized then that I would need to be REALLY careful moving places, especially if I used my superspeed. I could hear people walking around my prostrate body. I shut my eyes and listened to their conversations, waiting for the worst.

"Who in the world is this?" someone said.

"He's absolutely gigantic!" said another.

"I don't think he's from here," said a third.

"I agree. What if he's an alien. He could have been sent from a warring planet to wreak havoc and conquer Nordiaho! It has happened before many a time; it could happen again, despite the Supreme Court Leader's beliefs that it won't," mused yet another frightfully.

"What if he stepped on a town? Or anywhere populated? He could kill someone!" another person practically shouted.

At this point I began to get annoyed. I mean, heck, I'm not dangerous! I'm not gonna kill someone! And for Pete's sake! I'm not an alien from a warring planet sent to conquer Nordiaho! YEESH! Who are they *kidding?!* So what if I'm approximately thirty-five feet taller than everyone else here! It's not like I'm gonna deliberately step on someone or something! And, just to clear things up, I'm not cannibalistic either; that's just *gross!*

They continued talking, labeling me things that I will not repeat. I was getting madder and madder now, and just as I reached my boiling point, they said five words I hope I never hear again (Although I may not get that wish):

"Let's get rid of him."

They talked amongst one another about how to do that. Right away they nixed drowning me and dropping me off a cliff. (They figured they'd never be able to move me.) But then, just as they had reached an agreement on what to do, I heard someone yell, "WAAAAAAAIIIIIITTTTTT! *STOP!* You have to STOP!"

"Who's there? And why?" someone in the previous group asked.

They must have moved away from where I was lying because I couldn't hear everything that was said. But what I did pick up was this.

"My name......I represent......I know him......"

"Him?......the giant......you know the......"

"He isn't......won't hurt anyone...he's fine...... leave him be......good-bye now!"

I heard the first group leave, then I heard some other people hurrying over. I still had my eyes squeezed shut, and I held as still as possible.

"Hi-yai-ai! He really is huge!" someone said.

"So do ya really know him?" asked another.

"I dunno. I think so. I've gotta get a closer look to be sure. I just didn't want him to die."

"Well, that sure was sweet of... Hey! Where are you going?!"

"To get a closer look."

"You can't just do that! What if he picks you up or something?!"

"Ooooooooooohhhhhh *no*! Don't you even THINK about touching him!"

I had been listening to this conversation and trying not to laugh until I heard this last part. '*Touch me? Who?*' I thought.

All of a sudden something lightly tapped my eyelid. I suppressed the urge to swat it away (whatever/whoever it was) and kept my eyes shut.

"Ya know, he looks kinda familiar. Don't ya think?" somebody said.

"Kinda. I mean, his hair reminds me of John's. If only he'd open his eyes, I could tell," someone else said.

Something tapped my eyelid again, a little harder this time, and I considered opening my eyes. I decided not to, but then it hit me harder and I jerked my eyes open.

"Weeeeelll?" one of the people to my right said.

I didn't see anyone in front of me until I stared

cross-eyed down my nose. I could see somebody, squatting, staring up at me, but it was hard to tell who it was since I was cross-eyed and all.

"Can you back up so I can see you better?" I whispered.

"Uuuuuuuuuuh, sure," the person said, somewhat nervously.

The person backed up and we gasped collectively.

"Tim?" I asked.

"Oh, my WORD! John?! What the heck happened to you?" Tim exclaimed.

"That's a LOOOONG story," I said. "Where's everyone else?"

"Oh, they're over there," he said, gesturing off to his left, my right. "Come on guys; it's him; it's fine."

The others came around and stood next to Tim.

"Hi guys," I said, for some reason feeling a little shy. When they stood up straight, they were just a little taller than the top of my head. (When I am lying on my stomach, that is.)

"Hi John," Sarah said.

"How you doin'?" Priti smiled.

"Well somebody had a whopper, and boy do I mean

whopper, of a growth spurt!" Katie grinned at me.

"Why thanks Katie. I'm doing pretty well, how are y'all doi…," I started, only to be cut off by P&T's mom.

"All right, listen buster. I don't know you. I got to know Katie and Sarah quite well during the weeks you were gone. But you? You I don't know. I wouldn't even know your name except that they were talking about you quite often in your absence. So, especially since your body parts' sizes have been staggeringly exaggerated to possibly dangerous proportions, you may not touch my children. Especially Priti. I do not trust you yet. Is that clear young man?" she monologued.

"Ugh! Mooom! Come on!" Priti sighed exasperatedly. "That's just weird, and rude too! He's our friend! You may not know him, but *I* do, and *I* trust him completely!" And with that, Priti ran around to my shoulder, vaulted up onto it, and sat on the top of it.

"Ma'am, my name is Jonathan, but you can just call me John. I would not do one thing to harm your children. I swaratak. I am sorry you do not trust me yet, but I sincerely hope you don't hold anything against me for my size," I said politely, pouring on the Texas country manners and charm and ignoring the fact that P&T's mom was fuming at Priti's defiance.

Tim chuckled softly, and I could only guess that it was because of my use of the Nordiahoan word "swaratak." Then P&T's mom made a "harrumph" noise and turned her back on me. I felt Priti hop over my shoulder blade and lean towards my ear. "I am SO sorry about that!" she whispered, her breath tickling my ear. "That was so embarrassing! She's really over protective of us, especially me. For some reason she thinks I can't hold my own and Tim can. I guess it's 'cause I'm a girl. I'm not technically supposed to be around guys she doesn't know really well either," she sighed.

I was shocked. This was a side of Priti I had never seen before. I had no idea she had a rebellious streak running through her. No wonder she was so eager to be friends with the three of us; her mother didn't let her be friends with that many people.

"S'okay." I whispered back as quietly as I could.

Katie and Tim updated me on their progress in the battle. They had succeeded in getting 3/4 of the known serum and all the notes. They had made no progress on terminating the SCLs though.

We were all talking and laughing with each other when P&T's mom spun to face me. Walking towards me briskly, she stopped three feet from my nose.

"Stand up!" she ordered icily.

"What?" I asked.

"I said, 'Stand UP!'"

"Why?"

"Because I want them to see just how tall, how *dangerous* you are. Maybe that will change their minds about 'trust'," she smirked.

I got the feeling that it might take a long time, and maybe a height change, before she trusted me.

Priti hopped off my shoulder and Katie nodded at me while Sarah smiled her support. I sighed gustily, accidentally nearly bowling everybody over. They backed up and I slowly rose to my feet.

I heard someone gasp. I looked down and saw P&T's mom smirking. I laid back down and looked at them. To my shock and grief, I saw that Priti's face had paled. Sarah's face was also white; Tim looked a little worried; and Katie looked sad and sympathetic.

P&T's mom was smiling.

"So, now you see the dangerous potential he has, hmmm?" she said.

"Mom, I don't know what you have against John," Tim almost yelled. "Yes, I see that he could be dangerous." At this his mom smirked. "I know that if he isn't careful, he could hurt someone, but I also know that he is very careful and responsible. After all, he's my friend, and he's very nice. He would never do anything to hurt any of us."

"Yes!" Priti nodded enthusiastically.

Sarah and Katie agreed heartily. P&T's mom frowned.

"We shall see. I will give him a trial. We will see how he does." she said, and, turning around, she marched out of the clearing.

"Guys, you're not…um, I dunno… scared of me? Right? 'Cause I'm really the same; it's just me, John." I asked nervously.

To my surprise it took them a second to answer.

"No, of course not!" Katie said. "And I think I speak for all of us. It was simply kind of a…uh…," here she paused as if searching for the right word, "shock to see just how *tall* you really are."

"Oh good!" I said. "For a minute there I got really worried that...," I trailed off. "Why are you guys looking at me like that?"

"Well, um, John, please don't take this the wrong way, but... Priti's and Tim's mom, her name's Sharon BTW, she's kinda right," Sarah started shyly.

"About what?" I asked nervously.

"Look, John, you're our friend, and we'd never want to hurt your feelings, but, you're HUGE and, um, possibly dangerous, not to mention menacing, and, well, very... visible and a possible threat to the mission."

"*WHAT?!*" I shouted. They covered their ears and backed up quickly, with something like fear in their eyes. "Sorry, that was loud," I said quickly. "Look, I know I'm a little, well, maybe a lot taller, but I'm still me. Still the same John. I haven't changed. So answer this: *Why* are you scared of me? I know you are. I can tell. It doesn't make me feel very good, but please don't lie to me. That just makes it worse."

They fidgeted, shifting from foot to foot nervously, looking around. Finally, Priti stepped forward a little timidly. "John, we're not scared of *you*. It's just, your size is a little nerve-wracking. And, also, your voice is really loud."

"Well, how come you swung right up onto my shoulder just, like, ten minutes ago?" I asked softly.

"Um, you hadn't stood up yet." She grinned up at me.

"About my being visible, two things: one, with Sarah's power, how big a problem is that? And two, couldn't my size be of help? I could create diversions, scare the SCLs, reach things high up, et-cetera. Not to mention my powers have most certainly multiplied. I'm sure that now I can run faster, lift things of *incredible* weights, I mean, how cool is that?"

"You've got a darn good point there," Tim said.

"RUN!" someone screamed from the nearby town. "A giant has smashed the town hall! Run for your lives!"

"WHAT?!" we shouted (well, I didn't actually; that wouldn't have gone well) in disbelief.

Sarah darted up a ladder and looked. "Oh, my goodness! There really is one! He's destroying the town! John! Here's your chance to prove yourself to

Mrs. Sharon and Nordiaho!" she clapped giddily.

"Well, here goes nothing," I said, pretending to roll up my sleeves.

Sarah turned me invisible and I crept to the edge of town, being careful not to step on any of the fleeing people.

The other giant was approaching the capital building, smiling evilly. He had a very scruffy look about him. He wore a coarse brown shirt, a leather jacket without sleeves, thick-looking, blood-red pants, and big brown lace-up combat boots. He showed no care where he stomped those combat boots down, I might add. He had long brown hair, kind of like Tim's, and a long scar down his cheek. He also had a knife strapped to his calf and a holster on his other leg, *and*, strapped to his back, he had a lethal looking sort of machine gun.

"Hey!" I yelled. My voice boomed out over the town, and I noticed that several fleeing people covered their ears and grimaced. The giant turned my way.

"In the name of the Fearless Five, I command you to stop!" I continued.

I was still invisible, so I think the other giant

presumed I was a tiny person with a microphone.

"Ha! Right! Who's gonna make me? All the reg'lar people on this filthy planet couldn't stop me," he guffawed, speaking with a thick, nasally drawl, in, to my surprise, English.

"Oh, I'm not small; you must have misunderstood. But I am going to stop you, no doubt about that," I said. I stood tall and Sarah made me visible again.

"Oh no! Another one?!" someone shrieked from down below. Katie told me later that I was quite a sight to behold in my super suit, bristling with weapons, my hand resting lightly on the handle of my pistol, standing at thirty-five feet tall, ready to go. If you ask me, this reminded me a lot of the kind of stand-offs that my ancestors used to have to do out West a few hundred years ago, and I was doing my best to copy the stance they always used — that strong, proud, gun-fighting stance that my brother Jimmy taught me.

"Oh look. It's a little boy! What ya gonna do? Chuck your toys at me?" he taunted.

Inwardly I seethed, but outwardly I made my gaze remain as impassive and steely as before. I refused to let him see that his taunts riled me up and insulted me.

"Do you have a power?" I asked.

"A power? 'Course not; that's a stupid fairy tale!" he frowned.

'Good!' I thought happily.

"Let's go cupcake," he said, smirking.

"You're on!" I said.

"Prepare to be crushed!" he laughed.

I waited for him to make his move first. We stood in the town square, circling each other.

"You from this wretched planet?" he asked, spitting on the ground.

"Guess," I said, wrinkling my nose.

"I'm gonna go with no. I ain't from here either," he smirked.

Suddenly he threw a punch at me. I dodged it easily. I threw a weak punch at him and he laughed.

I had decided to pretend I was weak and a bad fighter to drop his guard. I knew that he had no powers and mine were superspeed (excellent for dodging sneak attacks and staying one step ahead) and super strength (makes you almost invincible and gives your punches and kicks a *lot* more power), so I knew I had the upper hand.

A few minutes later Tim contacted me over the headset and asked why wasn't I givin' it to 'im? I just smiled.

"Wow! You're worse'n my grandmam, and she's dead!" the giant taunted me.

"Why are you here?" I asked.

"Well, let's just say that I was sent here by my superiors to distroy this filthy, wretched ball of trash. Why? Because my superiors, one in perrrticulaaar," he drew out the word slowly, "has a score to settle with this place. Surely you are aware of the ongoing rivalry between our two planets? I was born in an alley and decided that I was going to right the wrongs that Nordiaho had committed against our shining jewel of a planet. So here I am, in all my might and strength."

"Hmm," I said. "And what 'shining jewel of a planet' would you be from, oh *mighty and strong one*?" I added sarcastically. By this point, he had hit me a LOT, and each time, I had pretended it hurt. I decided that I was ready to put my plan into action.

"Kimaniragashniga, not that it's any of your business.", He said. (He pronounced it: Key-mah-nee-rah-gosh-knee-gah. Yeah, I know; it's one heck of a mouthful.)

"Okay, then tell your superiors that if they send anyone to Nordiaho ever again, this will happen." And, with that I reared back and slammed my fist into him, sending him flying.

"*WHOOOOOAAAAAAHHHH!*" he screamed as he flew through the air. He landed with a ground-shaking thud, groaning, several thousand feet away in a (thank goodness) empty field. The only apparent damage was the fact that the farmer that owned that certain field *might* have a smaller harvest. Then, with a swirl of purple and a swirl of gold and a whooshing noise the giant disappeared.

"Whew! That was fun." I chuckled.

"HEEELP!" someone yelled.

I looked around.

"It's one of the cheraygah men! He's trapped under the glass dome that the giant flung off our town hall!" another person hollered.

"Cheraygah is our parliament." Priti informed me via the headset.

I strode over to the glass dome and easily lifted it up. The man underneath it looked up at me and smiled.

"Well, the others said you wouldn't fall for that, but I knew you would," he yelled up at me. "It was a trick; we've got you now!" And then I felt a "WHAM" as something hit my back. I twisted around. There was a tranquilizer dart about the size of a Labrador Retriever puppy right between my shoulder blades.

'*Oh no!*' I thought. '*If I pass out now, I'll kill people and ruin the town!*'

Fighting off the waves of sleep that were already washing over me, and cursing myself for getting myself into this, I stood up and ran. I ran as fast as I could, while still watching where I stepped. My strides ate up the ground as I tried to put as much distance between myself and everyone in the town. This got harder as I continued. My eyelids got heavier and heavier until I could no longer fight it.

I toppled, slamming down so hard that I literally saw houses jump off their foundations and then slam back down. I guess I weighed enough thanks to my size and my muscles, and I hit the ground hard enough to make them jump. It's kinda funny if you think about it.

Over my headset I heard Katie say, surprisingly

calmly, "John, they've captured me and the gang; don't let them get you! Stay strong, we'll be in tou…"

I went out cold.

CHAPTER 8

The Problem Becomes The Solution

'*My head!*' I thought. '*What happened to my head? What's going on? Where am I?*' Suddenly memory flooded in. The dart, my friends, thirty-five feet tall, CAPTURED! I could hear things now: Katie crying (Katie *crying*? What in the world. If Katie's crying, things must be really, really bad!), Tim yelling curses, then a door opening and closing.

"Is he unconscious still?" a deep voice asked.

"Ye-es," Katie answered, her voice cracking.

"Well then, we might as well tell you the plan, since he can't hear us," another man said.

At that remark I decided to pretend that I was still unconscious.

"What are you going to do? To us? With him?" Priti asked nervously.

"Well, let me tell you…," the first man chuckled lowly. "You see, your friend here; he's a giant. Now Nordiaho had had giants 'visit' before, but they've always wreaked havoc and then left before we could catch them. Plus, they've never had powers. But him, he has powers. As a normal human he has great powers, but as a giant, oh-ho! He becomes DANGEROUS! We can use that! Oh yes! And we will!"

"He's only around forty feet tall! Not to mention, John would never do something destructive!" Sarah yelled.

"True, but we've covered all that. We're not stupid you know. Do you see that big ray gun in the corner? Yes. Do you see that big needle attached to that humongous glass ball full of orange-ish mahoro (a Nordiahoan color) liquid hanging right above him? Yes, that thing is very hard to miss. And, furthermore, do you realize that your dear John is in the middle of a bridge that is over 50 cubitos long? That we are far from him, against the wall? That there is a seemingly bottomless abyss over 100 cubitos below the bridge?

That the roof is over 40 cubitos (a Nordiahoan measuring unit equal to 15 feet) above the bridge? Do you? WELL?" he said.

"Yes, yes, we see all of that! What's your point?" Tim asked exasperatedly.

"Let me just say that your friend is going to become our biggest weapon. He will become a monster, a nightmare from whom only we can defend the whole planet. Once we save the planet, we will become heroes! We will use that status to become the sole rulers of Nordiaho, then, when we rule everyone, we will show our true colors! Oh yes! Your giant here, he will force the entire planet to serve us. We will be waited on hand and foot. We will be the richest men in the galaxy! We won't ever have to lift a finger. The citizens will farm the land, make our clothes, our food, and military supplies. They will construct our palace, which will be the greatest architectural wonder in the galaxy, no, the universe! The building itself will sprawl over 100 egeans (a Nordiahoan unit for measuring land area: equals three acres), and it will be our everything. Anyone who refuses to serve us, slacks off, or opposes us, they will be EATEN!"

"Cannibalism? Really? That's just gross!" Sarah muttered.

"Oh no, not us; him! He, your former friend, will eat them! Rebels, slackers, people who complain about their place and treatment, they will become a tasty snack for our menace here. There will be no jail either. Instead, criminals will be publicly tortured for months, years even if the crime is bad enough, like a cat plays with a mouse, and then they will be eaten. If that doesn't discourage people who want to rebel or commit crimes, I don't know what will! Oh! How wonderful it will be to have a pet capable of wiping out entire planets! For I'm sure you can see that he would be completely unstoppable." He laughed maniacally.

'That's SO gross! I would never do that! Does he think that my size makes me a blood-thirsty monster? The idea! I oughta torture him! However, he does have a point. I might be unstoppable, but wait, I'm only thirty-five feet tall! That just doesn't work out right,' I thought in a rage.

"John would never do that! How dare you imply that about him!" Katie ranted.

"John might not now, but you know what, let me just show you," he said.

I'm gonna let Katie do the narration now since she had a better view.

Katie's Narration:

'The nerve! The audacity! Ugh! If only John would wake up!' I thought, with half a mind to kill this guy.

We watched, waiting, wondering what would happen. Suddenly, with a "WHOOSH!" the needle above John dropped down on a tube and imbedded in his arm! The tube started pumping the liquid down into him!

"What's happening?!" I yelled.

"You see, that liquid is growth serum. There are thirty ounceasos (a Nordiahoan unit for measuring liquids; equals two ounces) of it in that glass ball, and it will activate once we take the needle out of him. One ounceaso equals the growth of one cubito, and, honestly, since it's pretty much a cinch to make more, I think we'll put all of it in him!" He smirked. "Don't you think a monstrous giant over thirty cubitos tall would be enough to strike fear into the hearts of even the bravest army? Who would dare oppose something like him?" He grinned at us, a big, cruel, delighted smile.

After all the serum had been drained from the glass ball into John, the needle removed itself and the glass ball and needle retracted into the ceiling. The room started to shake. The shaking grew and grew in ferocity until we could barely stand, and a sound like a rushing roar of wind filled the room. It was so loud we couldn't even hear each other. Then, John started growing.

It's kind of hard to believe, but he grew; he really did! It's also kind of hard to describe, but, as he grew, as his body got longer, it also got higher and wider.

Like, from back to chest got higher, and from arm to arm got wider. That way his body stayed in perfect proportions. Fortunately, his clothes grew with him.

Soon his feet were at our end of the bridge and they were so BIG!!! I could see every detail in his shoes; every crack, crevice and detail were now HUGE. I swear I might've fit in every one of them!

"HUZZAH! It worked! He is HUGE!" the man cheered. "Now, bring forth the mind eraser gun!"

Three workers promptly rolled forward the gun that the man had pointed out earlier.

"What does that do?" Tim asked nervously.

"It does two things," the man said. "First, it erases all his memory; second, it gives me control over his mind."

I knew I couldn't let this happen! I wouldn't let it happen to anyone, but especially not to John! Not the sweet guy whom I've had a crush on since the time I (literally) ran into him once at the grocery store when I was thirteen! Oh no! Did I just say that?! AH! Anyway, I had to stop this!

While the men were distracted setting up the gun, I ran over to John. His feet were pointing straight up and they were smashed together, but, thanks to his size, I was able to slip through a chipped spot in the rubber lining of his shoes. I climbed, finding handholds and footholds by the threads of his jeans. (I could see the threads of his jeans!) Upward I climbed, higher and higher, for what felt like an eternity, until I reached the top of his ankle. I ran and scaled his tennis shoes until I reached the top, and then I laid down flat on top of them.

I looked below me. The men had just finished readying the gun. I prepared myself to stand up.

"FIRE!" yelled the man.

I leapt up, dug my feet into the weave of his tennis shoes, and held out my hands. The gun began to emit beams of light and I used my power to dissipate them. I knew the gun didn't have that much juice; I just hoped that I could hold out long enough, since both myself and my power's strength had never been put to such a test before. I also don't think the men realized that I was there.

My breath started coming in ragged gasps and I knew I wouldn't be able to hold on much longer. The control and exertion were draining more out of me than I had expected. Then, just when I thought I couldn't do it anymore, the gun was drained empty. I collapsed, and I could feel myself slipping off his shoe.

John's Narration:

"JOHN!" Priti screamed.

I decided not to pretend I was unconscious anymore and I opened my eyes slowly. I lifted my head up an increment and looked down towards my feet just in time to see Katie slipping off my toe. She started falling, and I waited for the right moment. When the time was right, I used my superspeed so I wouldn't be seen, and I sat up, grabbed Katie out of the air, and then lay back down.

I unfolded my fingers slowly, carefully, keeping her cradled in the center of my palm. Katie was curled up, shivering, and panting. I exhaled softly. My breath caused her bangs to flutter and she opened her eyes.

"John," she said quietly, smiling softly. "I'm sure you heard their plan. They think… the ray worked… if they ask you to eat the others," she shuddered, "put them in your breast pocket and say you're saving them." She struggled to get each word out. She looked exhausted.

'Oh my word! She's so small! She fits in the palm of my hand! What am I supposed to do? What if I accidentally kill one of them? WHY IS THIS HAPPENING TO ME?' was what I was thinking. What I said though was, "Are you okay?" I whisper-breathed, hoping I was actually quiet. And then I couldn't help myself. "You're so…small!"

"Ssssh! I'm fine." She grinned up at me.

Katie's Narration:

He looked… different. I felt like I was looking at him under a microscope, every detail was so clear. I could see every strand of blonde hair that was swept to the left across his forehead. I noticed he had a few tiny freckles across his nose too. His eyes though, oh, they were so deep and calm! Dark, dark blue with small swirls of gray-blue, and in them I could see a reflection. The reflection was of me, small, frail and helpless. Curled up in the palm of his hand. When he bent his fingers, I fit perfectly in the sort of cup in the middle of his hand. I've never felt so…so helpless, so… meaningless and small.

He smiled at me. It made his face light up, revealing laugh lines around his eyes and a deep dimple (from my point of view anyway) in each cheek. I knew, right then and there, that not a trace of the memory-erasing ray had hit him, that I was safe, and that we would make it through all this okay.

I was swept with a wave of emotions and I knew I was blushing deeply. I think he noticed I was blushing because, all of a sudden, I heard a low noise, and I started to vibrate a little. Startled, I looked up at him. His eyes were twinkling, and his Adam's Apple was bobbing slightly.

'*Oh, he's laughing!*' I thought. '*Very quietly, but he's*

laughing.'

John's Narration:

The fact that she was blushing, well, I couldn't help laughing a little. I noticed her kind of jump when I began to chuckle, which, sadly, only made me laugh a little more. I tried to be as quiet as possible, but, unfortunately, I think they heard it.

"He awakes!" the man yelled. Yeah, they heard me.

"Get in my pocket! Quick!" I breathed softly to Katie.

She nodded, ran across my chest, which took her a second (I think my chest is the size of a smallish parking-lot to her!), and slipped into my shirt-pocket. It kind of tickled. I could hear her outlining the plan to the others over the headset. Then she was talking to me, "John, I know you're not gonna like this, but you have to act scary and mean. You have to act like the ray gun actually worked and that you're under their control. After the first part of the plan plays out, and the men leave, we'll work out an escape plan. Ok?"

I sighed. "Ok," I whispered.

"Jonathan! Stand up!" The man yelled.

I grunted, frowned, and slowly stood up, trying to adjust myself quickly to maneuvering at my new height. When I was fully erect, I looked down, down, DOWN (WHOA! I had no idea they grew me THIS MUCH!) towards my feet. Standing at the far end of the bridge were the others, huddled together. I just stood there, feeling awkward, unwieldy, shy, and ungainly.

"Well?" the man said. "Go on. They're yours to do with as you please," he urged.

Carefully, I dropped to one knee, noticing them jump when I did, leaned forward, and slid my hand behind the others. (My hand practically dwarfs them. It could "swallow" them whole; yeesh this is weird!) Then, I turned my hand quickly so that they fell into it, wrapped my fingers around them and stood up. I could feel their hearts beating and their chests heaving. Over the earpiece I could hear their breaths coming in short, ragged spurts.

I held my hand over my shirt pocket and slid them in, carefully but quickly.

"Aren't you going to do anything?" the man asked.

Katie's Narration:

I could feel his heart beating through his shirt. When he was picking up the others it started racing so fast that I had to dig my hands into the weave of his shirt in order to avoid being bounced around like a popcorn kernel. Now his heart was racing again as he tried to think of something to say.

I helped the others hold on and waited to see what he would say.

It feels so weird being so small compared to John. Every time he stands or kneels or such (It might not happen to him. I'm sure it doesn't as a matter of fact, but it happens to me and the others.) from my/our point of view he moves so quickly that it feels like I'm plummeting to the ground or being thrown into the air. There's a "whoosh" of air so loud that I can't hear, and my ears pop (Yeah, he's that tall). Then I'm caught, I'm no longer weightless, and I hit the bottom of his pocket again. I feel like I'm in another dimension, another world.

At least there's no shortage of things to do in his pocket. There are all these loose hanging threads, which are as thick as sinew, that I've been reweaving.

The threads that have been "cut off" entirely I'm using to make a woven belt. The threads are quite thick and soft, and, since he's wearing a plaid shirt (blue, white, and green), the colors alternate and it's turning out to be quite pretty so far.

His chest rose up, and we with it, as he took a deep breath. Priti shivered a little.

"Later." he BOOMED. We covered our ears. I had no idea that his voice would be so... insanely LOUD. It seemed to echo off the walls and reverberate around the room, huge as the room was.

His heartbeat slowed a little, and we waited tensely to hear the man's reply.

"Ah, torture. That's good; they certainly deserve it." The man chuckled. "I'll be back. Everyone, clear out!" With that, I heard lots of doors opening and closing and then a loud clinking, sliding noise, which John said later was the floor expanding so that the "bottomless abyss" was all covered over.

John sighed gustily and sat down, causing our weightlessness to occur again. Then he must have lain down, because all of a sudden we were SMASHED against his chest. We were rising and falling with both his breathing and his heartbeat, which had finally started to become normal again.

After a moment, a loud, deep rumbling sound filled the room, and then it stopped.

"What was that?" Sarah asked nervously. "Are they coming back?"

The low, throaty chuckle and the vibrations happened again. (Although this time the vibrations and movements were more intense, because we were all lying on his chest, instead of lying in his hand near his chest, like I had been earlier.) The others looked around nervously, since they couldn't see what he was doing, and had no idea what the noise was.

"No, they're not coming back," John laughed slightly. "That's my stomach rumbling."

Priti gasped and her eyes widened. (I can't quite say I blame her, seeing the history that Nordiaho has with giants, but still, it's John! Hello!)

"Whoever that was, I heard that gasp," John said, thankfully keeping his voice more quiet. "I'm only a little hungry for Pete's sake."

"Who's Pete?" Tim asked, confused.

John started laughing at this, HARD. No longer

able to keep his laugh at a quiet chuckle, the laugh burst out of him like a caged animal escaping. Booming loudly, his chest shook violently as he laughed and laughed. Of course, since we were in his shirt pocket, we were tossed around like a bunch of rag dolls in a washing machine. Or maybe in a contained tornado.

"John! STOP! Please! We're all over the place here! OW!" we yelled at him. (Thank goodness for our headsets or he never would have heard us!)

The shaking stopped, as did the horribly loud noise, and his chest rose and fell beneath us as he took deep breaths.

"Sorry!" he said, almost shyly. "It was just so funny, and I needed a laugh, and I... momentarily forgot about...uh... sorry."

"S'okay," Tim said. "Hey, can we, uh, get out now?"

"Oh, uh, sure thing. Here," John said. He reached up to his pocket and lifted the flap so that we could crawl out.

The others crawled out before me, in a rush, as if they couldn't wait to get out of his pocket. While I waited, I looked around. Have you ever seen the detail of someone's fingertip before? I couldn't help noticing his fingertip since it was bigger than my head. It's so detailed that I can see every groove.

I grabbed the belt I was weaving and the small ball of loose threads I had made (that way I could keep weaving while we weren't in his pocket), and crawled out. When I got out, I saw the others just staring up at John.

"What are you guys looking at?" John asked.

"Uh… you," Sarah said.

John's Narration:

Ya know, I wish they'd stop acting so scared of me. I don't think Katie's scared of me, but the others are another story. I mean, it's understandable, I guess. I am *really, freaky, crazy TALL*, but I haven't changed! I mean, when my stomach rumbled and I said what the noise was *someone* gasped nervously.

Look, I'm not that kind of person, okay! I'm not dangerous! Really, I'm not! By most people's standards, I'm still a kid! I really wish they'd stop being so jittery around me. Like, right now for example, they're all staring at me like I'm a martian in an exhibit. Well, all of them except for Katie. She's sitting on my knee mumbling under her breath, and I think she's weaving something, but I can't really tell from all the way up here. (Hey, from my point of view, my knee is about one hundred feet away from my eyes, and the two to three-inch person is doing something with millimeter thick thread, or something like thread anyway...)

"Guys, why are you looking at me?" I asked.

"Um... I dunno. You kinda look, uh, different. It's kinda hard to describe, but, um, it's like looking at you through the world's highest-powered microscope since you're so, um, humongous!" Priti said.

"Like, all of your pores are completely clean! Dude! How do you do that?" Tim asked.

Katie snorted and flopped over on my kneecap.

"What's wrong with Katie?" Sarah asked.

Katie screamed quietly and started pounding her fists on my knee. This didn't really hurt, so I didn't care.

I shrugged, which sent them all flying forwards and then backwards as my chest moved along with my shoulders.

"Sorry," I mouthed as they stood up, then decided to sit down on my chest instead.

Katie sighed and then began to stab my knee with

her fingernails or something.

"Ow!" I said, and jolted my knee a little.

Katie looked up at me, shocked, almost like she had just broken out of a trance.

"Katie," I said softly, "Are you okay?"

She shook her head slightly and sighed.

"Come on Katie." I looked at her. "Come join the others."

I patted a spot next to Sarah with my finger. Katie hesitated.

"Come on; don't be shy. You know all of us Katie; we don't bite," I smiled.

She sighed and stood up slowly. She walked up my leg, climbed over my belt, and stumbled over the small creases in my shirt with uncharacteristic clumsiness until she collapsed in a heap next to Sarah.

Katie's Narration:

The others ran over and surrounded me.

"You know Katie, he's right; we don't bite," Priti said. "Honestly though, our biting wouldn't be that bad; it would be him you'd have to worry about. I mean with the size of his mouth, he could bite you in half with no effort at all…," she added quietly.

John sighed so gustily that we all toppled over, so loudly that we couldn't hear.

"Do you think he heard me?" Priti asked me timidly.

I sighed and tapped my ear. "Earpiece." I said.

"Fine," John forced out. "I get it."

He scooped us up gently and plopped us on the floor, then he rolled over so that he was lying on his side, his back towards us.

We sat for a moment in stunned silence. Then a loud, splashing noise began. We could tell John was breathing faster, and his shoulders started to heave.

"What's that sound?" Tim asked.

I gestured that we should all take our earpieces out. Everyone did.

"What is that sound?!" I almost exploded. "He's CRYING! Y'all made him *cry*! I've never *ever* seen John cry! How could y'all be so insensitive? Don't you think maybe it's weird for him too, being so tall? And here y'all are, acting like he's gonna *eat you*! Do you really think that John would do that? I mean really? *John*, who helps us study for tests, who's humble, who doesn't rub anything in! Not about how smart he is, or how athletic, or about how he's stronger than 3/4's of the guys at school! *JOHN! IS! NICE!* And if you can't see that, if you actually think he'd purposely destroy things or eat people, I don't know *what's* wrong with y'all!"

With that, I jogged off in a rage and started the long trek around John — past his shirt, his neck, the back of his head. By the time I reached the top of his head, I had to pause for a second.

I came around to his forehead and what I saw nearly broke my heart. His cheeks were streaked with tears and he was biting his lip like he was trying not to make any noise. He was breathing in rapidly through his nose and his chest kept heaving.

"John?" I said, tentatively, quietly. "Are you okay?"

He smiled wanly and brushed a tear off his cheek.

"I'm... fine," he struggled to get out. Then he sighed. "No, that's a lie. I'm really... not."

"What's wrong?" I asked. "Please tell me. You need to tell someone."

"All right. You of all people deserve to know." He blushed a little, which, of course, was very noticeable because of his size.

I blushed too, sat down, looked up at him encouragingly, took out the belt and started weaving.

John's Narration:

Katie is just so sweet! I'm really glad someone isn't scared of me.

"I'm just really tired of their comments. I mean, it's like I'm not even human anymore! They're all scared of me; none of them seem to want to be friends now. It's just exasperating! They act like I would actually *eat* them! I mean, come on! I'm just… sick and tired of being treated like… like a danger or a liability." I frowned.

"John, look, I'm not scared of you at all, and… I hope the others come around! You're NOT a danger OR a liability! You're amazing! I mean, how cool that you can probably now take this whole building and effortlessly pull it off of its foundation! Come on! If the others can't see how great you are, then that's their loss!" she finished breathlessly.

I smiled a little. "Being this tall isn't all fun and games you know. It's, well, it's kind of awkward and annoying too. For example, I can't do anything with y'all really. I can't participate in any games, give anyone a hug or a high-five, it's even hard to talk to people because my voice is so flippin' LOUD!"

"Will this help?" Katie asked. She stood up, ran over, and kissed me on my cheek by standing on tiptoes. (She didn't get that high, but who cares?)

We both blushed, then, when we saw that we were both blushing, we burst out laughing. Fortunately, I managed to keep the sound down by slapping my hand over my mouth.

After we both stopped laughing and calmed down, I looked down at her and saw her doing that thing she had been doing when she was on my knee.

"What are you doing?" I asked her.

"Weaving," she said, then she looked up at me with a funny expression on her face. "What's your waist measurement?"

"Uh… I don't know… 200 feet?" I ventured.

"Ha-ha," she smirked. "Not now silly; when you're your normal height."

"Oh. Twenty-eight inches, I think. Why?"

"It's a surprise." She smiled up at me.

I grinned back at her. Then, I heard a shuffling

noise up near the top of my head. I looked around.

"Hi John," Sarah said quietly, coming over to sit next to Katie.

"Hey big guy!" Tim said, flopping down on his stomach next to the others.

"Priti!" he hollered. "Where are you?!'"

"I'm coming! Hold on! I had an idea!" she yelled back.

She came into view digging through her satchel. "Ah-ha!", She said, holding something over her head triumphantly.

"What is it?" Sarah asked.

In response, Priti plopped down on the floor and spread the things in her hands out in front of her.

I squinted. I couldn't quite tell what the things were, so I leaned over towards them a little more. When my shadow fell on them, they looked up at me, startled.

"Uh, John, no offense, but if you were to lose your balance, since you're lying at such a weird angle, you'd fall right on us. So, if you could maybe, um, lie back the way you were, and just like, rest your head on your arm or something so that you can see, that would be great," Tim grinned at me sheepishly.

"Oh! Um, sure, yeah, sure thing," I said, and repositioned myself again. I did, however, in that time, see what the things were. In front of her was, I think, I still wasn't quite sure even though I got a closer look, an apple, a bag of cookies, and a gun.

"Uuuuuh, Priti? What is that stuff?" I asked. "You're not going to shoot me, right?"

"No! Of course not! This is food!" she announced triumphantly.

"You're going to eat a *gun*?" Katie asked her incredulously.

"No! No! This gun is one of my dad's inventions. It grows inanimate objects. I only had the apple and the bag of cookoos, which are like cookies by the way, on me, but at least it's better than nothing." She smiled up at me. "You said you were hungry."

She pointed the gun at the bag and pulled the trigger. A little bolt of lightning exploded from the barrel and hit the bag. There was a "POP" and the bag grew until it was the size of my palm. Then, she sliced the apple, and grew the slices. "POP" "POP" "POP" "POP", and then there were apple slices also about the size of my palm.

"Go ahead," she said. "They're all yours."

I think, because I was so hungry, I inhaled that food in about thirty seconds.

"Thanks Priti!" I smiled. "So, um, still friends, right?"

"Yeah. We're sorry for being skittish around you. I guess we didn't really think about how you might feel, being so tall and all that. We're sorry," Sarah said.

"Thanks guys. I'm glad y'all don't think I'm a bloodthirsty monster anymore." I smirked. They blushed.

Then I heard footsteps; then a door opened and shut.

"Hide!" I mouthed frantically.

"Where?" Tim whispered. "We can't reach your shirt pocket anymore because you're lying on your side! And if you move enough to either let us get in it or to put us in it the man or whoever it is will notice it and will think something's up!"

My mind raced. Where could they hide? My gaze fell on my hand, and I looked at my shirt sleeve.

'*Hmmmm,*' I thought.

"Hurry John!" Priti whispered urgently.

I brought my arm out from under my head and set it near them. Then, quickly, I unbuttoned the cuff.

"Quick! Get in!" I mouthed.

They ran in and I could feel them flatten themselves against my arm and wrist. I buttoned the cuff up again and waited.

Katie's Narration:

John's arm was slightly bent, and we were against the smooth inside of it. It was actually quite warm and comfortable. (Yes, I know that sounds weird, but if you feel the underside of your arm, you'll see what I mean.) I was closest to the opening of his sleeve, right up against his pulse. Since he was lying on his side and the arm with the sleeve in which we were hiding was partly underneath him and curled towards his face a little, we could hear him breathing. We could feel it too. (Which, honestly, was a little weird.) His breathing was so slow and even, I think he was pretending to be asleep.

"Wow! Earl! You were right! He's... fantastically FREAKISHLY HUGE!!!" someone said.

We shot forwards a little as a muscle in John's arm bulged.

"He'll work well in our plan. The key piece." The man from earlier said, "Stand up Jonathan! Show Jude how tall you are!"

We looked at each other nervously, then we braced ourselves. John stood up slowly, thank goodness, and actually managed to keep his arm kind of level. Of course, he couldn't help tipping it side to side a little, so we slid around a bit. At one point, I slid so far that I nearly fell out of his sleeve. It felt so weird, like we were free-falling in reverse. There was nothing under our feet but his shirt, and I could tell without even looking at them that the others were scared. Not of John, but of the fact that we were only separated from an over 450 foot drop by a maybe half-inch thick piece of fabric.

Then I felt something smooth and warm slide beneath my feet. I smiled, *'He crossed his arms! He's so considerate. He must have heard our breathing over the earpiece and realized what was going on and how scared we were!'* I thought.

"Thanks, John," I said.

His arm moved slightly, as if he was telling me he heard me.

John's Narration:

I'd never felt so responsible in my life! I was carrying

around four people, and I had to keep them safe.

I was most worried that my shirt would rip, they would go plummeting down to the ground, the men below me would see them, and, worst of all, I wouldn't be able to catch them.

I could hear their breaths coming fast and ragged over the earpiece. I could feel their hearts beating like a drum corp against my arm. Then I had the idea to cross my arms. The second I slid my left arm underneath my right arm, their hearts slowed, their breathing became more or less normal, and they kind of slouched against my arm.

"Thanks John," Katie said over the earpiece.

I knew I couldn't respond verbally, so I shifted my left arm a little, hoping she got the message.

"See! He's perfect!" the man whom I learned is Earl yelled. I tensed.

"Absolutely! We'll be back at 1:30 parmenuto tomorrow. Good night." The man named Jude shouted up at me.

Then they left. (Priti told me later that parmenuto to them is like P.M. to us.)

I lay down, slowly and carefully, rolled onto my

side, (slowly and carefully), and unbuttoned my cuff (slowly and carefully). They got out and collapsed against my chest.

"That was nerve-wracking!" Priti said. "I don't think I've ever been that high ever! Well, except in a Shuttle. Thanks for crossing your arms so we had something to stand on!"

(In case you are wondering, though some of you might have been higher than about 450 feet, the buildings on Nordiaho are a lot shorter than the buildings here on Earth, which is why she's never been that high before.)

"You're welcome," I said, through a huge yawn.

"Time for bed?" Sarah grinned up at me.

I nodded and smiled sleepily. They stood up and walked a bit away, then they lay down.

"Good night," I said.

"Night," Tim yawned. "Hey, you don't snore, do you John?"

"No," I chuckled.

"Good, 'cause if you did: A. we'd never fall asleep, and B. we'd probably get blown all over the place, like little leaves," Tim smirked.

Five minutes later they started shivering and I could hear their teeth chattering over the earpiece. I reached out and carefully wrapped my arm around them and slid them up against my shirt. Katie looked up at me and smiled as they got comfortable in the warm hollow I had made in the crook of my arm. I smiled back.

We slept like that all night.

* * * * * *

Katie's Narration:

I woke up first. When I woke up, I forgot where I was. I had a momentary panic attack. I looked around. There were Priti, Tim, and Sarah, curled up against a HUGE piece of fabric, and behind me… I turned around. A GIGANTIC (Like, seriously, crazy, freakishly, mammoth, gargantuan, HUGE!) rising and falling mass of the same fabric!

Then, my brain clicked. Last night! John! The men with the growth serum! DUH!!

I looked over towards John's face. His hair had fallen across his face like a curtain, and he looked so…serene. I can't believe he didn't move at ALL last night! Just to keep us warm! So SWEET! He might not have slept much at all last night. Poor guy. I'm sure the position he's in isn't that comfortable.

You know, anyone else who doesn't know John might see where we are as a trap, but it's not. I mean, sure, I can't get out without Sarah's ladder unless I woke him up, but that doesn't mean that it's a trap.

I sat down to continue weaving. By the time Tim and Sarah woke up, I had finished the one belt and started another. When Priti woke up an hour later I had finished the second one.

It's kinda funny. If you think about it, the pieces I'm using for these belts were probably less than 1/4 an inch long at his normal height, but now they're over four feet long and really thick!

I gesture we should take our earpieces out before we talk. Everyone does so.

"Should we wake him up?" Tim whispered.

"No, I don't think so. We should let him sleep," I said. "I don't think he got much sleep last night."

Priti nodded. "I woke up at midnight and he was just lying there, watching us sleep, almost sadly. The poor guy."

Sarah sighed. "I feel so badly for him! He can't really do anything with us; he's too big. He seems so left out!"

I frowned. How could we include him? I had NO idea.

* * * * * *

He woke up at noon. We were lying on our stomachs in a circle and I was teaching them to weave a community blanket out of threads from John's shirt when we heard a groan and a sigh from high up above us. We looked up. John was smiling down at us, but I noticed his eyes were dull.

"Morning John!" we chorused. That made his eyes twinkle with laughter and he looked better.

He swept his hair out of his eyes, sat up, and stretched.

"Good morning," he said. "What are y'all doin'?"

"Weaving a blanket," I replied.

"By hand?" he asked, surprised.

"Well, yeah. How else do you propose we do it in

this situation?" I teased him.

He laughed. We covered our ears. When he stopped he said, "You're right. And of course, you know how to weave a blanket by hand Katie."

"It's really fun!" Priti exclaimed.

"I'm sure it is," John grinned. "Say, where'd you get the yarn or whatever? D'you bring it? Looks like you have a big ball." He pointed at the ball I had made of all the loose threads I had found.

"Uhhhhh…," we looked at each other. "It's from your…um…shirt." I blushed and looked down at the blanket in the awkward silence that followed.

"My shirt?!" John asked unbelievingly. "Have you been picking it apart while I slept?!"

"NO! Of course not!" I exclaimed. "There were just, like, a bajillion loose threads in your pocket. That's what we're using."

"Oh," he said flatly. "Good."

He stood up and walked around the edge of the room a few times. We flew up in the air each time he put his foot down (yet another unforeseen complication, sigh). After his third step, Sarah made a platform of bars and we all sat on it.

Finally, he stopped. He was walking back over to us when one of the loudest noises I swaratak I've ever heard filled the room. We covered our ears and grimaced.

When we looked up again; he was bent over, holding his stomach.

"WHAT was THAT?!" Priti asked.

"John?" Tim asked.

"Ummm...," John didn't look at us. "That was... my... stomach. Please don't be scared!" he added quickly.

"We're not. Are you okay?" Sarah questioned.

"No!" he groaned sadly. "I'm SOOO HUNGRY!!! I've never been this hungry in my life! I feel AWFUL! And, NO, I'm not going to eat you guys!"

"John, we know you're not going to," I said softly. "How do we get you food though? I think the men intend to starve you so that you'll eat anything, but we can't let that happen."

Tim coughed. "Guys, I can teleport things, remember?"

John's face lit up. "REALLY?!!" he yelled, so happy that he not only forgot to keep his voice down, but he yelled. (Oh, I don't think my poor ears will ever recover! I mean, imagine taking the movie theater's speakers and then turning them all the way up, and then multiply that by about a hundred, *at the loudest part of an action movie! He's that loud!*)

"Er... yes. And if I'm not deaf I'd be quite happy to," Tim remarked, rubbing his forehead.

"Oh man. Sorry!" John turned beet red. "Was I really that loud? Be honest, how loud was I?"

"Uh, on a scale of one to ten, you hit fifteen million!" Priti grumbled.

John winced.

"Tim, can I have something to eat please?!" John fairly begged. "I am so hungry I could just about die. Because of that battle, and all the drama, besides that snack I haven't eaten in TWO AND A HALF DAYS!" As if to punctuate the fact, his stomach growled louder and longer than the first time.

"Yes. Yes. Hold on." Tim raised his hands a little. All of a sudden food started appearing in front of him. A plate of pirogies, mac-n-cheese, 3 loaves of bread, 5 one-gallon jugs of milk, a layer cake, and an unidentifiable bowl of something.

"NO WAY! You guys have mac-n-cheese on

Nordiaho? And pirogies too? Yum!" John bounced on his toes.

We laughed, and Priti grew the food while Tim explained that he brought most of the food from Earth, however the unidentifiable bowl of something was from Nordiaho. It was called Smormahnos, and it was his and Priti's favorite. (pronounced: Smor-ma-nose)

John sat down and rubbed his hands together. He picked up a loaf of bread, but then he paused, "Wait! Where are my manners?! Do y'all want some?"

"No, it's fine, that's for you," Sarah said shyly.

"But y'all haven't eaten for longer than I have! I mean, I had the cookoos and the apple last night and y'all had absolutely nothing! I can share! Really! There's a ton!" he protested.

"John, you eat that. Tim can teleport some more for us," I insisted.

"Go ahead!" Priti urged.

"If you're sure," he said, "Thanks for teleporting utensils for me Tim. That way I don't have to eat with my hands." He took a bite. "Mmmmm!" He closed his eyes and sighed happily.

In about ten minutes he had finished everything. (Have you ever seen someone eat who's both over 450 feet taller than you and starving? It's quite a sight to see.) He was lying on his back with his hands behind his head and his knees in the air. "Ahh, I'm full; that is a glorious feeling," he said contentedly.

We had eaten, and he had given each of us a (to him) teeny-tiny crumb of the cake with a wee bit of icing on it. It was really good. A moist, rich, chocolate cake.

* * * * * *

The days that followed began to take on a sort of routine. We would wake up in the morning and eat breakfast together. John would then walk and/or run around the room, then we would talk. Around 1:30 P.M. each day (I'm just going to use P.M., not parmenuto, to avoid any confusion) the men would come in and put John on display. Then we'd eat lunch, play around, plan our escape, eat dinner, tell stories, and then curl up together and sleep.

As those days passed, we all learned things. The

four of us learned to tell when John was going to be loud: his chest would rise up higher than normal and his Adam's apple would jerk. It was kind of scary if we were in his shirt pocket at those times, because, even when we couldn't see him, we would go soaring up into the air and then we would feel his chest rumbling as he spoke. Honestly, knowing this was really good, because, one day, a man called John a really dirty name as he was leaving the room, and John started shouting after him (REALLY LOUDLY!!!), and then he whipped off his tennis shoe and threw it at the wall so hard that it made a HUGE dent! Honestly though, the dent's being there is kind of nice, because John'll pick us up and set us on one of the ledges in the dent. As we sit on it then we're more or less eye-level with him (when he sits), so he doesn't have to lie down all the time to talk to us. We also learned better balance, so that we could ride on his shoulders when he ran around the room. We'd be going so fast and covering so much distance…it's really cool! (Let me tell you, the first time he picked me up to have a ride, the height and the speed with which he picked me up nearly made me vomit. Every time that I had been that high, or *nearly* that high before, I had either been in his shirt pocket, his shirt sleeve or other places where I could not *see* how high up I was. So, the first time that he picked me up and I was in his hand and could fully see everything, well, it was quite an experience, let me tell you! I nearly hyperventilated, but fortunately he noticed, and he slowly raised me up the rest of the way to his shoulder. I'm not scared of heights, per se, but if I'm in a situation like that, where I could fall *very* easily, it's kind of nerve wracking.)

John learned to keep his voice down better and how to walk as stealthily as one his height can. We also learned the best hiding places "on" him. So far, the top three are his shirt pocket, his shirt sleeve, and the stiff collar of his shirt at the back of his neck. Twice we had to hide IN his hair (the men showed up when we were on the ledges in the wall created by his shoe-throwing incident, so we only had the time to jump off of the ledges into his hair.), which was *okay*, but it was still a little weird.

We'd surprise each other, too. For example, one day, when Tim said he wished he could stop sleeping on the floor, John searched around in his pockets and produced a huge, unused tissue which he proceeded to fold over and over again until it looked like a thick soft mattress that was big enough for all four of us. One night we surprised John by secretly teleporting three pairs of his clothes from his dresser on the campus in the middle of the night. Then we folded them up, laid them sort of near his head, and grew them. We used Sarah's bar ladder to get back over his arm into bed. His reaction was the BEST! He started jumping around (so up onto Sarah's platform we went) and whooping and hollering (so we clamped our hands over our ears). Sarah turned him invisible and he changed into a clean pair of clothes (Jeans, red, white, and blue plaid shirt, clean socks, and cowboy boots.) almost immediately, going on about how good it felt to be wearing clean clothes. The other pairs of clothes and pair of tennis shoes we then shrunk and hid on one of the upper-most ledges of the shoe dent; that way the men wouldn't see them when they came in each day for either inspection or "show-and-tell." Honestly though, the men haven't even noticed that he has been wearing different clothes and shoes every time, so I don't think they would have even noticed clothes lying around everywhere, but whatever.

One of the most important things we learned was how to work well as a team with John. The others lost all anxiety around him and we even created games we could play with him!

Life was looking up (sort of), except for the fact that we were trapped, and John was over 450 feet tall (we kinda need to fix that). We were happy. But then, one day, everything changed.

John's Narration:

It started out like any other day. We had just eaten breakfast and we were talking quietly when I heard approaching footsteps.

"Hide!" I whispered urgently. "They're *way* early!" They leapt up and I put them in my shirt pocket. The door slammed open no more than fifteen seconds later and four men whom I didn't recognize dragged someone inside.

The person was screaming at them in words I couldn't understand. I looked down. They were dragging in a young-ish girl. She was fighting them and yelling at them in what I finally realized was a foreign language. She had black hair in a thick braid almost to her hips, and she had on an elaborately decorated shirt and jeans with something that very closely resembled leather chaps over them. I wondered why she wasn't using a power to fight back, but then I saw a thick, glowing, metal-looking anklet strapped around her leg and I wondered if that was one of those "power-restraining bands" that Priti had warned me about. One of the men said something to her and she looked up. She paled but maintained a brave composure. The men used her moment of distractedness to throw her to the ground, and then they left her there, laughing.

I watched her quietly. She was sitting on the ground, knees to her chest, and she was crying softly, which really hurt.

"Hey," I said softly.

She looked up and yelled something at me in that same strange language. I had no idea what it was, but based on the tone and facial expressions that accompanied it, I figured it was something along the lines of, "Go ahead! Eat me and get it over with!"

"I'm not going to eat you," I said.

She stared at me again with a look of complete confusion.

"Do you speak English?" I asked.

She shook her head.

"Do you understand English?"

She nodded, looking at me both cautiously and curiously.

"Look," I said, "I'm not gonna hurt you. The men think I'm harmful, but I really don't want to be. I'm not actually under their mind control; they just think I am, and I act like it when I have to to convince them that I am. You're safe in here. My name is John."

She sat there for a minute, thinking, then she nodded at me, "Kitaileeo." She pointed to herself. (Pronounced: Kit-i-lee-oh)

"John, can we get out now? Are they gone?" Sarah whispered.

"Yeah, sure," I said.

I placed my hand, flat, palm up, next to my pocket, and they climbed out onto it. I lowered them down to the ground and they went over to Kitaileeo. Katie knelt down and unlatched her power-restricting band using her power. Kitaileeo rubbed her ankle where the band had been and looked up at the others semi-nervously.

"What's your power?" Sarah asked.

Kitaileeo responded in the language and Priti's eyes got wide.

"TukaTapei?" Priti asked.

Kitaileeo nodded vigorously. "Sela! Kuten Larohey?"

The two of them started talking quickly. The rest of us looked at each other; Tim shrugged.

"Uh, Priti? What's going on? Translation please?" Katie asked her.

"Oh! Sorry," she said, "She's a ClanaTupek, a descendant of the original inhabitants of Nordiaho. My Dad is one, so I can speak their language, TukaTapei."

Katie screwed up her face. "Hey, Priti, I just wanna try something, I want to see if I can possibly speak TukaTapei. I understand a lot of languages, so I want to see if this language might match or parallel one of them. So how would you say 'Hello, how are you?' in TukaTapei?"

"Sure," Priti nodded. "Ahnero Katan Kikeepan."

Katie burst into a grin. "It's a blend!"

"What?" Tim asked.

"It's a blend of several different languages that

different groups of people on Earth speak! And I happen to know all of them!" Katie explained, then she took a deep breath. "Leeohora, Anilaphero."

Priti grinned, "Yes! Yes! That's it!" she shouted. "How did you figure that out?"

Katie shrugged. "Plentan Koa; I just guessed."

Kitaileeo clapped her hands and beamed.

* * * * * *

When one o'clock came around and it neared the time when I would be displayed (sigh), we started trying to adjust Kitaileeo to getting onto my hand. (By the way, if Katie or one of the others doesn't say the translation for what Kitaileeo says, I'll have Priti stick it inside of parentheses for y'all readin' this.)

"No, Kitaileeo, you have to hide! And there's nowhere else to hide in here but on me since there's literally no furniture or anything!" I tried explaining to her for the fifth time.

She looked up at me and yelled something.

"She said, 'No, John; I can hide on my own. For you do not yet know my power,'" Priti translated.

I sighed. "She keeps saying that! But she won't tell us *what* her power is! AGH!" I flopped onto my back.

"The ClanaTupeks all have rare and special powers, but they aren't allowed to tell anyone what they are," Priti explained. "It's a belief of their clan that if they tell anyone their powers will diminish."

"So, though we don't know her power, we're supposed to just leave her to her own devices? You know they're gonna make me stand up! What will she think? How will I keep track of where she is if she's HIDING?!" I stood up and threw my hands up in the air.

"Trastae ne," Kitaileeo tugged on my shoelace.

"She said, 'Trust me,'" Katie said.

I cleared my throat. "Fine," I said, "just... be careful, please!"

She nodded. "Ayellah." (She said "Yes." ~Priti)

I heard footsteps and I bent down. I held out my hand and the others jumped on. I put them in my pocket and then I looked down just in time to see a bright flash of light, and then I couldn't see Kitaileeo. The door opened below me and four men in robes filed in. I sighed. These "displays" of me are SO irritating! I mean, imagine that you were an exhibit in a museum because you looked different and you had to do everything you were told. I can't WAIT until we bust out of here!

The men who came into the room were leading another man who looked old and blind. The old man sat, and they sat around him in a semi-circle. The man looked at me. I squatted, resting on my heels, and looked back at him. He was definitely blind; even from my height, I could tell that his eyes were milky and clouded.

He cleared his throat. "Grant," he coughed, "tell me, how old is this giant you've brought me to see?"

"We don't know sir," Grant shrugged. "We're guessing over twenty-five."

"Over twenty-five you say, hmmmm?" the older man said.

"Yessir," Grant said.

"I doubt that. How old are you son?" he asked me kindly.

"Eighteen and a half," I said.

"Eighteen and a half? Why! He's only a boy you bald-headed dingbats!" he exclaimed, punctuating it by hitting Grant on the head with his cane (with incredibly accurate aim for a blind man). "Over twenty-five! HA!"

He sounded like George, Madame's lawyer in that old movie "The Aristocats"— scratchy voice, energetic, and kindly. The last trait something I would hardly have expected from one of…them.

"Are you feeding him? Giving him water? Did you even think to give him a blanket or a pillow?" the man asked.

"Um… no, no, and no," another man replied.

The old man sighed. "I work with a bunch of nincompoops. You have no idea how to take care of a child apparently. Leave, everyone. I would like to talk to with him, alone. And Grant?" Grant stopped on his way out the door. "If you eavesdrop, if *anyone* does, they will be FIRED! Am I clear?"

Grant and the others nodded and closed the door behind them.

"So," the man said, looking upwards. "How are your friends?"

I didn't know what to say. I bit my lip nervously. I heard several gasps over the headset.

He smiled at me. "Don't worry child. I won't tell. I'm only pretending to be a part of this operation so that they don't kill me."

"How did you know?" I asked softly.

"My power is extremely enhanced senses and the complete mastery of unarmed combat. So, for example, though it may look like I'm blind I actually have better sight than most people. I can see the small lump in your shirt pocket, and I can hear them too." He smiled warmly. "You are a good friend to have kept them all safe. Would they come out to see me?"

"Oh, uh, guys? Did y'all hear him?" I mumbled.

"Yeah, we'll come out," Tim said over the headset.

They climbed out of my pocket onto my hand and I set them on the ground carefully.

"Kitaileeo," Katie whispered.

She appeared. "Påpa!" she exclaimed. (Grandfather) They hugged each other.

"I thought you were dead, dear child! When I heard you were captured during the raid on Veloto I feared the worst! Once I discovered that you had been brought in here, I had to come find you! I am glad that you were put in with him. If you had been put in with Vashtir we wouldn't be together right now." He shuddered.

"Who is Vashtir?" Tim asked.

"Vashtir is the last of the Ganotas." He paused, and Tim and Priti gasped.

"What is a Ganota?" I questioned.

"A Ganota is a giant yellow cat with black stripes and a large mane of hair. It has great stealth, and strength, and large, powerful wings, and it breathes fire. They were thought to be extinct," Priti explained. "I'm assuming that Vashtir is Mom's Ganota, Sheelian, under the SCL's mind ray. Sheelian was captured last year. Ganotas are actually very gentle, and they only eat Varsheeras. That's it. But they were killed off because people thought they were dangerous because of how they looked." She sighed sadly, and I snorted and muttered to myself that I knew how they must have felt. "Mom and Aunt Catherine each saved one, a male and a female, to breed and restart the species, but in the middle of the night, the government stole Sheelian, my mom's Ganota, the male. Now all hope for the species is lost. Or so we thought."

Tim brightened. "Yes!" he shouted. "If Vashtir really

is Sheelian, what if we reverse the ray's influence and then get him back! Then we could restart the species! Both he and Rahastira, the female, are only two years old by now, so there's still a chance! You know, it was losing him that made Mom so cold and closed-off. I think it made her realize that if the government could get away with taking Sheelian then they might be able to get away with taking the rest of us. She worried all the time that they would take us away from her…," he trailed off sadly.

"Guys, what about our escape plan?" I asked quietly. "The Summer Solstice Eclipse Festival is in two days' time! I thought we were breaking out then. It's our best chance. And if we break *in* to get Vashtir, we'll give ourselves away and lose all chances of escaping! I mean, what if they realize that I'm not under their control, and take you guys to Vashtir's cell and then redo the mind control on me when y'all aren't around to stop it?"

"But! But! JOHN! Saving an extinct species! Well, not really extinct, but you get the POINT! How can you turn your back on this?" Priti yelled desperately, with a stubborn look in her eyes that I've come to recognize as a BAD thing.

"Priti," I lay down on my stomach and looked her in the eye (well, sort of), "I know this is important to you, but we have to get out of here first. We won't be able to rescue Shelan,"

"Sheelian," she corrected.

"Sheelian while we're trapped in here. We can come back for him, okay?" I said calmly.

"But…but…you… kanaki pleerohog!" she yelled.

Tim, Katie, Kitaileeo, and the old man stared at her in utter disbelief.

"Priti," I started.

"Don't you 'Priti' me, you klingoro hopodo!" she yelled.

"Young lady!" the old man said. "How dare you?"

By this point, I began to get the feeling that the things she was calling me were not only mean (which was what I had originally figured), but were also really, *really* rude! "Priti, what did you say?" I asked.

"Nothing, tutaretardor!" she taunted.

Tim's eyes got wide and his jaw dropped.

"Priti, what did you say?" I repeated, a little more forcefully.

"I said nothing, you...," she began.

"Priti!" Tim yelled. "Stop! How dare you?! John is way more important than Vashtir! Or Sheelian!"

Priti made a "harumph" noise, flipped her hair, stuck her tongue out at me, and turned around with her back to me.

I groaned and muttered underneath my breath. Priti can be almost unmovable when she puts her mind to it, and she has a small temper that can get her into real trouble when it flares, even though that rarely ever happens. "Priti, please don't make me use my size as an advantage!" I pleaded with her.

"Ha!" she turned around. "I don't believe you would!"

"Priti, what is the matter with you?!" I asked, struggling to keep my voice down and the semi-volcanic temper (that I happen to "share" with my brothers) in check.

Katie's Narration:

What the heck is the matter with her? I've never seen her temper flare in such an explosive manner before! I mean, even on the rare occasions when John has lost his temper (usually when another student is racist to me or something like that), he has never been dealing with someone being this flat out rude! For heaven's sake! She called him a… Okay, I'm actually not going to repeat any of it: it was that bad! But now, she's taunting him TO HIS FACE! He's turning red, she's been insulting him so much! Just the things that she's said in English that he can understand would be enough to make even the calmest, most emotionless person explode! So, if you ask me, he's doing a VERY good job keeping his temper under control.

Poor guy! Everyone just recently got over their nervousness around him, and now she's taunting him to do the very things that made her so scared of him in the first place! This is the stupidest case of irony!

Oh no! She just called him a really mean name! I can see small beads of perspiration on his forehead, and his lower lip is turning white, he's biting it so hard!

"You're too scared to do anything because you think everyone'll run from you, behemoth. So, ha!" she taunted.

What has come over her? I mean really?! His gaze hardened. Like the others, I backed up slowly, moving away from Priti.

In one fluid, lightning-fast movement he grabbed Priti and put her in his jeans pocket to shut her up.

Ouch! That's gotta hurt! His jeans pocket, no matter how big it may be, is probably really cramped, all smashed up against his leg like that. She's trapped too, if I had to guess. The pocket's probably too tight to get out of.

Frankly, at the moment, I can't say I pity her. She was far, FAR too rude. Curse words like that should not be used to label a person, no matter what language you say them in.

Priti started to scream. John sighed and put his hand over his jeans pocket. She stopped.

I can see the pain in his eyes. It's VERY obvious that he hates this, but, then again, he was kinda put up to it.

"What did she call me?" he asked us, almost threateningly.

"Uh… John? You probably don't want to know. I mean, I'll tell you if you just *have* to know, but…," Tim trailed off slowly.

John squatted. Priti yelled "OW!", but then she shut up.

John's Narration:

Really! Just the things she said in English were 'nough to make me boilin' mad. I mean, I feel a *little* bad for keepin' 'er in my jeans pocket. I'm sure it's uncomfortable, seein' as how ev'ry time I move she gets squashed, bend'd, contorted, and smashed up agin'st me, but you know what? I don't give a darn! She can stay in that dang thing for...

Why does my drawl always surface when I'm hoppin' mad?

"Was it that bad?" I asked tentatively.

"Um... yeeeeeaaaahh," Tim muttered.

The older man (whom I think had been totally forgotten about), coughed quietly. "I'd best be going kids. Godspeed to The Revolution!" he smiled at all of us, then he gave something to Katie and something to Tim and whispered to them briefly. He kissed Kitaileeo, told her something, slipped something into her hand, and then he left.

I lay on my back, thinking, my anger slowly subsiding. I paled suddenly. "Oh, my word! What have I done?!" I yelled jumping up.

Katie's Narration:

He leapt up, jumping into the air in a flash of motion. When he landed, we flew so high up in the air that we literally were thrown ABOVE HIS HEAD! (Don't ask me how that works exactly. All I can see as a logical guess is that it had something to do with super strength or something.) He gasped and, bending over, caught Tim, Sarah, and Kit. I tumbled down and down and down. *"Why can't he see me?"* I thought. *"What's wro…"* WHUMP!!!

* * * * * *

'I'm dead; I've gone to heaven; I'm surrounded by gold,' was what I thought first, after I became conscious again. I tried to stand up, but I couldn't. I was wrapped tightly in something, wrapped so tightly in whatever it was that I couldn't get free.

"Guys!" a voice below me said. "Wh-where's Katie?" It was John, sounding terrified.

'Excellent question,' I thought. *'Where am I?'*

"Oh no!" John moaned. "This is all my fault! What are we going to do?"

"John!" I wanted to scream, to shout, "I'm okay! I'm right here!" But I couldn't, because I had no idea where "here" was.

My arms were stuck but my fingers and hands weren't. I felt around. It was soft, and warm and also golden-ish. A flash of inspiration. Could it be? I think it is. But how do I tell? Maybe I…WHOOOAAHH!!! I plummeted down to the ground.

Yep, I am where I think I am.

CHAPTER 9

Katie, TRAPPED!

Stuck! Tangled! Pinned down! "And in what?" you may ask. Well, I'll give you a hint… actually, never mind. I'll just tell you. I. Am. Stuck. In. His. HAIR! Yeah! I know! How am I supposed to get out of this one? And guess what?! My blasted earpiece fell out! Now I can't use that! Agh!

At the moment, he's pacing the room, muttering to himself about how this is all his fault and if he doesn't find me, he'll be devastated. Sweet, but I wish he'd stop talking for just a moment so that he could hear me yelling at him instead of drowning out my yells with his voice.

Wow! Just wow! This is the oddest situation that

I've ever been in. How am I supposed to get out of this? My voice is kind of hoarse from yelling right now. He hasn't heard me either. Sigh! This is really awkward, for me anyways.

"Kitaileeo, do you think you can find her?" I heard Sarah ask.

No answer. I waited. Still nothing. All of a sudden, I heard a whooshing noise. I felt like I was being hit with a ferocious gust of wind. Then the noise stopped. I looked up. Kitaileeo was hovering a mere six inches above my head.

"Kitaileeo," I croaked. She jumped.

"Katie?" She looked around. "Walla Kutopana? Ahna seero kakena poto." (Where are you? I hear you but I don't see you.)

"I'm right here!" I said as loudly as I could. "Look below you!"

She did. "Katie!" she exclaimed. She landed in a crouch next to me. "Aroyo chickay anoto scope?" (Are you all right?)

"Yeah, I'm just trapped," I croaked. "Can you get me out?"

"Ayellah," she smiled. (Yes.)

She knelt next to me and began to untangle me from his hair. The whole time we talked rapidly.

I learned a lot about her in that time. She is nineteen summers old and has lived all her life in the ClanaTupek town of Veloto, a secret village hidden from the whole planet. The ClanaTupeks live in many villages like Veloto, protected by a force-field-like bubble that turns everything inside of it invisible. They created villages like these almost two hundred years ago to escape persecution and to keep their traditions. She has three younger sisters, two younger brothers, and four older brothers. Her older brothers had been delighted when she was born and taught her to hunt, ride, and craft her own weapons before she could walk. She learned how to make anything out of her surroundings and soon became not only the only female hunter in the clan, but the best tracker and crack shot in the whole village — well, besides her older brothers that is. Two weeks ago, an SCL patrol was making its rounds in the forest surrounding the force field when Salateesha, a two-month old, started crying, even though they are all taught not to cry for this very reason. The men charged and discovered

Veloto. They wouldn't have caught anybody, since all of the ClanaTupeks fled, using their special, extremely powerful powers, but, when Kitaileeo's three-year-old little sister got stuck in a Tractoray (basically a mini tractor beam), Kit slammed herself into her sister and was captured instead.

She was put in prison on a false charge, denied a trial, and sentenced to execution by John. She said that she was jailed on a false charge because her family clan had the rarest, most powerful powers on the whole planet, and the SCLs had been trying to get rid of them for years. She alone had *seven rare powers*!!!

Her favorite things to do are to go hunting, weave things, make beadwork or leatherwork, ride horses, and best her siblings (or try to anyways) in athletic feats. Her village, Veloto, covers over 250 egeans. The village is in the middle of the land and is surrounded by lush, thick forests, full of streams, animals, and hideouts. The reason no one had ever found Veloto before was because it is technically in another dimension. The force field sphere had shrunk everything inside of it, and then the sphere itself was hidden in the knothole of a tree. You could enter Veloto only by touching the knothole. Because you had to climb the tree to get to the knothole, and since no one other than the ClanaTupeks climbed the tree, no outsiders had ever found Veloto before. However, since the SCLs had climbed the tree because they thought that there was someone up *in* the tree, they got into the portal completely by accident.

She missed her family and Veloto. She said that the worst part was that they had most definitely relocated the portal by now and she had no idea to where!

* * * * * *

Twenty minutes later she had just finished untangling me, and I had just stood up and stretched, when the scariest thing happened.

"WHOOSH!" John stood up. We steadied ourselves. All of a sudden he leaned forwards and flipped up into a HANDSTAND! Kitaileeo and I barely managed to grab his hair in time to avoid plummeting several hundred feet to the ground and certain death.

We heard clapping below us. We risked a look

down. Tim and Sarah were below him, as was Priti, who had made up with John during my "de-tangling."

"Hey John," Tim yelled. "Can you do a front flip?"

Kitaileeo looked at me in horror, returning my terrified expression.

"Yeah," John said. He sounded like he was smiling. Kit and I, on the other hand, were about as far from smiling as possible. We wrapped our hands in his hair and held on for dear life.

He jumped to his feet, landing with a "BAM", and did a front flip.

I groaned. We were pretty much trapped up here. He couldn't hear our shouts, Kit didn't have an earpiece, they couldn't see us, and apparently John was doing a gymnastics demonstration. We held on tight, waiting, and hoping for the best.

"Can you do a…back flip?" Sarah asked.

"Sure can," John said.

"SHOOM. FLIP. BAM!" He flipped backwards.

Twelve tricks later, I was beginning to feel a little nauseous, when Tim asked John if he could do a trick that would be VERY bad for Kit and me.

"You know the trick where you do a handstand and

then fall into a backbend?" Tim asked.

"Yeah," John said.

"Can you do that from a headstand?" Tim grinned.

OH. MY. GOSH!!! We are going to die!!! After all, John probably weighs, let me see...

He weighed 187 pounds when he was basically six feet and five inches, so he weighs, estimatedly, at more than 450 feet, over 14,025 POUNDS!!! So, if he were to do a headstand, with us "on" his head, we would be crushed in less than half a second!!!! I mean, really, imagine over seven tons on top of you!

Kitaileeo grasped my hand and squeezed it. John flipped up into a handstand. He started dropping himself into a headstand. I held my breath, hoping that, at the last moment, one of the others on the ground would see one of the two of us.

'I can't believe it! He's going to kill us, and he doesn't even know it!' I thought. *'This is the first time I've ever been scared by him! Right now he's terrifying me!!!'*

At just the last second before his head touched the ground however, Kitaileeo pulled me away into another reality. (I know, whaaa?!)

* * * * * *

I'm not sure how long it was until I woke up, but suddenly I felt something warm around me and a warm breeze on me. My eyes fluttered open. I looked up apprehensively. Black, ringed with a blue circle, blue, blue, blue, ringed by tan. What is this? Why is my brain so foggy?

"She's up!" a foggy sounding voice said.

"You did it!" another voice said, muffled.

"You can stop crying, she's fine. You saved her; you didn't kill her. How were you to know?" another voice comforted.

"Nnnnnnnn...," I groaned. "What happened?"

My vision cleared and my thoughts sharpened. *'That's John above me, but what are they talking about?'* I wondered.

"Katie!" Sarah gave me a slightly uncomfortable hug. "Oh, I'm so glad you're okay! When Kitaileeo told us what happened we felt so badly!"

"Oh Katie! I'm so sorry! If I had, you know, smashed you…I…I wouldn't know what to do!" John said. "I didn't know you were on top of my head. I…I…I…," he trailed off, blushed, and looked away.

"What happened?" I asked again.

"Well...," Priti said, kneeling beside me. "After Kitaileeo atom-bounded you, the transportation process was too harsh for you, so when you re-materialized you were out cold, and your heart was barely beating. We tried everything that we could to get you to wake up, and then John had a brilliant idea! John! Tell her!"

John stuttered shyly, "Well, I...I read a book once abo-about some tiny people like y'all compared t-t-to me, and one of them got hurt like you K-katie. They, well, their heart wasn't b-beating, so the...the giant thumped them on...on the chest w-with his finger, and...." He paused, breathing hard.

I could tell he felt awful, like this was all his fault. His cheeks were wet, his face pale, his eyes dull, and his lips without color from his biting them so hard.

"John, John, it's not your fault! Really!" I insisted.

He grimaced. "Yes, it is! If I hadn't fallen asleep in the forest and lost my guard, I wouldn't have been transported back to Earth. If I hadn't been transported, I wouldn't have had to bring myself back. If I hadn't had to bring myself back, I wouldn't have grown. If I hadn't have grown, I wouldn't have been sedated and captured. If I hadn't have been captured, I wouldn't have been grown even more. If I hadn't been grown more, you guys wouldn't have been scared of me; I wouldn't be dangerous; I wouldn't have been turned into a man-eating monster; I wouldn't be a threat; I wouldn't be the kind of person you all have to exercise caution and restraint and be alert around; and, most importantly...," His voice kept getting louder and louder, and now he was nearly yelling. "I wouldn't have nearly KILLED YOU!!!" he yelled deafeningly.

He was boiling mad now, almost the maddest I've ever seen him — mad at himself, but still BOILING mad. I didn't know what to do or what to say. I knew that if I said the wrong thing, it was entirely possible he might explode.

I looked at him. He was kneeling, sitting back on his heels, hands in tightly clenched fists on his knees, scowling, his face red, his muscles straining against the fabric of his shirt, jaw clenched in anger, staring at the small group of us in his shadow below him.

"John, that is NOT true!" I said. "None of that is

true. You're just not thinking straight. Stop beating yourself up and think."

"Oh really?" he said, as a muscle in his neck clenched so hard that we could see the large ridge it made even from all the way down below. "Who nearly crushed you? Who caused you to nearly be eaten? Who alerted the SCLs to where you were because of his size? Who terrified an entire village? Me! I! AM! NOT! HELPING! AT ALL!"

"JOHN!" I yelled. "Take a deep breath! Please, stop talking and listen to me!"

He shut up, livid.

"John, look at me." He looked down at me, and I propped myself up on my elbows. "I'm serious; stop beating yourself up! While SOME of that stuff may be true, you're leaving out a lot of things! For example: Who has two phenomenal powers? Who DIDN'T eat us? Who saved us from the SCLs? Who is an amazing, smart, caring, fantastic friend? You are! So, STOP acting like you are horrible!"

He turned beet red, then stood up, and went and sat in a corner of the room and put his head on his knees. I saw my earpiece on the ground and grabbed it, putting it in my ear again, safe and sound. Kitaileeo started walking over to him.

"Go away!" he mumbled through his arm. "Leave me alone!"

She kept walking anyway.

John's Narration:

I feel like a complete idiot! How could I be so stupid! This is so hard! I hate my height so much! I cannot wait until this ends, that's for sure.

"John?" Someone whispered behind me. "Hyejo Kinowa?" (Can I talk to you?)

"What?" I asked.

Kitaileeo sighed, coming around me into my line of sight.

"Hinde!" She commanded, pointing at my headpiece.

I put my headpiece in front of her; she smiled. She pointed at my headpiece's side tech panel and handed me a tech chip that enlarged in my hand and looked at me expectantly.

"You want me to put that in there?" I asked, perplexed.

She nodded vigorously and pointed again at the chip. I put the chip in a slot and put the headpiece back on my head.

"There, much better," she said.

"Ack!" I yelled, jumping several feet in the air.

She laughed. "Well, I can see that it worked."

"Kit, you're... you're speaking English!" I exclaimed. "How... how is that possible? I can understand you!"

She screwed her face up, confused. "I'm not speaking English; you're understanding TukaTapei."

"What?" I squawked. "How is *that* even REMOTELY possible? I wouldn't know a word in TukaTapei from a character in the Chinese alphabet!"

"Well, it's kind of hard to explain, but I guess you can understand me because, well... it's complicated, but basically the chip allows you to understand any language anywhere! Anyway, I need to talk to you."

"About what?" I asked nervously.

"You."

"Me? Why me?"

"Because you need to know why you are here, why you are the way you are. Three hundred years ago a wolf gave the eldest member of our tribe a leather-bound book. The book contained a detailed prophesy concerning Nordiaho. It went like this:

Kitaileeo's retelling of the prophesy:

Nordiaho, a fair planet in the Grindian galaxy, would be overtaken one day by a group of evil men who would worm their way into the near-highest levels of The Government. These men would stop at nothing to rule the universe. They would appear too powerful to be stopped, but have hope! For a force would come that WOULD stop them!

The force would seem unlikely to be able to stop them, just a group of youngsters, but, do not be fooled! Although there would also be brave helpers to arise in dire times of need, the force would mainly consist of seven individuals who would take the following traits:

One would be Smart, Unprejudiced, Caring, Master of her powers, Calm under duress, an Earthling, and Water-Cay. (Katie)

Another would be Quick on his feet, rough around the edges, Master of his powers, Master of any weapon EVER created, from any planet, from any galaxy, any universe, Strong-Willed, Dare-Devilish, a Nordiahoan, and Fire-Cay. (Tim)

Another would be Sweet, Shy, Quiet, Agile, Clever, Well able to use her powers, an Earthling, and Flora-

Cay. (Sarah)

Another would be Brilliant, Caring, Calm, Certain, Definitive, Using her powers carefully for the Greater Good, a Nordiahoan, and Fauna-Cay. (Priti)

Another would be Smart, Master of her many powers, an Excellent Tracker, Shot, and Hunter, Clever, Agile, a ClanaTupek, and Wind-Cay. (Kitaileeo)

Yet another would be Silver-Tongued, Rough, Agile, Defiant, Slightly untrusting, Clever, Tough, Dare-Devilish, Quick, a BackStreet/BackWoods Boy, a Hunter, Tracker, CrackShot, a Nordiahoan, and Blood-Cay. (Yet to come)

And the last one would be Agile, Caring, Kind, Generous, Brave, Strong, Quick-On-His-Feet, Clever, Noble, a True Leader, a Moral compass, a Master of his powers, an Earthling, Extraordinarily Tall for a Reason, and Earth-Cay, The Foundation. (Guess all you smart people. Extraordinarily tall... Who *could* this be?)

These seven individuals would find each other and bond. They create the seven "elements," that, when put all together, become an unstoppable force: Earth, The Foundation; Water, The Map; Wind, The Free

Spirit; Flora, The Knowledge of The Earth; Fauna, The Help of The Animals; Fire, The Courage And Blazing Strength; and Blood, The Driving Force, The Life Giving "Sustenance."

Three Earthlings, three Nordiahoans, and one ClanaTupek would stop the injustice and save Nordiaho.

The last one listed, the Earth-Cay, who would be grown to an unfathomable height of over thirty cubitos, about 646 cubitos below the edge of Nordiaho's breathable atmosphere, would, because of his height, at first be shunned, used, feared, run from, laughed at, and scorned. But he would save his friends and help defeat the SCLs, and, in the end, be loved, celebrated, and honored.

This prophesy has been waiting to be fulfilled for over 300 years now!" she finished breathlessly.

"Wow!" I said. "That's…amazing! But…we're missing the seventh element, the last piece."

"I'm sure we'll meet him soon enough. Now, come back over and join the others and stop being a grump."

I laughed. "Oh, thanks." I stood up, and we walked back over to where the others were sitting and waiting.

* * * * * *

"So, you all are planning to escape during the La Chartararia then?" Kit asked us later, adjusting her new earpiece.

I nodded. "Since a total eclipse during the Summer Solstice hardly ever happens, it should be easier to slip out and much easier for the others to blend in with the crowds."

"John, how come you understood what Kitaileeo just said?" Katie asked me curiously.

"It's a long story," I shrugged.

"Do you have a solid plan yet?" Kit probed, redirecting the subject, blushing slightly.

"We think so," Priti said, "however, we don't know how to get past the guards."

"Why, that's simple." Said a voice from above us. We all jumped and looked upwards. I stood up slowly.

Along the ceiling ran huge, industrial-style air ducts. One of the vents had a hand sticking out of it, unscrewing the screws at the corners with a knife. I was out of sight of whoever was in the air duct, so, without anything for a size reference, I don't think whoever it was realized that the ducts were over 600 feet from the floor.

I reached up and slid my fingernail a tiny bit beneath the vent. I pulled a little, and the screws shot out as I pulled the flimsy vent away. I had done this so that I could see who was in the vent, but, of course, I had forgotten that the person's hand was stuck through the metal slats of the vent.

"AAAAAAHHHHH!!!" The person yelled as they got pulled out into the air with the vent. I leaned forwards and snatched whoever it was out of the air, saving him/her from certain death.

CHAPTER 10

The Seventh, Blood

"LET ME GO!" the person yelled. "Make this robot-thing let me go or I *will* disintegrate him!"

I gulped a little, not in the mood to be disintegrated, and set "it" on the floor.

"Sorry about that," Sarah said, "but you would've died from the fall had he not caught you."

"Hmmm," the person muttered, turning to look at me. "He's very realistic looking. How'd you get enough parts to make him so big?" For some reason he thought I was a robot or something.

"Um... he's not a robot; he's real," Katie said quietly.

"What?!" The person jumped. "No, no, no, no, giants aren't, no, you wouldn't be here if he were real;

you'd be dead. All the giants I've seen or unfortunately run into have tried to eat me. He can't be real! It just isn't possible."

I lay on my stomach behind him. "Turn around," I breathed.

Katie's Narration:

John's breath blew the boy's lion's mane of hair forwards and it swirled around his face and in front of his eyes. He became rigid, fear in his eyes like none I've ever seen. He turned around slowly, uncertainly.

John's Narration:

He stared at me for what seemed like hours, taking me in.

He had *dark* black hair, sort of long, untidy, swept to the side. The most startlingly blue eyes I've ever seen stared up at me from an almost perfect face. He was tall; he came up to the bottom of my nose (when I'm lying on my stomach anyway) instead of, like the others, to my upper lip or below. He wore black jeans with a hole in the right knee, heavy-duty, black, lace-up, combat-style boots, a red shirt that was a little too tight, showing off his rather large abs and biceps, fingerless black gloves, a leather jacket, black with a little red "piping" on the sides and arms, a utility belt *chock-full* of weaponry, and quick draw holsters hanging from his belt on either hip, tied to his leg with "piggin' strings", complete with black pistols with engraved silver plates on their grips and barrels.

I blinked. That was all it took. He whipped his hands forwards, blue bolts shot out of his gloves, and I went flying backwards and slammed, *hard*, up against the wall.

"Should I kill 'im?" he asked in a deep voice, with a tone that implied he'd be pleased to do just that.

"Put him down!" Katie commanded, in the most authoritative voice I've ever heard her use, *ever*.

He dropped his hands, the bolts ceased to flow from his gloves, and I slammed to the ground. I untangled my arms and legs and then stood up.

"HEY!" he shouted below me. "Are you trying to intimidate me? 'Cause it ain't workin' bud."

I sighed, well, half-way between a sigh and an extremely suppressed laugh. "If I were trying to intimidate you, I would pick you up and dangle you by the collar of your leather jacket," I replied.

"Are you gonna eat me or not?!" he yelled up to me.

"Of course I'm *not* going to eat you! Why would I do that?" I said.

"Uh...," he stuttered, confused, "Beeecause that's what giants DO."

I laughed. "I may be tall *now*, but I wasn't always. Just two weeks ago, I was as tall as you are. I may have even been a little shorter," I smiled.

He looked at me oddly. "You mean *you're* The Definitavidito?" he asked incredulously.

"Yes, he is," Kit said.

"The what?" Sarah mumbled.

"NO WAY! REALLY?! I never thought I'd get to meet him! To think! I'm alive during the prophesy's unfolding!" he said, grinning.

"What's your name?" I asked.

He stiffened. Why I don't know. Maybe he was the seventh element, and was, as the prophesy said: "Slightly Untrusting...a BackStreet/BackWoods boy."

"Why should you care?" he snapped.

"Well, how else are we supposed to get to know you if we don't know your name? Do you want us to address you as 'it' every time we talk to you?" I countered.

He sighed, mumbling under his breath. "You can call me Virgil. Happy?" he flippantly returned.

"Nice to meet you, Virgil. I'm John," I said sarcastically.

"Yeah, I know. You're Jonathan 'John' Matthew Phillips. She's Katie Eagle Cross; she's Sarah Faith Powers; he's Tecumseh 'Tim' Sollema Lordsworth; she's Priti Kitania Lordsworth; and she's Kitaileeo Winnipehoe Chickoreeah," he said, pointing to each of us in turn.

"Oooookay, how do you know that?" Sarah asked.

"The prophesy says your names. At the very bottom, you know, like in the 'post-script' as you Earthlings call it," Virgil said, confused slightly.

Kitaileeo nodded. "I remember reading that once, but then it disappeared. I think my parents got rid of that part in our family's scroll after I asked them if I was a part of the prophesy."

"What was the last name?" Katie asked.

"Peyton S. Catske," Virgil said, blushing.

"Really?! We get to meet a Catske?!" Priti exclaimed. "No *way!*"

"Um, forgive me for asking, but, why is that important?" I asked.

"Catske is *the* royal family! They have been for over *seven hundred years!*" Priti explained.

"Can y'all keep a big secret?" Virgil asked. We nodded. "I'm only telling you this because you're six of the seven elements. You're talking to a Catske right now."

Priti's jaw dropped so low that it practically touched the floor. The others just stared at him in dumbfounded shock. I looked at him curiously.

A member of the royal family was standing in front of, well, really below me, dressed in ragged clothes, weapon loaded, open carrying, with an accent, using slang and shouting up at me. If he really was Peyton, how did a member of the royal family fit the character description: "Silver-Tongued, Rough, Agile, Defiant, Slightly untrusting, Clever, Tough, Dare-Devilish, Quick, a BackStreet/BackWoods Boy, a Hunter, Tracker, CrackShot, and Everything in between, a Nordiahoan, and Blood-cay?"

I was picking up these vibes from him right now, that was for sure, but how did those vibes fit a *prince*?!

I mean, can you see a *prince* as "Silver-Tongued, [and] Rough...Tough...a BackStreet/BackWoods Boy?" I sure can't.

"No way," Priti said incredulously. "*You're* a Catske? I don't believe that *at all*! What's your name?"

He sighed. "Peyton S. Catske."

"What?!"

"No *way*!"

"You're the seventh element?"

"You certainly fit the bill."

"Sweet!"

"Welcome to the group dude!" we all exclaimed over each other.

Everyone gave him high-fives. Well, I didn't, or I would have squashed 'im.

Suddenly we heard something (or rather someone) behind us. "What the blazes is going on back here?"

We stiffened. We knew that voice all too well. It was Earl, my "warden." And, judging where the sound came from, he was walking alongside of my prone body and had been around the area of my lowest rib when he spoke.

Peyton pulled a technological screen out of his

glove in front of him and scrolled across the screen. He was momentarily enveloped in a blue light, and then, when it disappeared, he was no longer dressed like a ruffian, but was standing in front of us in royal garb.

Katie's Narration:

He had on a dark, royal blue velvet shirt with puffed sleeves, finely embroidered with a shield and crest on the front. His pants were the same color and fabric, one leg embroidered all the way down the side. His red leather belt was inlaid with precious stones, and the buckle was solid gold, gilt with silver, and gorgeously engraved. He wore a red velvet cape, edged with white fur, and tall black boots, polished to a high shine. His hair was combed smooth and slicked back, no longer appearing long. He wore rings of precious stones as well, and the chain that secured his cloak was gold, with a clasp of a HUGE ruby, ringed with diamonds. Around the diamonds were alternating emeralds and sapphires. (At least, I assume they were those particular gemstones, although it's highly likely that they were different gems, gems from Nordiaho, that I don't know the names of.) He smiled at us and winked; Priti swooned.

John's Narration:

The others were hiding in my sleeve when Earl appeared. All of them were hidden except for Kitaileeo. Because she was the last to hide, she was still out in the open when Earl appeared. Earl saw her. His gaze hardened, and, before she could even run, he spat on her. I grimaced. I knew I couldn't do anything or I'd ruin my "cover." She looked at him, pure hatred rolling off of her in waves. She raised her hands, threw him into the air, and slammed him to the ground. She pinned him there, and then she looked at me. Her eyes were glowing slightly, and I both realized that she was not herself and wondered if she had some sort of power like shooting lasers from her eyes.

She looked at Earl, then at me, her gaze traveled over me and eventually landed on my mouth. She looked at Earl, then back at my mouth again. I shut it quickly. She raised her hands and jerked them apart; Earl disappeared.

'Oh no! She atom-bounded him!' I thought anxiously.

'But where to?!'

I looked around, wondering, when, all of a sudden, I felt something. I jumped up. There was something in. my. MOUTH! I felt something urging me to swallow. I couldn't! I wouldn't! I fought the urge, which I assumed to be Kitaileeo manipulating my atoms, but I wasn't sure. Finally I beat "it" and spat Earl out. He hit the ground, livid. (Thank goodness he can fly, or he might have died from the fall. Not that I wouldn't wish that on him, but it might raise some questions from the other men in charge. Earl's powers are flight and "multilingualism." He can speak, read, and understand *all* the languages in at least the galaxy, possibly even the universe.)

Earl jumped to his feet and stared at Kitaileeo in complete rage. For a moment or two he seemed to be making up his mind as to what to do exactly about the predicament. Then his gaze hardened. "Jonathan!" He spun towards me abruptly, "Pick her up THIS INSTANT!" he roared.

I gulped slightly, but then did as he asked, so as not to ruin my cover.

He smiled diabolically. "Good. Now, I want you to

put her in your mouth. Right. This. INSTANT!"

I paled slightly. Kit looked up at me from the palm of my hand and winked, assuring me that she would atom bound herself away at the last second. I blew out a breath of relief and did the most horrifying thing I've ever done. I slowly started to raise my hand to my mouth. But then, just when she was about to atom bound herself away, Earl flew up behind her and shoved her into my mouth. She screamed, I gagged, Earl laughed. I threw my tongue up behind her to prevent her from…gag… falling down my throat. I felt her hit it and shuddered with horror.

Earl laughed again, as though he were having the time of his life. "Now, close your mouth."

I had felt Kitaileeo crawling slowly up towards the front of my mouth, but as soon as she heard this she stopped abruptly where she was. Slowly and carefully I closed my mouth. Though weird, it was almost a relief to be able to tell where she was in my mouth. That way I knew that by closing my mouth I wasn't going to, say, bite off her hand by accident or anything. As soon as my mouth shut all the way she screamed. I've never heard anyone scream like that, but then again,

I've never seen anyone in this particular circumstance before. She started pounding at the inside of my cheeks violently and it took all I had to keep from swallowing, slapping my tongue down, spitting her out, or gnashing my teeth, which she was right next to. Earl laughed as she continued to scream. I could hear Katie and Sarah and Priti over the earpiece doing their best to calm her down, and finally she did stop hitting me and screaming, which was a relief.

Earl looked at me. "Now, swallow her." He was smiling and laughing so much and looked much too smug and joyful over poor Kitaileeo that I had half a mind to step on him or somethin'.

I decided not to swallow, but then Earl narrowed his eyes at me. "You know, your Adam's apple, as I believe they call them on Earth, is about the size of a small shuttle, so I can very easily tell that you have not swallowed at all. Now, SWALLOW!"

I slowly, carefully, disgustedly swallowed. I felt her fall back against my tongue again and scream. I shuddered again and resisted the very powerful urge to start dry heaving.

"Good job!" Earl crowed. "Now there are some

things I need to discuss with you."

I nearly freaked out. There was absolutely no way that I could talk when I not only had a person "hiding" in my mouth, but also that person was in front of/under my tongue. If I were to talk and bring my tongue down from being pressed up against the roof of my mouth, either she could fall down my throat or my tongue would crush her, neither of those options good.

"Kit," Katie said frantically over the earpiece. "You have to atom bound. NOW!"

"I can't!" Kit said.

"You can't?! What do you mean you can't?!" Priti yelled desperately over the earpiece, echoing the thoughts that were racing through my head. I could feel the others pressing themselves against my arm, their hearts pounding with the distinct beat of fear.

"I only just learned of my power to atom bound about a week ago. I still haven't quite mastered it yet. That was why I was so hesitant to atom bound you Katie, when we were on top of John's head. I'd never atom bounded two people at once before. I...I can't atom bound when I'm, uh, wet," she said, sounding embarrassed.

At her mention of being wet, I nearly dry heaved again. My mind was also racing at about thirty miles an hour, trying to figure something out.

"John," Kit said. "Just swallow me. You have to."

"NO!!!" Katie screamed before I did (fortunately). "There has to be another way! There has to!"

I know that I was only going to have Katie and myself narrate the story, but, then again, I never expected this to happen, so I'm gonna let Kit narrate here just this once.

Kitaileeo's Narration:

Never, ever have I been in a situation so scary, dangerous, and… disgusting as this! All I can say is, thank goodness he had just brushed his teeth like fifteen minutes ago! I'm not gonna lie; it's still really weird in here. I never expected to have it all end up like this, being swallowed and all. He's done his best to keep me from falling down his throat and from being bitten or anything, which I really appreciate. I can only hope that traitorous dog Earl doesn't expect John to talk back to him or carry on a conversation or

I'm really almost as good as dead.

Earl had been revealing to John his plans for unveiling John to the public, and during that time the others had been working out a plan. Unfortunately, I couldn't atom bound since I was wet, and Tim couldn't teleport live things. So the plan that they came up with was that if Earl asked John a question or asked him what he thought of the plans, I'll sort of tuck myself in the hollow on the inside of his cheek, hold on by sliding my fingers in between his last molars, and hope for the best. I don't think he really liked this plan. After all, he shuddered quite violently when the whole plan was proposed (he can't really *talk* to me, now can he?), but then Sarah asked if he had a better plan and he stopped. Unless he absolutely has to talk though, he'll either nod or shake his head, grunt, or make noises that he can make with his mouth shut.

All of a sudden, I was pitched forwards and nearly deafened. I had never realized that it would be so loud, but then again, I am in his mouth, so I guess I should have figured. He said, "Hmmmm?" basically. But the noise was so loud and the vibrations so intense that I'm still not quite recovered. His whole mouth vibrated, and his teeth moved a little too. I fell onto my hands and knees on the 'floor' of his mouth. Ugh.

Then, horror of horrors, Earl asked him what he thought of the plans. John paused, and I scrambled up and moved into position.

"Sounds great," John lied. I felt like I was in a seatless rollercoaster or something. The mouth movements required to say "sounds great" smashed me up against his teeth, threw me around, and nearly me pitched me into his mouth on top of his tongue. Not to mention, it was so loud that it sounded like he was yelling, even though I knew he wasn't.

"What will you do to the populace to make them truly terrified and make them step in line?" I heard Earl yell up to him. I gulped, for this question would require a much longer answer. I felt John swallow and was drenched with a little saliva.

"I think," John hesitated, "that it would be best just to stomp around and roar a little, just to...," he stopped immediately in mid-sentence. I had lost my grip and had fallen onto his tongue right as he had said "to", and, since his tongue was moving because he was talking, I had landed dangerously close to his throat and was slipping towards it.

"Jonathan, are you all right?" Earl asked.

I felt John nod, right as I grabbed the thing hanging from the back of his throat to pull myself up. All of a sudden, he bit his tongue so violently that it started to bleed, and I realized my mistake. You see, Nordiahoans do not feel any pain when this thing is prodded but humans *really* do! For some it's even something the elders called their "gag reflex." Fortunately for John (and for me) it didn't appear to be. But I imagined I had just caused him an immense amount of pain and he had bit his tongue to prevent himself from crying out. He started to grind his teeth together, and he was also sort of running his tongue in between his teeth, over and over again. The result was that the grinding was both deafening and dangerous, and the result of his running his tongue in between his teeth was that his tongue was moving so much I couldn't get onto it!

"JOHN! STOP!" I yelled. "Grinding your teeth is deafening me and whatever you're doing with your tongue is making it move too much! Also, grinding your teeth is really basically deadly for me! Please stop!" I sobbed the last sentence out. As soon as the sobbed sentence escaped my lips, though I hadn't meant it to, he stopped immediately. I felt myself beginning to grow weak and a little dizzy and for a second I couldn't figure out why. Then, I realized. "John, I need you to breathe through your mouth, not your nose. I know it sounds weird, but if you aren't breathing through your mouth then I don't get any air other than what was in here when you shut it. I'm running out of air in here as I speak. It will also give me a little bit of light. It's dark as the devil's heart in here."

He complied, and I was suddenly able to breathe again as air rushed over me. Heck, even his breathing was loud from my position.

Then, I heard Earl yell up again. "Jonathan, are you all right?!"

I felt John shake his head, then I heard Earl yell up. "Whatever is the matter then?"

I heard John thump his chest and Earl said, "You?" John nodded. Then, I felt John shake his head, and Earl said, "No?" John shook his head again, and Earl said, "Can't?" John nodded again. Then, John opened his mouth wide and pointed to it, and Earl said, "Breathe?!" John shook his head, and Earl said, "Talk?

Is that it? Have you lost your voice?" John nodded vigorously.

'Genius!' I thought. 'He's a complete genius! I just hope Earl will buy it.'

"Well then, I'll just come back later then," Earl said. "Goodbye for now." Then he left, and I heard the door shut behind him.

As soon as the door shut, John doubled over and opened his mouth all the way, holding his open hand underneath it. "Get out," he said, however, since he was talking very carefully and almost painfully because I was still in his mouth and still hanging onto the thing at the back of his throat, it sounded more like, "Git owt." Happily I complied, letting go of the thing, and I fell, sliding down his tongue. But, like a complete idiot, I forgot about his teeth, and I slammed into them hard and fast, for I had built up a bit of momentum during my slide. John and I both let out a cry of pain, but his was more of a yell and mine was more of a cry. He only rubbed his jaw, but, since he's so big compared to me, it probably hadn't really hurt him that much. Because he's so big compared to me it REALLY hurt me, and I lay there curled up into a ball, in pain and unable to move.

"Kit! Are you okay?" Katie and the others yelled over the earpiece. When I didn't answer they yelled, "John, is she okay?!"

I heard and felt John say, "I dunno," and then I saw him reaching carefully into his mouth. I whimpered as he felt along his teeth and his fingers, which were as big as me (or bigger even) and able to crush me in an instant if he wasn't careful, got closer and closer to my prone form.

"Ssssshhhhh. S'okay, I ain't gonna 'urt you Kit," he said, his fingers getting closer and closer. I bit my tongue, trying not to whimper. But when his fingers brushed right past me and he continued feeling around, I started to cry a little, worried that, because I was so small, he'd never ever find me and I'd be stuck in his mouth forever. That thought alone was enough to make me nearly start sobbing, because as kind and thoughtful and amazing and all as John is, being stuck in his MOUTH forever would be AWFUL, HORRIBLE, and DISGUSTING! He heard me crying and realized something must have happened, so he started to backtrack. I kept my mouth shut then and hoped that I wouldn't end up swallowing any of his…

ugh...saliva. His gigantic fingers were now so close to me that, since I was so small compared to them, I could feel the heat radiating off of them. I shivered and began to whimper again. He paused, and then moved his fingers a little closer so that they were right in front of my face. I began to worry that, if he moved them any closer, he'd hit me in the face and smash my face in or something even worse. I managed to get out the words, "Almost there," and then I fainted right as I felt his fingers tap me tentatively. When I woke up I was somewhere with blinding light and he was positioning me onto his palm. I lay there, curled up into a fetal position, freezing cold, sopping wet, and shaking like a leaf.

John's Narration:

"Kit! I'm so, so sorry!" I said. "There was nothing I could do about it; you know that. I'm really sorry about all you had to go through though. I really am! I would never ever do something like that, I swear! I'm sorry that I'm...I'm so scary a-and that I had to...to do that to you. I wish...I wish I wasn't such a... such a...a monster."

She continued shivering constantly, and she showed no sign that she had even heard what I had said. I held her against my chest sadly, trying to warm her up. I felt her "unroll" in my hand and then she sagged against me. I could feel her teeny-tiny heartbeat faintly thumping through my shirt.

We spent thirty minutes like that, dumb in shock and horror and disgust — Kit snuggled against me, me leaning against a wall, Peyton, still dressed in his princely outfit, leaning against my shoe, and Katie, Tim, Priti, and Sarah still in my sleeve, leaning against my arm. I realized then that I had actually never touched Kitaileeo before! The whole time I'd known her (which, admittedly, was not *that* long…), she had insisted on hiding on her own. She refused to ride on my shoulder; she rarely even touched me of her own accord. Yet, now I'd held her…*in my mouth!* And I've been holding her for over half an hour by now, and all she has done is whimper occasionally!

After thirty minutes though Kit whispered, "John, you're not a monster. I forgive you."

I smiled softly.

* * * * * *

We still had not moved when the door opened and shut. This was when everything started spiraling out of control.

I was, as I said, leaning against the wall, the wall opposite the door, and Peyton was leaning against my shoe. I looked down at the door, saw Earl come in, and quickly slid Kit into my pocket.

"Ah, *my* glorious giant," he smirked. "I have…," he trailed off, staring in awe at my left foot.

I looked down and shoved a groan back down my throat. *'Agh! Peyton! How do we explain this?'* I thought.

"Your… your Majesty?" Earl stuttered, bowing low in front of Peyton. "How came ye to come and with thy glorious self grace our humble abode with your divine being?"

Peyton laughed, a deep but light and refined sound. "You flatter me. I was simply here, talking to this giant that you have locked up in here." He waved a be-jeweled hand in my direction. "That is all right with you." He said the last part like a demand or a statement, not a question. What surprised me most was how his voice had changed. It was no longer deep and rough, with a slightly menacing tone to it, but it was light and cheery, rich, and he spoke each word like it was coated in honey.

Earl grimaced. "Of course, Your Highness. But… but he could kill you!"

Peyton laughed again. "Oh no, he is only dangerous when you tell him to be. He's perfectly human and harmless otherwise. As a matter of fact, I enjoy talking to him, so you may add it to your schedule that I shall come here to converse with him every day at around ten. Thank you."

Earl squirmed uncomfortably, at a loss for words. It was hilarious.

"Now, about what I saw you have him do earlier. I am extremely disappointed in you, a council man *and* a government official! And don't look at me like you have absolutely no idea what I'm talking about. I saw you."

"You saw what?" Earl coughed.

Peyton stifled a sigh. "I saw you make him eat her. Sentencing someone to execution by him without the consent or decree of a royal personage? Having him swallow a *girl?!* Whatever came over you? You of all people should know that we do not do things that way on Nordiaho. I am appalled, absolutely appalled! As you know, we on Nordiaho strive to uphold justice and righteousness. Imagine what the public would think if they found out about this. Consider yourself warned, *Earl*. Now, I fear I must go; duties await me. I will see you tomorrow." With that he strode purposefully towards the door and then exited after shooting me a wink and a smirk.

As soon as the door closed after him, Earl snarled. "Jonathan, tomorrow when he comes over, I want you to get rid of him. I don't care what methods you use, as long as they're excruciatingly painful and as long as they get rid of him before tomorrow's ceremonies end! Whatever you have to do, do it. I. Want. Him. Dead. And. GONE! Am I clear?"

I nodded, and he left the room, muttering under his breath the whole way.

* * * * * *

Later, we were discussing and refining our

escape plan thanks to Peyton who, being apparently very knowledgeable about the ins and outs of the compound, had helped us figure everything out. (He had "briefed" us while we were all in our state of shock.) He had provided us with a way to get the others out without their having to worry about being seen by any guards or security cameras. However, we did have one problem… me. My size would be a huge problem (no pun intended). Even if Sarah turned me invisible, it would still be impossible for me both to break out of the building undetected and to walk among the crowds safely. Heck, I'll bet I couldn't even fit through some of the hallways!

But Peyton had, thankfully, helped us think up a way around that as well. He knew of a secret underground passageway beneath the city. It was once used as a water-way to transport huge cargos of goods without clogging up the city. The water was gone now, and the ceiling was high enough that I could crawl along it comfortably enough. There was even a branch of it that ran beneath my "room" (ha-ha, right), so, if I broke the floor, I could just slip into it. Peyton had warned me though that if I was too loud it would never work. He also warned me about the Sojotos, a rebellious group that lived down there, striking back against the SCLs.

Armed with our new information, and satisfied with how our plan had developed, we lay down for the night.

Katie's Narration:

John fell asleep first, then the others drifted off. I lay awake, thinking. My mind swirled with "What ifs." "What if John never shrinks?" "What if we can't escape?" "What if we can't defeat the SCLs?" "What if we never get home?!" and more. But most importantly, and most terrifying, "What if, after we escape, and John has to wait awhile to give us a 'head start', the SCLs decide to give him an extra dose of the mind-wipe serum?! What if I'm not there to prevent it from affecting him, and he turns into a dangerous, bloodthirsty MONSTER?!!"

I stared at him. *'How could anyone think that this sweet person looming above me could be a monster? He's so peaceful, and good looking too. How could anyone this good looking be considered a monster? Who would even mistake him for a monster? Size matters not, in my opinion,*' I thought. His chest rose and fell with each breath he took. His hair had fallen over his eyes, and his lips were slightly parted, revealing a small bit of three perfect, white teeth. It was right then that it struck me just how BIG he really was. We're like teeny-tiny little buds next to the tallest, broadest redwood that ever was. Sure, he hates that we're scared of him sometimes, and I know that he doesn't look or act like a monster, but he could be one. He'd be a terrifying one too. If he were to fall under the influence of the mind-wiping serum, we'd be dead. Possibly the whole planet would be. I mean, imagine if he were to fall under it and then be told to kill us. Peyton, any opposers, no one would stand a chance, not even Kitaileeo! And, even worse, if he were to lose us, the ones who provide him food, and the SCLs refused to feed him to "keep him hungry for people" (ewww!!!), even the mind control serum couldn't keep him in check I'll warrant.

It's kind of hard to show you, but here's a size reference: When John has on cowboy boots that would normally have a heel of about an inch, we aren't even taller than the heel! It would take two of us on top of each other to make the height of his thumb, from the knuckle to the tip. If we were to lie on our sides, we'd barely be longer than the width of his eyes. We're shorter than his jean's belt loops. His fingernails are bigger than our heads. One of us could curl up and fit snugly in the hollow in his palm that appears when he folds his fingers up really tight. I can fit my whole hand underneath his fingernails. *His teeth are bigger than our heads!*

John is so humongous and we're so... so puny, he could literally do anything and get away with it, even, like the SCLs long to do, take over the world, even the galaxy, even the whole entire universe maybe. He could probably do it without a fight also. I mean, do you really think any army would try to fight John? Over 450 feet tall, one look from him would make even the bravest man turn and flee. But John's not like that; he's a truly good guy. If you ask me, he's like a modern-day Captain America, who is one of his idols. I have a feeling that even if eating someone would end the war, even if it was the worst man ever, he wouldn't do it.

I miss having him our size. His being so tall is a

great advantage, and it's cool and all, but I miss the normal John, the real John. I miss the John I can almost see eye-to-eye with when talking. I miss the John who doesn't have a deafening voice and earth-jarring footsteps. I miss the John that I can play board games or card games with. I miss the John with whom I don't have to constantly be alert and fully aware of where all of him is so that I don't get crushed. I miss him so much. We can barely even have normal conversations anymore, and forget about trying to have a private conversation with him. The sheer volume of his quietest voice he can possibly pull off makes that impossible.

As I was thinking all of these things, I heard a rustling noise. I looked up. John was slowly and carefully standing up, trying as much as possible not to shake everything. I thought he was asleep, but I guess not. I think he thought I was asleep as well. I ran as fast as I could and vaulted onto his left shoe. I held on tightly to the laces and looked up, up, up at him.

He moved slowly. I flew up, forwards, and down every time his left foot took a step. He walked slowly over to a corner, stretched, and stood on tiptoes. I heard a rusty scratching noise, like metal on metal. Then, he jumped. I almost lost my grip on his shoelace. The bow came undone because of my weight on the end of the lace, and I went soaring out through only air, holding onto the end of the lace for dear life. It then came sailing back around towards his shoe, and I collapsed on top of his tenni and grabbed onto the laces that were actually attached to the shoe. He pulled himself up, spun around, and landed outside on the roof.

He started to pull his legs into a crisscross position, saw me, let out a yell, slapped his hand over his mouth, and nearly toppled off the roof in surprise.

"Hi," I waved timidly, tamping down laughter.

John's chest heaved. "Katie?!" he panted. "What in the world are you doing?"

"Um... wondering what in the world you're doing," I responded.

He sighed. "Hang on."

He reached over me and hit a button on the other side of the gap he had created. I ducked reflexively as his arm and his torso arched above my head. What looked like rays of light ran up and created a dome over the roof; then they cleared away.

"There," John said. "Now nothing can get through to us, and no-one can see or hear us, er… me."

I laughed.

He slid backwards a little. "Hey, uh, do you want to, uh, sit somewhere more, um, comfortable?" He blushed awkwardly.

"Where do you mean? I would like to get off your tenni though. It's rather bumpy." I smiled up at him.

"Uh, I don't know," he hedged. "You could sit here." He sat up straighter and patted his leg over his pocket. I climbed up and sat down. I looked up at him again. He was staring off at the horizon, at the stars.

"So why did you come up here? And how did you even know this was here?" I asked.

He smiled softly. "I come up here to look at the stars, to think, and, well, I like to be alone. Tim told me about this place. His Dad told him about it, and Tim told me a few days ago because he figured I might enjoy the solitude."

"Oh. So, should I leave then?" I asked.

"No! No. You're fine," he sighed. "Tomorrow we're out of here. It'll be so nice not to be a caged specimen." He paused. "Today was one of the worst days of my entire life. I mean, poor Kit. I really, really hate my height. Do you...do you think that she is scared of me after the, uh, events of this afternoon? 'Cause I know I'd be scared of someone if they nearly... you know... ate me."

I smiled sadly. "No, John, I don't think she's scared of you. It's fine."

He cleared his throat. "Katie, is it weird at all for you?"

"Is what weird?" I asked, confused.

"You know, me. Is it weird for you to be around me? 'Cause it seems to me that anyone around me is in constant peril, possibly staring death in the face. I mean, I could kill someone accidentally, maybe even just by touching them too hard!" He pounded his fist on his knee. I jumped and flew backwards, slamming, hard, into his hip bone.

"Ooohh, OW!" I groaned, falling sideways onto his leg.

"Katie! Katie, are you all right?" He picked me up, laid me on his hand, brought his hand up near his face, and leaned over it anxiously. "Katie! Say something!"

"Stop! Stop!" I laughed. "Your hair tickles!"

"Are you okay?! Please tell me I didn't kill you!" he said, panicked.

"Of course, you didn't kill me you goof!" I smiled. "After all, I'm talking and breathing and all, aren't I?"

"Oh, thank heavens! Did I hurt you?" he asked.

I bit my lip. What could I say? I mean, yeah, it hurt like fire, but he felt bad enough I didn't want to make him feel worse. I took a deep breath. "*You* didn't hurt me...," I started slowly.

"Oh good. Wait... what do you mean, *I* didn't hurt you?" He asked, staring at me in what appeared to be a mix of confusion, amusement, and anger.

"I mean I hurt myself. If I hadn't jumped backwards, I wouldn't have hit your hip bone," I stuttered nervously.

"Ha-ha-ha, right," he smirked. "Very funny. Nice try."

He set me back on his leg. I realized I hadn't ever answered his question. We sat there silently, unsure of what to say to each other.

"You know," he said suddenly. "It may have been annoying, and it may have been weird and awkward, but, all in all, it wasn't half bad. We had some good times, made some good memories. Didn't we?"

"Yeah. Some good times," I said through a yawn. I leaned back against the cool leather of his belt. Lulled by the slow rising and falling movement of his breathing, I yawned again.

* * * * * *

I woke up late the next morning. To my surprise, I was carefully tucked underneath the community quilt. I must have fallen asleep on John's leg last night and he must have "tucked me in." I rolled over, wincing as my back screamed at me. To my amazement, the others were still asleep. But…John was gone. I looked up. Two looooong legs swung from a gaping hole in the roof.

I heard a deep voice singing low in the bass range. I continued to look up, now startled. I used my power to float up and I grabbed onto John's pant leg near the knee. I carefully climbed up, then sat down next (well, sort of anyways) to him. He hadn't seen me.

He was singing "Edelweiss." Quite well too. I had no idea he could sing. He'd never said anything about singing, and honestly, I had naturally assumed that he had never brought it up because he didn't sing well. Boy, was I wrong!

He finished "Edelweiss" then he switched to "Deep in the Heart of Texas," a song which (pardon the pun) I know by heart. He sang it quite soulfully, and the way he sang sounded almost like he was homesick.

I couldn't help myself; I joined in. "The stars at night are big and bright…"

John jumped. "Katie! Stop! Doing! That! Agh!"

"Sorry," I smiled shyly. "Can you believe that today's the day?!"

"No, I can't," he sighed. "Katie, I… I'm worried. What if something goes wrong?"

"John, we'll be fine. Now, we'd better go wake the others, eat breakfast, and prepare. The others and I have to leave in 45 minutes. You have to leave in two and a half hours, during the eclipse," I said.

"Yeah," John said. He 'swung' me up onto his shoulder. "Hold on tight!" he cautioned as he hit the button, jumped down, and closed up the roof.

The others woke up when he hit the ground. "Oh, thank goodness it's just you and Katie!" Tim exhaled, after leaping to his feet groggily and assuming a battle position. He relaxed when he saw who it was.

"Guys, we have to get ready; we only have 45 minutes until we bust out of this horrid place!" I said energetically.

They nodded and we began to get ready. First we ate; then we got dressed in our super suits and loaded up on our weapons. John, who couldn't get dressed in his super suit just in case the SCLs came in, paced around nervously. Finally, we had to yell at him to stop it. He kept launching us into the air with every footfall, and we were handling firearms! He blushed, then he sprawled out onto the floor, mumbling into his arm what sounded like a prayer and a few nervous what ifs.

Once we were all prepared and had rehearsed our plan in detail, John knelt in front of us. He held out his hand, and we all hopped aboard. He held us up to the air vents, to the certain one that had no cover on it, thanks to Peyton and John, and we pulled ourselves up through the hole. I went last. I paused, turned back, and firmly squeezed his thumb. He smiled at me and winked. Then I climbed into the air vent.

Once up in the vents I hesitated a second. Tim

noticed. "C'mon Katie! No sweat; he'll be fine! He can take on anyone. Trust me." I smiled. We had a plan and we were ready to execute it.

CHAPTER 11

Escapes And A Complication

John's Narration:

Bored, bored, bored, bored, bored, bored, BORED! This is going to be the longest two hours of my life! They left half an hour ago and now I have almost nothing to do! There's no-one to talk to, and this blasted room is so bare that there's nothing to do at all! I groaned. I'd been lying on my back, staring at the ceiling for about fifteen minutes, when I heard the door crack open. I jolted up and stared at it. Peyton strode in, and I exhaled in relief.

"Good morning John!" he said softly, closing the door behind him.

"Peyton, you have to leave! Now!" I said nervously.

"Why? What's wrong? Don't you want me to be here?" he asked, sounding hurt.

"No, it's not that. I'd actually love the company, but…," I hesitated, "they, Earl anyways, wants me to… to kill you."

Peyton went rigid and all the color drained from his face. "Well, that would be… easy enough for you, wouldn't it?"

I reddened. "Please don't say things like that."

He blushed a little, although not enough to bring all the color back to his face, "Sorry. So, should I be running right now?"

"Ha-ha-ha. Very funny; you're hilarious," I said sarcastically.

"No, I'm serious. Are they going to kill me? Are you going to?" he gulped.

"Peyton," I said softly, "I…I thought we were friends."

"No, we are, but… well, don't take this the wrong way John, but you're a…a." He swirled his hand in the air, as if searching for the right thing to say. "A possibly, um, dangerous friend to have…," he trailed off.

No one's perfect, and I'm no exception. I have a

slight temper (that same semi-volcanic temper that I "share" with my brothers whom I mentioned earlier), and what he said... hurt. I bit my lip and shoved a growl down my throat. Before I did anything rash, I spun on my heel, ran, jumped, and climbed onto the roof. I pulled my legs up, hit the ray-shield-generator button, spun around so I could see through the hole in the roof, and looked down.

Peyton was running towards the corner. He was going at quite a good clip, *however*, since from the door where he was standing to the corner was *at least* over two miles to him, I figured it would take him a while.

* * * * * *

"John?" Peyton yelled up at me.

I had been watching him "progress" for a *long* time. It was really hard not to laugh actually. What took me like five strides took him like 30,000 strides!

"Peyton, I already told you; I'm not coming down, and you're *waaaayyy* too short to come up," I said, annoyed.

"Look, John, I'm sorry I said what I did okay? Now would you please come down?" Peyton pleaded.

"No," I said.

"John, please! It's urgent!" Peyton desperately cried.

"Yeah, right. Because whenever something's urgent, the first thing the messenger does is freak out that their *friend* is going to KILL THEM!" I shouted sarcastically.

"Ow, that hurt. I'm sorry! Please, you have to listen to me! They're getting suspicious of you! They're going to install security cameras tomorrow, after the festivities end! You have to leave soon!"

"I <u>AM</u> leaving soon! As a matter of fact, as soon as the alarm on my watch goes off, I am *literally* breaking out of here," I sighed. "I'll come down *if* you stop being such a fraidy-cat. Deal?"

Peyton nodded, "Deal. And I'd shake on it, but…." I laughed. I turned and hit the the button. "Move or get squished," I warned, then I jumped down and landed in a sort of ninja-like crouch "next to" Peyton.

"Well, you weren't kidding big fella," Peyton chuckled, "but I feel like you should've added something like: And be sure to brace yourself against

SOMETHING because when I hit the ground it'll jar the earth and throw you over 50 feet in the air! So be careful!"

We both laughed. "Sorry," I said.

"By the way, what's a watch?" Peyton asked me.

I laughed again, a little loudly. Peyton clapped his hands over his ears. "Sorry!" I whispered. "A watch is a time-keeping device. They're very popular on Earth." I took mine off and laid it on the ground in front of him. "Of course, they're not normally this big, but…yeah."

He clambered up on top of it and stared down through the glass. It was a self-winding watch with an exposed mechanism, and he appeared to be enchanted with the spinning gears and inner mechanisms. Of course, the normally minuscule pieces of the watch were about as big as his head, but he seemed enraptured by it.

"This is the most advanced technology I've ever seen in my life!" he exclaimed. "This is incredible!"

I couldn't help laughing again, I couldn't believe that he thought this was more high-tech than Nordiahoan tech. I mean, just from what I'd seen, his tech made

Iron Man's tech look almost Stone Age, but I decided to play along. "If you think this is great, just wait until you see a cell phone or a computer."

"A what?" he asked. His face was glowing as he stared down at my watch; he seemed to be drinking it all in.

"Here, I'll show you," I said, pulling my cell phone out of my shirt pocket. "They're also not normally this big, but this is a cell phone."

I set it on the floor next to my watch and lay down on my chest near it and pulled it nearer to me. Peyton ran over and climbed up onto the screen. I turned it on, and he let out a cry of delight when my screen lit up, revealing my lock screen photo, a picture of my older brothers and myself imitating a photo from the Young Riders TV show we loved. The three of us were in old western style clothes, standing in front of some old western style buildings that sort of resembled those in Sweetwater. We were pointing our six-shooters at the camera so that they half concealed our faces.

"Is that on Earth?" Peyton asked me. He was sitting cross-legged on my phone screen, and it was all I could do not to laugh at him. "Is it a photo-taker?" he asked.

"Well, yes, it is on Earth, and yeah, it's sort of a photo taker. It's also something that you can play games on, and read things on, and listen to music on, and stuff like that," I replied.

"Can you show me pictures of Earth?!" he asked. He was sort of bouncing in his "seat," and it was cracking me up. He reminded me of my friend Nick in an Apple store.

I chuckled. "Sure." I opened the photos app and started scrolling. The first picture to appear was a photo that Katie had taken at the college basketball game. It was a great one of me halfway to the hoop in a slam dunk (yes, I play basketball BTW). Then a picture of Katie, Sarah, Jimmy, Kid and I at a park. Then a photo of a field by the college, wildflowers all in full bloom. (Texas has some amazing wildflowers; y'all should see 'em!) A photo my brothers sent me of my bronc, Dead Ringer (He's not really a bronc anymore, but that's what we call 'im) in a majestic rearing pose. The college Christmas party decorations. The decades dance. Football in the snow with a bunch of friends. The arboretum "field trip." And many, many more. Peyton, of course, had questions about every single one.

We spent the hour with my showing him photos and answering his questions as best as I could. He sat on the corner of my phone screen, near the bottom and I lay on my stomach with my chin propped up on one hand, sort of lying partly over the phone, using my other hand to scroll through photos for him. It was awesome and hilarious and fun all at the same time.

"Oh, John, guess what?" Peyton asked excitedly at one point.

"What?" I responded.

"When I cut the rope to start the festivities, before I came over here, I happened to look at the right spot in the crowd and saw Katie and Kit! They waved and pointed subtly at the others. They all made it!" he grinned.

I heaved a sigh of relief. "Oh, thank heavens!" I muttered.

We talked and looked at photos and other things on my phone for about an hour total, then Peyton had to leave. "For two reasons," he said. "One, I have to be present for the eclipse, and Two, I don't want to be here when you start smashing things; that could go very badly for me."

We both laughed, then I carried him to the door.

"Be careful out there!" I warned him. "Stay alert!"

He nodded. "Thanks! See you later! Good luck!" Then he snuck out the door.

* * * * * *

Fifteen minutes later my watch "dinged." I smiled, rolled my shoulders back, and walked over to the floor's "weak spot." I paused and listened, checking that the coast was clear. When I was satisfied that it was, I "reared back" and slammed my fist into the floor. There was a jolt, then a groan, then an ear-splitting crack. The floor started to cave in, and I leapt up, ran, and jumped up and grabbed the edge of the roof to avoid falling in with the floor.

After the dust cleared, I carefully swung down to the ground. I walked cautiously towards the gaping hole in the middle and looked down. Way below the hole was a smooth, paved road! Quickly and excitedly, I changed into my supersuit, loaded on my weapons, shrunk my other clothes (Priti had left me her father's invention, that gun that shrinks and grows inanimate objects), and put them in one of my many pockets. Then I slid through the hole and pulled a metal sheet that I *might* have torn off of the roof over it. It would be way too big and heavy for a normal size human to move. Even if they had superstrength, it would be too thick for them to even get their hands around, if you know what I mean.

Once down below I flipped on my headlamp and looked around. The bright light illuminated the cramped space around me. To a normal human, this would be a yawning cavern, insanely ginormous, but to me it was cramped, tight, small, and extremely uncomfortable. I crouched low on my hands and knees and began to crawl along the tunnel in the direction Peyton had indicated.

* * * * * *

Well, it has been half an hour, and I haven't met anyone or even seen anything living, and so far, the only damage I've done is to accidentally smash my foot through a thirty-foot-thick brick wall. Whoops!

At least I'm not bored. These walls (and the floor in some places too) are too well decorated to be boring. Apparently, Kit's chip allows me to not only *understand* any language but also to *read* any language too! (I wonder if I can *speak* any language…?) So, I'm learning all about the myths, legends, and history of Nordiaho and its people groups. Who knew I would find myself written into so many of the legends!

* * * * * *

It has been an hour now, and I've reached the point where I'm sick of crawling. Not to mention, my neck is starting to cramp something awful. Ack. I have heard a bit of rustling, and I thought I heard voices a few times, but I haven't seen a *single thing*! Is it possible that the Sojotos are really a group of really tiny people and that's why I can't see them? WHERE IS THE END OF THIS TUNNEL?! I didn't think it would take this long! And, I don't want to sound whiny, but I've been crawling with my head down for over an hour and it hurts *really* badly. I didn't get any sleep last night, and I can't even see the end of the tunnel! And the light of my headlamp stretches for at least 500 feet, 'cause of its size, *and* this is a *straight stretch* for crying out loud! It just goes on forever and ever and ever and ever and ever and ever and ever and ever and… where was I? Oh yeah, my strides, even when crawling, are looooooooong!

I'm pretty sure no Sojotos live in this branch of the tunnel. After all, like I said, I haven't seen anything living down here. Although, again, there is the possibility that I just can't see them. I sure hope not though.

Creaks, groans, whispering voices, the pitter-patter of tiny feet; please tell me I'm imagining things right now! Then someone screams, and a "rope" (to me it's more like the thinnest of dental floss) tightens around my leg. Darn! So NOT my imagination! I started to crawl forward slowly. As soon as I moved my right foot, the one with the rope around it, however, I heard a cacophony of screams. I stopped and craned my neck around.

There were about fifty people holding onto the rope. Do they really think they can restrain me? Really people!

"Do you really think you can restrain me?" I asked without thinking.

Another, louder, cacophony of screams erupted. I grimaced. Shoulda thought of their reaction first. Someone yelled shrilly and within seconds I was bound to the ground with "ropes."

I toyed with the idea of breaking the ropes and bolting, using my superspeed to get away as fast as I could, but then I figured they were terrified enough of me already, so I stayed put. I felt people scrambling over me, shouting in victory. I shuddered involuntarily. They screamed and ran to get off my body. I relaxed.

"Why am I here?" I asked.

An elderly man began talking near my right ear in a foreign tongue. My earpiece quickly adjusted to let me understand it. "…You are a trespasser, for one thing, and for another, you are a giant, sneaking underneath the grand capital city of Nordiaho. We do not trust giants, thank you very much. So, we shall take you to our camp prison, and…"

A young woman interrupted him. "Granpapa, I don't think he understands you. Hardly anyone knows, let alone speaks our language anymore."

"Oh, no, I can understand you perfectly," I said quietly.

Many of them gasped; others screamed. A man stepped forward from the crowd. "A giant who understands and *SPEAKS* Catishope?! (pronounced: Cat-ih-show-pea) How can this be?" he exclaimed, aghast.

A murmur rippled through the crowd. They all dropped their guard and I used that to my advantage. They were all on my right, so I slowly began to rip the "ropes" on my left. The whole time I was thinking: *'What did he mean, I spoke Caticho-whatever? Does that mean Kit's chip allows me to speak any language?! Yes!!'*

The man turned back to me, "How can you understand us and speak our language? What is this?" He demanded.

I bit my lip. I could think of one thing that would get me out of this mess: That thing Peyton called me that got him all excited. What was it again? Uh… Oh! The Definitavidito! I crossed my fingers on my left hand, "I'm the… the Definitavidito."

They all gasped collectively as one body, and I think a few of them even fainted. A tall, burly man forced his way up front. "If you truly are the Definitavidito," he boomed, "I have some questions for you. Where are the other elements? What are their names? Why are you down here? What are your powers? Who is…?"

"Donald!" the elderly man at my ear interrupted. "For heaven's sake! Give the boy a chance to answer!"

I smiled, tamping down the urge to laugh. "I'll tell you only if you swear on your life not to tell anyone else." Everyone nodded. "Good, okay then. The other elements are blending in with the crowds above, doing recon. Their names are Katie, Sarah, Tim, Priti, Kitaileeo, and Peyton. I'm down here because I had to escape from being held captive by the SCLs, and this was the safest, easiest, and smartest escape route for someone my size. What are my powers? Isn't that private? Why do you care? They're strong enough to whip you though, even at my normal size. I'll give you that."

The elderly man choked back laughter. "He's got a point, Donald."

Donald frowned, folded his arms, and said, "Harumph."

Slowly I rolled onto my side so I could stop using

my peripheral vision and actually see them all directly. Everyone was so busy watching or participating in the current argument that, surprisingly enough, none of them noticed but a little girl of about 12 or 13. She smiled up at me and winked.

"Will you let me go now?" I whispered. "I need to meet up with my friends."

They jumped, as if they had forgotten I could talk. The men looked at one another; then the elderly one stepped into my line of sight. "Chicoyrah, tie him down securely; everyone else, council!"

The 12 or 13-year-old stepped forwards. "Yes Granpapa." She walked towards me and, with a flick of her wrists, shot maybe 1,000 ropes into the ground and flung them over me with another hand motion. Then she shot a rope into the ceiling and swung over me. She dropped onto my ear lobe. I shuddered.

"Listen carefully," she whispered into my ear. I jumped slightly and nearly flung her off in surprise. "I am not going to tie you down. I know you are a good person, giant or no. After all, most giants would have broken free of these flimsy ropes and eaten everyone about ten minutes ago. I have some advice for you though. I will make sure that they let you go. But, when they do, move slowly; do not touch anyone; try not to breathe on anyone. Do not talk unless they ask you a question or unless they tell you to. Try your best not to laugh, cough, sneeze, or clear your throat. And, most importantly, do *not* look them in the eyes! Got it?"

I nodded slightly, nearly throwing her off again.

She smiled. "Good. And don't worry, I won't let them hurt you." She laughed at her own words, "Ha! Like they could!"

I rolled my eyes in spite of myself.

"Hey," she said. "One more thing. Do not be ashamed of your size. Not one bit. It's totally cool. Also, your size makes you immune to the power-stealing powder. The SCLs would have to use all they have just to weaken you powers by a fraction. So, since growing probably multiplied your powers 100 or more times, what harm could they do with that stuff? Oh, and if you're up against a lot of troops, just clear your 'allies' off the ground and tap the ground forcefully. But, though at normal size you'd punch it, since you're huge, do NOT punch the ground, whatever you do."

Then she swung back over me and disappeared into the crowd.

I smiled softly. *'Spider girl.'* I thought.

Donald turned to me, frowning. "The vote is unanimous, well, nearly unanimous. You are…free…to go."

Moving slowly, I sat up, then I rocked back onto my heels. Chicoyrah pulled the ropes away from me, and I started to crawl. I had only crawled two "steps" when I heard shouting from down the tunnel…in English, "We've got 'em now boys! Bombs away!"

Around the corner ran a group of people, fleeing in terror. They ran *right in between my legs* and merged with the other group. I heard an explosion, and, without thinking I threw myself in front of the bunch. They (probably also without thinking) ran up against me and lay down in an orderly line along my "body barricade." I heard larger explosions and felt things like tiny feathers brushing against my back. (I learned later that those "tiny feathers" were actually huge, deadly missiles. Thank goodness my size plus my superstrength gave me invincibility!)

I heard shouting from behind me. "Drat! The

tunnel's blocked! Those pesky Sojotos got away again!"

'Thank heavens my supersuit has camo-mode!' I thought, grinning.

* * * * * *

A while later the attackers left, and I slowly uncurled from around the group. They looked up at me cautiously, then Donald sat up. "What was that for?!" He bellowed. "You could have crushed us all, you behemoth!"

"Oh, Donald, be quiet!" Chicoyrah yelled from somewhere on the bottom of the pile. "He saved our lives you dimwit! Um, hello, duh!"

I laughed, pressing my mouth into my sleeve so I didn't scare them with the noise. Chicoyrah wiggled her way out of the pile and grinned at me. I smiled back.

"Y'all should get somewhere safe," I said softly. They nodded. "I have to go."

They stood up, thanked me heartily, and then dispersed and disappeared through several hidden doors in the walls and floor. Chicoyrah turned and waved at me before being hustled through a doorway. "Good luck!" she shouted.

I grinned. "Thanks!" With a groan I lay on my back and stretched out as far as I could (which is *QUITE* far). "I am so tired." I mumbled. I got up and continued crawling down the tunnel.

Fifteen minutes later I saw a prick of light ahead of me. *'Please be the end of this blasted tunnel!'* I thought. I crawled towards it hopefully, my efforts renewed. The light began to grow bigger and bigger until eventually I could tell that it was, most definitely, an exit.

I reached the exit, then I paused and listened. When I heard nothing, I stuck my head out a little way and looked around. I heard cheers below me, "Yay! John, you made it!"

"Finally, dude! We had begun to think you were napping!"

"No, Tim, *you* thought that."

"C'mon out, the coast is clear!"

I looked down. On the ground outside the hole, Katie, Tim, Priti, Sarah, Peyton and Kitaileeo were looking up at me. I smiled and slid out of the hole.

As soon as I was out, I promptly flopped down on

the lush, green grass.

"Oh my goodness, that tunnel is *so cramped*!" I exclaimed. "Where are we?"

"We're outside the city," Peyton said from near my ear, "in the Peyotano garden. It has been here for centuries. It's one of the seven 'element gardens' that are scattered around Nordiaho. And for the record, the tunnel isn't cramped; you're huge."

"Elements? Like us?" Sarah asked.

Peyton nodded. "There's one named after each of us. This one's named after me. Then, for example, there's the Sarteah (pronounced: Sar-tea-AH) garden, named after Sarah."

"Mmmmm-hmmmmmm," I said, as I fell asleep.

* * * * * *

I woke up maybe an hour later and rolled onto my side. The others were sitting in a circle, playing a game with sticks and coins. It looked like Tim and Peyton were trying to teach the others. (Which was not going very well. They kept interrupting each other and then kept hitting each other on the heads with their sticks. I'm not sure whether they were doing the latter playfully or otherwise...)

For example:

Peyton: "So you take the marker stick and..."

Tim: "Place it over your largest..."

Peyton: "Eh-HEM, largest coin and..."

Tim: "YOU USE THE STICK TO..."

Peyton and Tim, simultaneously yelling: "FLIP THE COIN! WOULD YOU BE *QUIET?!*"

"I told you they were both head-strong personalities," Priti whispered laughingly to Katie and Sarah, who both giggled.

I lay there watching for around 15 minutes before letting them know I was awake. How did I do that you may ask? Simple. I laughed.

Peyton and Tim jumped, then they both relaxed when they realized it was just me.

"Hey guys," I said quietly. "Um... remind me. When are we planning on staging our attack on the SCLs? You know, the big one that should hopefully change everything."

"In two days," Priti said.

"Oh great!" I groaned.

"What's wrong?" Tim asked.

"Well, where on earth…er…Nordiaho am I going to sleep and stay for two whole days?" I asked.

"Oh shoot," Peyton bit his lip, "That's a good point. Another point: I bet it's pretty obvious how you got out, so shouldn't we be on the road right now?"

"Oh man, you're right!" I exclaimed. "However, …um…where do we go?"

CHAPTER 12

Some Of The Most Fun Two Days Of My Life!

"I know where we can go!" was all Peyton said. And I am glad that's all he said, or I never would have agreed to his proposal. Why? Because the certain place he had in mind was the palace's main ballroom, which was big enough to hold the entire city's population inside of it, hence making it big enough for me.

He had Sarah turn me invisible and then he carefully led us through town. Let me tell you, it would have taken me forever just to take one step through that crowd. Thankfully, however, Sarah made me a bridge, a long, very wide bridge. After about ten minutes of careful traveling we arrived, and Peyton hustled me inside before I really realized where we were.

"Wait a minute…," I said slowly. "Uh, Peyton, where are we?"

He coughed uncertainly. "Well, you see, we are in the…."

He was cut off by someone at the door. "Peyton! There you are! Who are your friends?"

'Thank goodness I'm still invisible!' I couldn't help but think.

A tall woman with fiery red hair and sparkling green eyes stepped through the door, still talking a mile a minute. "Darling, you missed the bonfire lighting! I thought you were coming and…ACK!" Her "monologue" was cut short by a yelp of surprise as she ran into my invisible knee. (I was kneeling facing the door) I winced.

"Mom!" Peyton shouted. He jumped and ran at a breakneck pace towards his mom…and ran into my leg.

I groaned. Peyton's mom sprang backwards, trembling slightly. "What was that?!" she cried.

"What was what?" Peyton asked after shooting me a look.

'I am SO stupid!' I thought.

"Peyton, I am not an idio...," she trailed off and began touching my knee. I held my breath. She gasped. "Peyton! Run! Now! As soon as I get out, I'll get the guards! What are you waiting for? GO!" she spun around towards the door.

Thinking fast, I leaned over and slid my hand in front of the door. She ran into it and screamed.

"No, wait, please calm down! You can't leave! Please," I pleaded quietly.

She screamed louder. Peyton ran over and backed her away from the doors and I shut the doors with my thumbs. Peyton squeezed her hand and tried to calm her down.

"What are you doing here? Who are you?" she asked, her chest heaving beneath her dark green gown.

"Mom, Mom, relax," Peyton coaxed. "You're not going to get hurt! Please chill!"

"Peyton," Sarah whispered. "Should I make him visible?"

Peyton shook his head. "No, we should let him talk to her first."

Sarah nodded, then she looked at me. (She can see anyone who is invisible)

I carefully sat down crisscross and crossed my fingers. "Ma'am?" I started.

She let out a yelp at the sound of my voice and hid behind Peyton. (Peyton's gotta be at least 7'3" in Earth terms.) "Who are you?"

"My name is John," I said, keeping my voice quiet and calm. "I mean you no harm."

"If you mean me no harm, then show yourself! Come out from wherever you're hiding. Where are you hiding anyway? Behind the organ?" she said, a little less nervously.

I bit my lip. "Er...nooo, not exactly. I'll come out if you swear to keep quiet and calm, okay?" She nodded and I saw her gulp.

"Sarah?" I whispered and nodded at her.

She nodded back and gave me a thumbs-up. "Good luck!" she whispered.

She turned me visible and I waited for a scream or the thud of someone fainting, but I heard nothing. Perplexed, I looked down. Peyton's mother was staring at my knee, laughing.

'Ok, wait, what?' I thought.

"You said you'd show yourself silly," She said

through laughter. "You can't hide behind a curtain."

"Um, ma'am?" I said. "That's not a curtain, it's…."

"It's what?" she asked. "A stage prop?" She walked forwards and touched it, "Hmmm…it's firm, and…and warm. Is it a…a…uh…," she trailed off.

"Ma'am don't faint; look up," I said softly.

She looked up and promptly screamed. She propelled herself backwards until she was pressed up against the door, still screaming. Then, to my surprise, she started to cry softly. "If this is an assassination attempt, please make it quick."

I carefully laid down on my stomach in front of her. "Shh, please don't cry!"

She looked up at me with a tear-stained face.

"This isn't an assassination attempt," I said quietly. "I swear on my honor that you won't get hurt! I promise. I wouldn't dream of hurting anyone! Please stop crying!"

She sniffed, "How do I know that?"

"Mom!" Peyton cut in. "Trust him! You have to! He's the Definitavidito!"

She shook her head, "No, no, nonononono NO! This wasn't supposed to happen!"

"What is it Mom?" Peyton asked.

She sighed. "We, your father and I, named you, Peyton, before we read the prophesy. When we found out that your name matched the name of one of the elements in the prophesy we worried. You were bred for palace life, and you've never left the palace except for ceremonies and such!"

At this Peyton choked a little and began to cough slightly. I raised my eyebrows at him.

The Queen continued. "We didn't want you to go from a prince to a warrior, so… that's why we never told you about the… prophesy. How did you know about it anyway?"

Peyton opened his mouth, shut it, then he opened it again, "Mom, as your son, I was subjected to *years* of court gossip. How exactly do you think I learned about it?"

She sighed, "We should have thought of that."

I coughed. "You don't mind our staying here for a while, do you?"

She smiled wanly. "Well, since it would impossible to force *you* to leave, as long as you don't eat us out of house and home, or turn my son into a back-streets rag-a-muffin, you can stay."

Peyton gave his mom a big hug. "Thank you! Thank you! THANK YOU! You won't be sorry!"

She grinned. "We'll see about that. Well, now that you're staying, we might as well get to know each other. I am Queen Catherine Kartia Catske. Please just call me Cathy! Who are you?"

Katie's Narration:

Wow, she's pretty! She has thick red hair, bright sparkling green eyes, she's tall, and just absolutely gorgeous. And yet, even though she's tall, she's still completely dwarfed by her son. She comes up to his ribs!

I stepped forwards. "I'm Katie. I'm from Earth," I said, curtsying.

Cathy pulled me up. "Please don't do that. It makes me feel higher up than people."

I smiled at her. She smiled back, her face lighting up.

Tim stepped forward. "I'm Tecumseh, but please just call me Tim. Everybody does, well, unless I'm in trouble," he grinned cockily.

She laughed warmly. "I'll keep that in mind."

Sarah took a shy step towards her. "I'm Sarah," she said quietly.

Cathy stepped towards her and smiled warmly. "What a beautiful name. Pleased to meet you."

Priti moved up. "I'm Priti, Tim's sister; our father manages, well, he managed your stables."

Cathy smiled. "Oh! So, you are Sharon's and Chicoyah's (Pronounced: Shi-coy-uh) children! How lovely! I've heard so much about you from your parents before…," she trailed off awkwardly.

Priti blushed.

Cathy looked up at John. "Now remind me of your name young man."

He smiled slightly. "My name is John." He bowed deeply. "I can bow, right? I doubt you could feel…er… higher up than me."

She laughed aloud. "You, sir, are very clever."

He grinned and chuckled.

* * * * * *

We spent half an hour talking and getting

acquainted, then Cathy excused herself so that she could go oversee the preparations for the big feast that evening. The second she closed the door behind her John turned to Peyton. "Soooooo, Peyton…How come your mother has never noticed that you've been gone?"

Peyton blushed. "Well…you see… my powers are the ability to control technology, and also to shoot fire out of my hands and control it. So, I created a 'living' copy of myself. So, whenever I'm out there, incognito, my copy fills in and everyone thinks I'm here. It's genius really, if I do say so myself, because it gives me the opportunity to actually get some freedom!"

We all laughed.

"What?" he asked. "Is that not allowed? I mean, you have no idea what it's like to have been brought up like this, in the spotlight, living the regal life, yet trying to be a normal teenager. I mean, I know Earth isn't set up like Nordiaho and that you have many different countries and each of the different countries basically has its own ruler or monarch or whatever you all call them. Here on Nordiaho, however, there is one country, even if it's split into different parts, and there is one ruling family over the entire planet. My family being that family, and myself being the eldest son and heir to the throne, I have had to live under the watching eyes of THE ENTIRE PLANET!" Peyton groaned softly at this. "I mean, everywhere I go people worship me. Half of the people can't even say more than three words to me without swooning, fainting, or running away out of shyness and/or fear! It's absolutely exasperating!" he sighed. "All my life the one thing I've wanted is just a little freedom. That was why I was so excited to meet you guys. I thought I might actually get it for once in my life."

"So that's why you dressed and talked and acted like you did the day we met you. You didn't want us to find out who you really were!" Sarah exclaimed.

Peyton nodded. "Exactly. Hey, I have to go. My parents will be expecting me at the feast tonight and I have to 'freshen up' first." He smirked at us, then he slipped out the door.

* * * * * *

An hour or so later, Peyton came tearing back into

the room at maximum speed, "Hey guys! Guess what!" he panted.

"What?" we chorused, feeding off of his excitement.

"Peyton, you look fantastic!" Sarah remarked, blushing slightly. (He really did.)

Peyton blushed. "Why thank you! Anyway, my parents, King and Queen of Nordiaho, have invited you to join them at the royal table at tonight's feast! Can you come?" He bounced around like an excited five year old.

We laughed.

I looked up at John. He was biting his lip and twisting his utility belt in his hands. "Uh, y'all know *I* can't go, right?"

Peyton inhaled, opened his mouth, closed it again (It's something that seems to be a habit of his when he doesn't know what to say. It's pretty funny; it makes him look somewhat like a fish.), then sighed. "Ooohhh! I forgot! Ugh!"

John knelt lower. "Hey, y'all go ahead and go! Have fun! Seriously!"

We smiled up at him. "Thank you!" we said.

He grinned then gently shooed us out the door.

Peyton, however, ran back in, and I paused to see what he was doing. He had a quick conversation with John, and then he seemed to hand him something and John did something with it that I didn't see. Then Peyton exited the room and joined us again.

"What was that about?" I asked him.

"You'll see. You'll see in a while," he said, grinning at me.

* * * * * *

We followed Peyton through the castle.

"What do we wear?" Sarah asked.

Peyton grinned. "Oh, don't worry. Mother will take care of that. She's ecstatic to dress you all." He led us to a door and opened it a crack. "Mother, they're here."

Cathy came bustling out of the room, gown billowing around her. "Come in! Come in! Welcome!" she led us through the door into a large room filled with clothes and yards and yards of fabric. "Now, shall we get you dressed for the feast and ball my dears?" Cathy asked us excitedly.

"There's a BALL?!" I asked, both nervously and

excitedly. "It's too bad John can't participate," I said, more to myself than the others.

We looked around in awe at the sheer amount of clothes before us. I looked at the dress on a mannequin in front of me. On Earth people haven't dressed like this in at least two hundred years! But oh! Is it gorgeous! Dark blue silk in shimmering folds, a high waistline, puffed sleeves, and lace at the neck. I sighed, enraptured.

Cathy put her hand on my shoulder. "Yes, it is gorgeous, isn't it? Now!" she clapped her hands excitedly. "Let's get you dressed!" she began sizing us up. "Let's see, Priti dear, you'd look amazing in this, simply stunning; do try it on dear!" She handed Priti a long emerald green silk with a wide black sash. Priti slipped through a door to try it on. She came out several minutes later, during which Cathy had chosen dresses or outfits for the rest of us.

I had that gorgeous dress I had been admiring, the blue one. Sarah had an absolutely lovely rose-pink satin ball-gown. It had long tight sleeves, a white sash, and a full skirt. Tim had a blue "bib shirt" (those sorts of bloused shirts that have frilly rectangles buttoned onto the front that almost cover the whole front. They're from the Victorian era originally, but The Monkees (look them up) wore them a lot). He also had red embroidered pants, black boots, and a black leather belt with a gold buckle. Kit insisted on wearing her own clothes, so we all went to change.

When we came out Priti was waiting for us. We all gasped and exclaimed. The dresses fit the others beautifully, and Tim looked great, although a little uncomfortable. The only one we were missing was Kit. We waited a moment, and then she came out.

"Oh, my goodness! You look amazing!" I exclaimed.

She blushed. She was wearing a dress the likes of which I've never seen before! The bodice looked as if it was made of water. It was blue and it shimmered and rippled, and it had little pearls all over it. The skirt and the bodice were separated by a line of tiny black jewels. The skirt, oh! the skirt, was completely made of roses, creamy white roses! The skirt was full and long; it came past her feet, and it was stunning! Her hair cascaded down her back like waves and it was full of tiny flowers, red, pink, white, and blue.

Cathy clapped her hands. "Oh, you look wonderful

darlings! Now! Off to hair and make-up!"

Tim made a choking, gagging noise, and we all laughed as we followed Cathy to another room. She led us into a room with mirrors and tables everywhere. A few aides rushed up to us, "Oh darlings! How divine!"

"What beautiful dresses!"

"What gorgeous ladies!"

"And what a handsome young man!" they all exclaimed.

They sat us down in chairs and did our hair, then our make-up. It took them fifteen minutes just to get Tim to sit still, and then he refused to let them put any make-up on him, but he did, surprisingly, let them comb his hair. We all nearly died of laughter as he dodged powder, mascara, lipstick, curling irons, and even a wig! Finally, we were all finished and Cathy led us to the grand dining room.

"Are we late?" I asked, since no-one else was outside and we could hear conversations from through the door.

"No dear. You're with me, and the Queen is never late. Everyone else is simply early." Cathy stuck her tongue out at us and crossed her eyes. We all giggled.

Two guards opened the doors and everyone in the room stopped talking and stood at attention behind their chairs. Cathy dipped her head at them all and went to the Royal Table. She showed us to our seats and then sat at the head of the table. Once she had sat down, everyone else did. Her husband sat next to her. Their two daughters, who introduced themselves as Liliana and Katiana, sat on either side of them. Peyton's two younger brothers, Virgil and Jameson, sat next to the girls, and Peyton sat in between Virgil and myself. Sarah was next to me.

Peyton leaned towards Sarah and me. "I'll tell you what utensils to use when. Tim and Priti should know, so they can teach Kit." He gestured at the others sitting next to Jameson on the other side of the table. "You'll use this fork first for the Selano, er…salad course." He pointed at a small, ornately engraved golden fork. "Don't touch it until everyone is served and my mom takes a bite."

We nodded. I looked at the others across the table. Tim and Priti were sitting on either side of Kitaileeo and Priti was instructing Kit on cutlery.

* * * * * *

The food was amazing, but what came next was even better. We headed towards the palace's other ballroom. When we went through the wide double doors my jaw dropped. The room was gorgeous! Marble pillars, walls, and floor, and huge, tall windows. The orchestra was already playing, but on instruments I've never even seen the likes of before.

Once all the guests were inside, the orchestra struck up a slow dance. Priti sidled over towards Sarah and me. "Do you see that young man over there?" She pointed at a maybe 18-year-old talking animatedly with Peyton. "That's Grand Duke Nathan! Isn't he handsome?"

Kit nodded. "Yes!" she breathed.

I jumped. "Kit! That was English!"

She blushed. "I decided I'd finally learn it since I was trapped in there with you and all you guys spoke was English. Well, basically, anyways." She smiled. "Am I doing it right?"

I grinned. "Yes, you sound like you've always spoken it."

She grinned back at me and blushed.

All of a sudden Priti squealed and clutched at my arm.

"Priti! What in the world is wrong?" I asked, startled.

"He's coming this way! With Peyton AND Virgil!" she squeaked.

I struggled not to laugh. She was correct, however, that they were handsome. Peyton, with his bright blue eyes and thick black hair. Virgil, with grey-green eyes and red hair. And Nathan with thick brown hair, green-blue eyes, and the brightest, most dazzling, easy smile I'd ever seen. And he was probably six foot two.

They stopped in front of us and bowed; we curtsied back.

"Good evening ladies. You look beautiful tonight," Peyton said, smiling down at us.

As Nathan came up out of his bow, his eyes fell on Kit. His eyes lit up. "My lady, you look stunning! Have we met?"

Kit blushed. "No, Your Highness, I don't believe we have."

He smiled. "Please, my name is Nathan. What is

your name?"

"Kitaileeo, but you can call me Kit," she smiled dazzlingly at him.

"Well, Kit, may I have the next dance?" he blushed.

She beamed. "Yes, that would be delightful!"

His face lit up like a streetlamp, and he offered her his hand. Priti sighed and leaned against me.

"Lucky," she muttered.

"Aw, Priti, don't be jealous," I nudged her. "Besides, I believe someone else would like to dance with you…."

Virgil cleared his throat. "Um, Miss Priti, may I have the next dance?"

She straightened up and beamed at him. "Why yes, my lord, that would be delightful!"

He offered her his hand and they waltzed over into the middle of the dance floor.

Peyton shifted awkwardly from foot to foot, staring at Sarah. He cleared his throat, opened his mouth, then shut it again. It made him look like a big fish; it was kind of funny. I looked at Sarah. I could tell she wanted to dance with him. I nudged her softly and winked.

"I'm going to go get some punch," I said, smiling

graciously.

Peyton smiled at me and nodded. "Thank you!" he mouthed.

Standing next to the punch and cake table I watched the others dance. They all looked so happy. (I have to admit though, 5' 8" Sarah dancing with *at least* 7' 3" Peyton was kind of funny...) Suddenly I was aware of someone standing next to me.

"They sure look nice together, don't they?" a familiar voice said, although I couldn't quite place it because I had been hearing it a lot differently the past few days.

"Yes," I said. Then I thought to turn around. I nearly fainted. "JOHN! But how? I mean...you're... how did...you're normal!"

He laughed. "I bartered with Peyton for a temporary shrink. That's what we were talking about when y'all left. I have until tomorrow morning, 0900 sharp," he grinned, "so here I am."

I smiled. "Oh, I'm so glad!" I thought of something. "Since you're here and all fancied up, um...do you want to dance?"

He smiled. "The pleasure would be all mine my lady." He bowed.

I laughed, and he led me onto the dance floor.

* * * * * *

We danced for about three hours, switching partners every now and then, so I got to dance with the other boys too. Then we stopped for cake and punch. When we broke for refreshments, I noticed Peyton excuse himself.

"What did he say?" I asked Sarah.

"He said, 'I apologize, but I must go do my duties as prince and, ugh, socialize,'" she said, imitating him.

We laughed.

We were talking happily and getting to know Virgil and Nathan when the double doors slammed shut. We heard a scream. Out of the crowd stepped three men, one of whom I recognized as Earl. I heard John grind his teeth together.

We politely excused ourselves from Virgil and Nathan and dashed behind a pillar.

"Guys! We have to do something!" Tim exclaimed.

"Agreed! But in these clothes?" Kit said, fingering her skirt. But then she smiled. "Hold still," she said and tapped each of us on the forehead. "Now, think of your supersuits, and spin!"

We did, and each of us kind of glowed, and then we were in our supersuits, weapons and all.

"Whoa! No way!" Tim sort of yelped. "Is that how ClanaTupeks, you know, change their clothes?!"

Kit smirked, "Yes."

"Cool!" Priti said.

We leapt out from behind the pillar, and (literally for John and Tim) ran smack into Virgil and Nathan.

"Ack!" John grunted as he and Nathan's heads clacked together. "What are you doing here?"

"We want to help! We can help! Please let us!" they pleaded.

"Didn't you hear? They plan to unleash the power-stealing powder tonight! We have to hurry!" Nathan exclaimed. "If they get the powers of just the people in this room, there'll probably be no stopping them! My power is the control of thunder and lightning, and Virgil's is flight and shooting fire. We really can help!" The rest of us looked at each other and then we all nodded.

"Okay, you can help," Priti said.

Nathan and Virgil high fived each other and waved Peyton over. He ran over and Kit showed him how to "spin-change" really quickly. Then we all stood in a circle and "stacked" our hands in the middle of it. "Freedom for N.!" we cheered.

We broke the circle and ran through the frightened, anxious crowd towards the orchestra stage (where the men were standing). When we reached the stage, we paused and listened.

"We will rule over Nordiaho! We will then take over the entire universe! If you even think that you will be able to stop us, you are wrong…" Earl was saying. "You will *never* stop us, no one is powerful enough to defeat us, to defeat *me*!"

We leapt up onto the orchestra stage simultaneously, and Tim declared in his loud, deep voice that he loves to use, "Oh we'll see about that!"

Earl screamed in frustration. "You! I thought you were dead! I told my giant to kill you!"

At that statement two things happened: First, a ripple of exclamations went around the room at Earl's mention of a giant, causing John to wince, and second, Sarah laughed. In a surprising show of courage for her

(She's pretty shy) she said, "Well, that's the thing; you can't kill us. You're too dumb and weak."

Earl growled and let out a whistle. When he whistled, two hundred or more soldiers came bursting through the doors.

"Everyone! Please! Against the walls!" Peyton yelled.

All the guests complied quickly and pressed themselves up against the walls of the ballroom. We assembled ourselves in front of the squadrons of soldiers. Priti started muttering her chant to call the animals and John flexed his muscles.

We waited. There was a moment of tense anticipation, and then it was like a bomb exploded. We surged forwards with a fierce battle cry and met the charging ranks of men head on.

"I'll take the left flank," John said. "Sarah, can you cover me? Nathan, Virgil, Peyton, can you take the right flank? Tim, Priti, Katie, can you take the center? And Kit, can you help Sarah and me take the men on the left?"

Everyone nodded. "On it!" they all said.

We flew into action. I *want* to say we worked together like a well-oiled machine, but, sadly, that is not exactly what happened. You see, we had all learned to master our own powers, but, especially with three new teammates, we hadn't learned quite yet how to use our powers in a group fight. As a matter of fact, one of the first things that happened was that as Virgil and Peyton were making a wall of fire one of the troopers shocked Virgil in the leg with a "wrist sting-ray" and he tripped and nearly roasted Kit, except she atom-bounded just in time.

"Sorry!" he shouted.

"Guys! Watch out for their wrist guns! We don't wanna get shocked!" Priti yelled.

I sized up the men in front of me. Their armor was very detailed and looked extremely strong. The breast plates looked like overlapped circles of white metal. They had armor on their arms (the rerebrace and the vambrace, also the couter, or elbow armor if you want me to be technical. Yes, I know, that's old stuff though.) that looked like a cross between scales and chain mail that went from their wrists to their shoulders. They also had armor on their legs (if you want the technical stuff, the cuisse, the poleyn, equipped with fan plates, and the greave) that looked like a glowing, loosely-woven lattice. To top it all off, they each had "wrist sting-rays" (they're stun guns that attach to your wrists, basically, but, fortunately, they're not very good at stunning people), and they were surrounding a large cannon-like thing that had a see-through barrel FULL of the power powder. (Where they got some more, I'm not sure. I thought we got it all, but maybe they had a secret stash.) I was surprised that they had no more weapons than their poor excuses for stun guns, but I guess, since they thought we were dead, they were not expecting much of a fight.

Sarah created a bar that she jumped up to stand on. However, Tim was running to the center group of the men, and, as he jumped to the side to avoid a beam from the men's stun guns, he smacked his head on the bar and fell over. John dashed over at maybe thirty miles an hour, creating a gust of wind, and helped him up. Nathan tripped over a cheetah preparing to pounce on one of the men, and the cheetah growled at him. Virgil bumped into Nathan as Nathan leapt backwards from the angry cheetah. Virgil backed away and bumped into Kit, since she was atom-bounding everywhere and appearing in random places. Sigh.

I leapt forwards, sending a wave of my energy forwards and bowling over thirty men. Priti then stepped in, and, using the power of a pegasus (changing minds), she turned the fallen men into good guys. The men leapt up, realized what was happening, and ran over and pressed themselves up against the nearest wall, stripping themselves of their "uniforms" as they went (which proved they were just normally good men under the SCLs mind control). Tim let out a war whoop and high fived his sister.

Virgil and Peyton were working well together and had trapped about twenty men in a cage of fire. Priti ran over and changed those men's minds. They realized that they were inside a cage of fire and freaked out, dropping to their knees and begging for mercy. Peyton nodded and he and Virgil released them.

"Guys!" I said over the earpiece. "Don't kill anyone! Just hold them down or still until Priti can reverse the SCLs' mind control! I don't even think they have powers!"

"Got it!" everyone responded.

We leapt back into action. This time we worked better together. We fought side by side, as well coordinated as a team of figure skaters. After about fifteen or twenty minutes we began to overwhelm the men. We had changed eighty of the men back into "good guys," some of whom began to fight alongside of us.

One hundred and twenty left, and we were still going strong.

"Peyton! Virgil! John! Over here!" Nathan yelled.

John ran over first. Nathan whispered in his ear, John nodded, and then he took off like a shot, running around the edge of the room, I presume talking to the people along the walls. After he passed, the people hit the deck, like a wave.

Peyton and Virgil jogged over to Nathan and the three of them talked for a moment. Then, Peyton's face lit up like a lightbulb, and all three of them punched their fists in the air. Right after that I noticed Peyton pull three earpieces out of his pocket and give Nathan and Virgil each one, and then he stuck one in his own ear.

All of a sudden over my earpiece I heard Peyton say, "Everyone, listen up! When I count to three, HIT THE DECK! Got it?"

We all nodded, "Okay." He took a deep breath, "One…Two…THREE!!!"

We dropped simultaneously. I rolled over onto my stomach to see what was going to happen. Peyton and Virgil shot out fire from their hands, and then Nathan shot a bolt of lightning that met right in the middle of the stream of fire… "BOOM!!!!"

A ginormous blue and red shockwave exploded across the room. It stunned the troopers, and they all collapsed to the ground. Priti darted amongst them all, her hands glowing, humming to herself, and changed their minds back to good again, breaking the SCLs' mind control over them all for good.

"How did you DO that?" Sarah asked in disbelief.

The three of them blushed. "It's a trick we learned a long time ago, um, completely by accident actually," Virgil smirked. "We knocked Dad and the siblings out for thirty minutes!"

The doors exploded behind us. We whipped around and stared. A hulking man with glowing hands stood in the doorway. He had armor more advanced than the other men, and he looked like someone who was truly evil, not just someone under the SCLs' mind control.

We backed into a group, and took battle stances. He rocked back into a crouch, and then he sprang!

John's Narration:

He leapt at us. Katie threw up a force field in front of us. He battered that with shots of flame and bolts of lightning. Then he landed right in front of Katie's force field and just walked right through it. We leapt backward as one. I noticed Peyton and Nathan exchange a glance. This man had more than one power, and more than two, at least three. It was possible that this man had used the power-stealing-powder to acquire powers for himself.

I ran towards him at great speed and threw a punch at his stomach. He dashed right and dodged the hard blow completely. All of a sudden, he shape-shifted into a different looking man. He went from having greasy dark hair and shifty, beady black eyes to having light blonde hair and sparkling blue eyes. He looked like a perfect copy of…me.

Katie let out a cry of astonishment. Then she shouted for us to form ranks and attack. We did. A few minutes into the battle we realized that it was hard to keep track of which person was the right John, me or him. He looked so much like me that occasionally the others would think that I was him or he was me, and then they wouldn't realize that he was the bad guy we were fighting until he attacked us or used his powers. Then he shape-shifted into Peyton's lookalike. At least, he tried to. He was shorter than Peyton, which was too obvious a difference, so he quickly shape-shifted to look like Nathan.

Kit crept up behind him and grabbed his atoms. Katie held him from the front, and Peyton and Virgil created a cage of fire around the man. The man shape-shifted again. Priti let out a cry and stumbled backwards. So did Nathan, for some reason. The man he turned into was none other than Lord Johansson. He smiled wickedly at them all and nodded. "Yes." he whispered. "It is me." Then, he disappeared. Just vanished in midair.

Katie's Narration:

We did it! I mean, yes, Lord Johansson got away from us, but we can always fight him another day. And it is helpful to know what his powers are. Or what some of them are anyway. But hey! We won the battle, defeated the whole army and sort of defeated Lord Johansson!

We were all laughing and congratulating each other when I realized that normal-sized John still hadn't stood side by side with Peyton. Whenever that happens, it should be very interesting, let me tell you! Let me also tell you, we REALLY shouldn't have taken our eyes off of that cannon with the power powder in it. Or off of Earl for that matter.

We heard a whirring noise behind us; a loud whining, whirring noise accompanied by a cackling, maniacal laugh. We whipped around, half in astonishment, and half in rage, both at our stupidity and at Earl.

"John, evacuate all the civilians! NOW!" Peyton frantically whispered over the earpiece.

John did so, emptying the room in thirty seconds flat.

"You know what you have to do?" Peyton whispered over the earpiece.

"Yeah, I do," John sighed as he ran back to us and moved in front of all of us.

Earl cackled as he saw John move in front of us. "You'll never hold up against this, boy! No matter how strong you are!"

"Oh really?" John taunted, while motioning subtly with his hands for us to back up. We did.

The cannon finished charging and Earl smiled cruelly. "I told you so."

John just laughed. Earl hit the button and the powder shot out.

"REVERSE!" John yelled.

Peyton moved his hand, and all of a sudden, the second before the powder would have hit John, there was a flash of blinding light. When I opened my eyes John was huge again, and he was lying in front of the cannon, calmly blowing the powder back into Earl's face. Earl spluttered, coughed, and then screamed.

"MY POWERS!" he screamed. "YOU...YOU TOOK THEM! YOU MONSTER!!!"

John flinched and I winced.

John's Narration:

Okay, that is just not fair! *I'm* a monster?! He's the one who made me this size! I mean, *come on*! That is just so... AGH!

"*I'M THE MONSTER?!!!*" I said, possibly a little too loudly. Earl flinched. "May I remind you that it was YOUR idea to make me almost 500 feet tall? Or did you forget? 'Cause this did not happen by some sort of freak accident! OH NO! YOU did this to me! THIS ISN'T ON ME AT ALL!"

Earl began backing up toward the open doors. I swung them shut with my thumbs. Earl began to panic. I could see him hyperventilating and his face was ashen, his eyes brimming with fear.

My mind raced. There was no way I could kill this guy in cold blood. Well, ok, it wouldn't be cold blood; he actually quite deserves to die, but I can't *kill* someone! I just can't! (I'm probably going to have to work on that if I ever want to be a real, full-fledged superhero, I know.) I don't know what to do with him though. I looked back at Earl. He was still freaking out. IF the power powder had worked, I had just gotten all his powers. I wonder - what were his powers. I know he had flight and multilingualism, but I wonder if he had more. Anyway...

"Don't. Move." I growled.

I rolled over towards the others. I noticed Nathan and Virgil flatten themselves up as close to the wall as possible and I could see their chests heaving. I had forgotten that they had no idea about, um, me. I kind-of decided that for the moment I would simply ignore them.

"What should we do with him?" I whispered. Virgil and Nathan jumped at my voice, "'cause I'm NOT going to kill him! That just isn't gonna happen."

Peyton cleared his throat. "We *could* put him in the palace dungeon. I mean, his powers are gone right? So there's no way he could get out unless someone broke him out."

"But we have no idea whether his powers are gone or not! We don't even know if flight and multilingualism were his only powers," I said.

"Well," Peyton said, "let me check that out." With that, he reached down to his, uh, basically a wide, glowing, technological bracelet (kind of like a *super duper advanced* computer on your wrist), tapped a few buttons, and then, literally (like Iron Man does in Avengers!) *pulled a screen made only of light out of his bracelet and threw it up so that it hovered in midair right in front of him!! It was so cool!*

"What are you doing bro?" Virgil asked him.

"Hacking into the National Power Tracking Database," Peyton said matter-of-factly, his fingers flying over the screen in front of him. (Somehow, though it was only made of light, his fingers seemed to be hitting something solid! I wish we had tech this advanced, but I kind of feel like only Peyton does… and somehow, he thinks my *watch* is the most advanced tech he's ever seen! Ha!)

Nathan, Kit, Priti, Virgil, and Tim's jaws all dropped at Peyton's matter-of-fact statement.

"You can DO that?!" Priti squawked. "I though the NPTD was the most secure compusite, or a website, for you humans, IN THE ENTIRE UNIVERSE! And access to it is only granted to three people in the entire galaxy!"

Peyton snorted, "Of course I can hack it. No code is too hard for me to crack. Plus, I am a techie." A few seconds later he grinned triumphantly. "I'm in!"

Tim stared at him in open mouthed astonishment. "You just cracked the most secure compusite in the entire universe in under thirty seconds, dude! How many people have this power of yours? 'Cause if any SCLs do… let's just say we're DEAD!"

Peyton smirked, "I'm the only one. Control of technology, or being a techie, is the rarest power ever, because I'm the only person who has EVER gotten it! Now, as I was saying, Earl has flight and multilingualism; that's it."

"How are we supposed to find out whether or not he still has them?" Sarah asked.

"Oh, that's the easy part," Peyton grinned.

"Oh no. I don't like where this is going!" I groaned.

"John picks him up, throws him into the air, and, if he doesn't fly, John catches him, and if he does fly, we need to figure out something else," Peyton said.

"I'm not doing that," I said.

"You have to!" Peyton retorted.

"No way!"

"Yes."

"Absolutely not."

"Do it."

"*No!*"

"Yes."

"What! You think you can just tell me what to do

because you're a prince and I'm not?!"

"You. Have. To. Do. This! For Nordiaho!"

Katie's Narration:

This might not go anywhere anytime soon. They've been arguing for *ten minutes* now for crying out loud! I'm just waiting for one of them to snap. Finally, someone does: *"I! AM! NOT! DOING! THAT!"* John yelled, sending Peyton flying and slamming into the closest wall, pretty hard honestly, and the rest of us trying to plug our ears against the horribly loud noise. I think he yelled that as loud as he possibly could, because he practically screamed it! His voice went so low it just about rumbled like thunder. I could even almost see the sound waves coming out of his mouth thanks to our comparative sizes and the sheer volume at which he yelled.

Peyton jumped up and brushed himself off with as much dignity as a person can muster after being thrown through the air by the air accompanying someone who's more than 75 times your size yelling at you. He walked back over to stand in front of John again. John was blushing and looked a little bashful,

"Sorry." he whispered.

Peyton nodded "Well, if you're not going to do that, then what else are we going to do?"

I stepped forward. "We could simply tell Earl to tell us."

Tim frowned. "But what if he lies to us?"

I shrugged. "We can always threaten him…"

John frowned. "Don't you mean *I* can always threaten him?"

I looked up at him, "John, look, I know you don't want to act threatening, but. You. Have. To! Just for now."

He sighed gustily, a warm breeze that caused Nathan and Virgil to flinch. "Fine," he groaned. "Are you going to ask him, or am I?"

"That's up to you," Tim shrugged.

He thought for a minute. "How about one of you ask him and I'm just a sort-of backup plan."

We nodded. He held out his hand and we hopped on. Virgil and Nathan hesitated. I jumped down off of John's hand and walked over to stand next to them.

"Is he normally like this?" Virgil whispered.

I shook my head. "He's normally like how he was

at the ball earlier."

"Well then, why is he this big?" Nathan muttered.

"The SCLs grew him," I replied.

"Oh," Virgil grimaced. "Is he safe?"

I nodded. "He's perfectly safe; he wouldn't hurt a fly."

"Are you sure?" Virgil whispered.

"Like, absolutely positive?" Nathan added.

I nodded again. "Absolutely! I mean, you met him earlier for crying out loud! Now come on."

They nodded. I turned and leapt up onto John's palm and then turned around to look at them. They walked forwards and paused by his fingers. Virgil laid a hand on John's pointer finger and then looked carefully at John's face. John pretended to be very interested studying the fancy carvings on one of the pillars. Virgil moved forward, and, all of a sudden, John twitched his pointer finger *ever so slightly*. Virgil jerked his hand off as if John's finger were a pile of hot coals and let out a yell, panting.

John burst out laughing. "Got you!" he smirked down at Virgil.

Virgil frowned. "Oh ha-ha. Very funny. You're the

most hilarious *giant* I've ever met."

John smirked. "All right, all right; hurry up and get on my hand. We don't have all day."

Nathan and Virgil looked at each other warily.

"Only if you don't do anything sudden or dangerous," Nathan said.

John nodded.

The two of them took a deep breath and then leapt onto John's hand. When they landed, however, Nathan shuddered.

John rolled his eyes. "And what was that for?"

Nathan smiled bashfully. "Sorry, it's just old memories resurfacing. The last time I was in a giant's hand it was during a raid, and that hand was on a direct route to a HUGE mouth!"

"Well then, I firmly swear you will be going absolutely nowhere near my mouth," John said.

He lifted his hand into the air, and, careful to keep his hand level, he rolled over so that he was facing Earl once again and set us down. Earl, probably cowed by the tone of voice John had used, hadn't moved.

Peyton drew himself up to his full height (which is really quite impressive for a "normal" person) and strode forward towards Earl. "Earl, I have a question for you. It's very simple, a yes or no answer really, so here it is: Do you still have any powers?"

Earl hesitated.

John's Narration:

Oh, I hate this. Hate, hate, hate it. Hate my size, hate the SCLs, hate how everyone (well, mostly everyone anyways) is scared of me. I AM SO SICK OF THIS! And now I have to act all big and mean and scary. That is so not my strong suit. I probably need to get better at it, since I'm kind of getting the feeling that I'm going to be doing quite a bit of this terrifying giant interrogator thingy. Ugh.

Earl still hasn't answered Peyton's question, which is both annoying me and scaring me, because no answer from Earl = Terrifying Giant Interrogator Act. Again, ugh.

Finally, Earl shook his head. "No comment."

Peyton looked at me expectantly. Inwardly, I groaned. After a moment's pause, I let out a low growl. "Answer him," I rumbled.

Earl paled as he stared at me, or, more specifically,

my mouth. I sighed, inwardly.

"I don't know," he stammered. "I probably don't, but I have no idea whether the power powder worked or not!" he said quickly.

Peyton frowned, "Well then figure out the answer *very quickly* or he'll figure it out for you!" He pointed back at me, and I tried my best not only to look terrifying but also not to roll my eyes or groan, which got a small chuckle out of Katie. When I was sure Earl wasn't looking, I glanced down at the others and stuck my tongue out at her. She grinned and stuck her tongue out right back at me.

Earl nodded timidly, and then he jumped up into the air in a way that was probably supposed to look like a heroic and dashing leap into flight but ended up only looking ridiculously stupid and hilarious because he promptly fell to the ground and landed on his butt.

He frowned, well he started out frowning, but then turned it into a groan of what I assumed to be pain. "Say something to me in another language."

"Chich-chich iko lekino ainea," Kit said. (You're a mindless, infuriating pig.)

Earl paled even more. "I have no idea what you

said! I can't fly either, and that means I've lost my powers!" He began to panic. "What do I do?! What am I supposed to tell the others? This is terrible! I truly am powerless! I was supposed to bring them news of great success at the next meeting! I mean, they didn't like that I would be the first one to acquire hundreds of powers if the powder worked, but they...," he trailed off, as if he suddenly remembered we were all right there.

Tim cleared his throat. "So, where and when is this meeting Earl?"

Earl took a step backwards, "Oh no! Nononononono NO! I am NOT allowed to tell you that!"

Peyton turned to me and raised his eyebrows.

"When and where? He asked you; answer him," I said, dropping my voice as low as I could possibly get it, until the walls shook. "*Truthfully!*" I thought to add.

Earl hesitated, but then he shook his head, "No."

"Tell us," I growled.

Earl shook his head.

Katie slipped over to my ear. "John," she whispered.

Katie's Narration:

"John," I whispered. "You're just going to have to be more threatening. I know you don't want to, but remember, he tried to make you kill us!"

John's gaze hardened. I had had a feeling that would do it. He stood up slowly, unfolding himself until he loomed (and boy do I mean LOOMED!) over us, his head nearly bumping the roof. He bent over, and, before any of us could blink, he had snagged the back of Earl's collar between two fingers and swung Earl up into the air. Earl screamed as John once again stood up to his full height.

"WHEN AND WHERE IS THE MEETING?!" he roared, so loudly that we all had to cover our ears so we didn't become deaf from the volume of his voice.

John's Narration:

I hate this, but I have to do it. Besides, to be honest, I think it serves him right.

Earl squirmed as I lifted him up to be level with one of my eyes. "It's at the headquarters, the day after tomorrow!"

'Perfect!' I thought. *'That totally fits with our plan.'*

"Do I know you're telling the truth?" I asked.

Earl gulped. "Yes, I swear it on my life!"

"Where is the headquarters?" I asked.

Earl swallowed so hard that I could see his (to me anyways) teeny-tiny Adam's apple move. "Put me down and I'll tell you! I swaratak!"

I leaned over and dropped to one knee, setting him on the ground unceremoniously, glad for an excuse to stop being terrifying.

"Thank you, thank you, thank you!" Earl said gratefully. "Now, as I promised, the coordinates. Does anyone have a piece of paper and a pen?" he asked shakily.

Nathan dug around in his pockets, produced the items, and handed them to Earl. Earl hastily scribbled down two strings of numbers and handed the paper back to Nathan. Nathan put them in his pocket and then he looked at Peyton.

Peyton walked up to Earl, and he and Nathan each took one of Earl's arms and escorted him out of the room.

"We'll be back in a minute," Peyton called over his shoulder.

I lay down on my side in front of the others. "Thank goodness that's over!" I mumbled.

The others lay down on the floor and stretched, yawning quietly.

"Why are battles so exhausting?" Tim yawned.

We all yawned somewhat simultaneously and shrugged.

"Peyton better hurry back or I might fall asleep right here," Virgil said, lying on his back and staring at the intricate murals on the ceiling of the ballroom.

We laughed. "I'm sure he and Nathan will not fail to wake you up should you truly fall asleep," Sarah giggled.

We chatted for a few minutes and then Peyton and Nathan jogged back into the room, both of them looking pleased with themselves.

"How did it go?" Kit asked, propping herself up on her elbows.

Nathan grinned. "He put up a bit of a fight once he realized where we were taking him, but we, uh, solved that problem. He's in the dungeon, solitary confinement, cell 11A32." He cracked his knuckles and smirked.

They lay down with the others. We decided that, though Nathan and Virgil weren't elements, that they could become a part of our group. We had started to fill them in on the plan we had made for our "climactic battle," revising it as we went along to fit them in, when Nathan cleared his throat,

"Um, guys, if you don't mind," he paused. "I have two little siblings, Andrew, who's sixteen, and Leilani, who's fourteen, and, well, they have great powers, and I was wondering, could they help? 'Cause they really want to, and I quote, 'Sic it to those evil traitors' as best as they can."

We looked at each other.

"What are their powers?" I asked.

"Leilani can fly and control weather, and Andrew, well, Andrew's power is kind of complicated to explain. Basically, he can shoot bullets out of his fingers, and he has *deadly* accuracy. BUT! The bullets themselves are special, because he can turn them into anything he needs or wants to. Well, sort of, anyway. He can turn them into bombs, fireballs, smokescreens, sleeping gas dispensers, electric shock dispensers, mind control tabs, on and on and on and on," Nathan finished.

We looked at each other again.

"Are they here? Can we meet them?" Tim asked.

Nathan nodded. "They went off with Jameson to his room since the three of them share a similar dislike for and disgust concerning dances. I can go get them if you want me to."

We all nodded. Nathan got up and turned to leave the room. Peyton followed him. When the two of them reached the door, Peyton grabbed Nathan's arm and started speaking to him quietly. I strained to hear what he was saying. I could barely make it out, but this is what I heard. "Look, Nathan. Andrew I'm fine with; he's great. But LEILANI? You have just got to be kidding me! I mean, you know what she's like! Especially around other girls! And, if you haven't noticed, we are working with four girls here! What do you think she's going to do when she sees them? 'Cause I doubt she's going to give them all hugs and get along well with them. You know just as well as I do that is just NOT her thing Nick! Why can't you just bring Andrew?!"

To which Nathan responded, also in hushed tones: "Look, she has improved, Peyton. Maybe this time will be different; who knows. Just give her a chance, okay pal?"

Peyton snorted. "Do I need to remind you of all her previous fiascos, Nick?! The gala charity ball. The court fiasco with the visiting dowager princess from another planet. The carriage parade where she had to sit with the daughters of other Dukes and Duchesses, even if they weren't the daughters of the Grand Duke and Grand Duchess. The Freedom Day March. The Memory Day Flag Placing at the Soldiers' Cemetery. On and on and on and on and on and on and ON! GIRLS AND LEILANI JUST DON'T MIX!!!"

Nathan sighed. "Just give her a chance! Please!" Then he turned and left the ball room.

Peyton groaned and headed back to the rest of us. Sarah touched his arm lightly. "What was that all about?"

Peyton just gave a little strained sort of laugh. "Oh, you'll see." Soon enough Nathan returned with two people following him. The boy and the girl stepped toward our group and introduced themselves.

Katie's Narration:

Man, we just keep getting more and more people every day!

Andrew is tall, taller than me but shorter than Nathan (And DEFINITELY shorter than Peyton), maybe six feet tall on Earth. He has light blonde hair that looks like gold in the sunlight. He has gray/blue/green eyes that, oddly enough, look dark blue when he turns his head, and they sparkle with an unquenchable sort of fire. His hair is swept to the right, and it keeps falling into his eyes. He's wearing (I guess since he didn't go to the ball) a dark blue shirt that's almost black, jeans, and a plain red tie. He's rocking back and forth on his heels and smiling widely, his grin lighting up his face and revealing perfect white teeth.

Leilani also has blond hair with whiteish highlights, and hers is short, barely to her shoulders. She has bright green eyes and pale skin. She's kind of short, but she has a wiry frame and broad shoulders and a strong jaw. She's pretty, but in an outdoorsy sort of way. Her eyes sparkle like emeralds, and I saw them light up when they landed on each of the boys, but when she looked at Priti, Sarah, Kit, and me, she looked almost confused.

"You want me to work with girls?" I overheard her ask Nathan, in a half-disgusted, half-amused tone that I didn't like.

Nathan sighed. "Leia, you are a girl. Stop acting like girls are inferior to you. These girls might just surprise you too."

"Well, I'll try," she smirked.

They walked up and stopped directly in front of us. Leilani looked at each of us girls with a cold hard stare, then she spat. As Nathan pulled her aside and lectured her, I decided I didn't like her that much. I tuned back into their conversation in time to hear Nathan say, "Leilani Kashnikov Peterson, behave!"

To which she responded, "Of course, dear brother, or should I call you by you real name? Lord Nathan Violence Johansson." She smiled, slapped him, and flounced back over to stand next to Andrew, who was blushing violently, staring at the floor.

We all looked at each other in shock (Well, everyone except for Nathan, Andrew, Leilani, and Peyton that is. I noticed Peyton mouthing, "See, I told you bringing her was a bad idea!" or something like that, to Nathan.). Was Nathan really Lord Johansson?!

I mean, I know Lord Johansson can shapeshift, but that still couldn't be right!

Tim strode over to Nathan and led him back to us. Nathan just stood there, staring at the floor, rubbing where Leilani had slapped him. (We discovered later that her hand had been crackling with lightning when she had slapped him.)

"Are you Lord Johansson?" Sarah asked with a quiver in her voice.

Nathan looked up at us, opened his mouth, then shut it abruptly, and dropped his gaze back to the floor again.

Kit stepped toward him shyly and took his hand in both of hers. She walked away from us with him and they started talking quietly.

I strained to hear what they were saying. When I had no luck, I thought about seeing if John could hear them (because he probably could), but I decided not to.

I went over to where Andrew and Leilani were standing, determined to learn more about them. Andrew and Tim had obviously already hit it off and were animatedly discussing weaponry and heavy artillery. Leilani just stood there glaring at me, so I went and engaged in the conversation that Andrew and Tim were having.

About five minutes later Nathan and Kit walked back over to us. We broke off our conversations abruptly. Nathan looked at us with uncharacteristic shyness.

"Um...," he cleared his throat. "I need to tell y'all something."

"Are you Lord Johansson?" Tim asked straight up.

"No!" Nathan said quickly. "I'm not! I swear!"

"Then who are you?" I asked.

He blushed, "Let me tell you a story:

Once upon a time, there was a little boy. That little boy was trained in all sorts of martial arts tactics and defense. He was building bombs before he could walk, and by the age of three he was educated in nearly every form of martial arts there is. But, at the age of five, he was bound and gagged and tied to a column on someone's front porch in the middle of the night. In the morning the door opened and out came a husband and wife with cups of commonatea, I think you Earthlings call it coffee, to watch the sunrise. When they saw the boy, they leapt about three feet in the air. They untied him, read the note that had been left with him, and took him inside. They adopted him as their own son, and he became their oldest child. His name went from Nathan Violence Johansson to Nathan Pietrov Peterson. As I'm sure you can guess, that little boy was me. I used to be Lord Johansson's middle son." He stared at the floor awkwardly. "I've been living with the, er, good guys for fourteen years now. I'm not an SCL; I swear it on my life!"

We looked at each other, unsure of what to do.

John cleared his throat awkwardly. "Are you saying you have other siblings? Lord Johansson has more kids?!"

Nathan almost smiled. "Oh yeah, and they're, like, much worse than me. My younger brother is constantly making the news for, uh, things, and my older brother…," He paused for a moment. "My older brother, oh boy, he's… complicated, to say the least. Because not only is he like Peyton, well, he has gigantism anyways, but he's *much* taller, and he's *DANGEROUS*! He's three years older than I am, and he'd kill you as soon as look at you. He's the most skilled and terrifying assassin in the entire galaxy, not to mention...," he sucked in a breath nervously, "he has *the best powers from every single power category* — well, all of them except for Peyton's techie power, and the power to shrink and grow! *That means he has over fifty powers!*"

"*WHAT?!*" Tim shouted. "*How is that even possible?!!!*"

Nathan sighed, "Dad, er, Lord Johansson, experimented on him when he was younger. He was originally born with fifteen powers, which is still higher than anyone else in the history of Nordiaho, but then Lord Johansson manipulated his DNA and gave him all the powers he could, which were the best of the best. He has 58 powers! The only reason that he couldn't give him the techie power, was because no one had been born with that power when he did the experiments. No one actually knew that power existed until Peyton was born two years later. And the only reason that Lord Johansson didn't give him the power to shrink and grow was because it was such a rare and special power that dad, er, Lord Johansson, couldn't unlock its, eh, code. I mean, he tried... but something went wrong, something went really, *really* wrong. Also, Lord Johansson put a mind control chip in the back of his neck that allows Lord Johansson to take control of his mind whenever he's in a close proximity to him. Not only that, if Lord Johansson ever dies, Lord Johansson's 'brain' will be downloaded onto the chip, and then Ben, my brother, will become Lord Johansson, only a thousand times more dangerous! I know Ben was trying to figure out how to get it out of himself safely, but, then again, I haven't seen him in almost seven years. I do know one thing though; if Ben really likes you, like as a friend or whatever, Lord Johansson's chip is so 'old' technology-wise, that Ben is able to fight the chip's influence so that he won't kill you. That is, if Lord Johansson hasn't fixed that. Anyway, I highly suggest you stay clear of him!"

"How... how many people has he, um, killed?" Sarah whispered.

Nathan paused to think for a moment. "At least two hundred and eighty-four, although my numbers aren't really up to date on that. He could have killed more than that by now. He's taken out entire governments in one night. The only person he's ever liked enough not to kill though... was me. I was in my room one night, in the Peterson's house, and all of a sudden he came crashing through the window. I was only twelve. Lord Johansson came in after him and ordered him to kill me. Then Lord Johansson left, probably to make it look like he had no hand in the killing. Ben could barely stand up in my room, and the ceiling was nine feet high. He looked at me, sitting on my bed, paralyzed by fear, crying. It was the perfect night because everyone else was out of the house. Andrew, then nine, was at a friend's house; Leilani, then seven, was at another friend's house; and Mom and Dad were out on a date night, if you will. I was all alone, and Ben knew it, and I knew it too. I knew what he could do to me, and I was so terrified, I started to beg him, to plead with him, to please, spare my life, not to do this monstrous act, and to act like a human. He paused in moving towards me. I was terrified, but I just started saying, 'Ben, please!', over and over and over. All of a sudden, he jerked. He started to strain; it looked like he was pulling against invisible ropes. Then, he started to scream — not a high scream, but a sort of anguished, pain-filled, terrifying yell, as his chip started to spark and crackle. This went on for five minutes until at last he collapsed to the floor, panting and groaning. I crawled to the edge of my bed. I had always been terrified of him as a little kid, probably because he was almost nine feet tall, but he seemed to have liked me when we were growing up. I don't know why, but the fact that he liked me saved my life. He looked up at me finally. 'Nate! Did I hurt you?' he managed to get out in between gasps.

'No. Did I make you mad or something? Why did you come here? Why would Dad make you kill me, Ben?' I had said, trembling. Ben looked at me, and I'll never forget the look he gave me, ever. 'I don't know Nate. I just don't know. But I'm not going to kill you. I like you too much to do that.' He smiled wanly up at me, then he stood up. Before I could think, I ran over and gave him a hug. Well, I kind of hugged his knee, if you know what I mean. Then he left me, and I haven't seen him since that horrid night." He sighed. "I know it sounds weird, but I do miss him, a lot, even if he is an assassin and a murderer."

Tim coughed, and we all looked at one another again.

* * * * * *

After fifteen minutes of tense discussion, we decided that Nathan could stay in the group. Then after that we took a vote on whether Andrew and Leilani could join. Andrew's staying was a unanimous "yes!", but Lcilani (after some pleading on Nathan's part) was eventually given a "trial."

Then we decided to go to bed. Lying down in complete exhaustion, we all fell asleep almost instantly.

* * * * * *

The next morning, we woke up almost at noon. When I woke up, I was surprised to see that I was one of the last people awake. John was lying down in a corner talking with Andrew, Nathan, Peyton, and Tim. Kit and Sarah were talking quietly to each other, and only Priti and Leilani were still asleep.

I sat up and stretched. Sarah saw me, and, smiling widely, beckoned me to come over and sit with Kit and her. I walked over and sat across from Sarah. Kit had apparently been telling Sarah about herself, now that Kit could speak English and all.

We were talking together quietly when someone

cleared her throat softly behind me. I looked at Kit and Sarah, who were both sitting across from me, and noticed Kit's expression go from open and happy to dull and reserved. I twisted at the waist to see who was there and saw Leilani standing behind me. I stood up cautiously. Leilani looked at the floor and cleared her throat again,

"Um, thanks for agreeing that I should stay, Katie, even if only on a trial. I thought about it really hard last night, and I'm willing to give you girls a trial, you know, since you're giving me one," she said, with uncharacteristic shyness.

We looked at each other, surprised.

"Okay," Sarah said. "Deal."

Leilani smiled and sat down with us. I noticed that Andrew saw all of this, and he nudged Nathan, who nudged Peyton, and the three of them stared at Leilani in utter disbelief for a moment or two. I tried my hardest not to laugh out loud.

Leilani, obviously taking the deal to heart, began asking Sarah and me loads of questions about Earth and Kit dozens of questions about life as a ClanaTupek. We, in turn, asked her questions about how she grew up. Kit asked her, at one point, why she didn't like girls? To this Leilani responded that she had been raised around boys all her life, so she was used to boys, and most of the girls at court were "weak and boring, always preferring to play with dolls and clothes rather than with swords and guns." So, she decided that boys were more fun and that girls were weak and lame.

Finally, Priti woke up, and we all ate breakfast together.

John's Narration:

You know, I just can't wait until I'm my normal size again. I mean, this is ridiculous! Agh! I could just scream! I hate this! One more day, John; just one. More. Day. Of. This. Torture!

I wonder how our battle will go. It is honestly kind of making me nervous, all this planning and re-planning and re-re-planning. At least now we have a solid plan.

Andrew doesn't seem to care that I'm almost 500 feet taller n' he is. Which is nice. Leilani doesn't even acknowledge that I'm here really, which is not that nice.

Breakfast was good. I've never before eaten any of the things that were served, so that was kind of fun. Of course, I couldn't eat in the dining room, so we had a picnic in the ball room and Priti grew my food again, since I gave the gun back to her. Now, at almost noon, Andrew is demonstrating his power for us. He has been for the past few minutes. He told us to call out the names of different weapons, and he tried to make a bullet for each one. The most popular type he has done so far is a gatling gun. (We had to explain to him and the other Nordiahoans what a gatling gun was, which was kind of funny, but whatever.)

Lunch'll be soon, and then Jameson and Virgil are in a play at court, and Virgil has invited us to come watch them. I'll be invisible of course. Palace life sure is fun, although I bet I'd have more fun if I were my normal height; but, oh well. At least the palace, being a palace and all, is big enough for me to fit semi-comfortably in several of the rooms.

At least I'm kinda used to being this tall now. The one thing I might never get used to though is being stared at and being feared. I can only hope I'll shrink at the end of all of this! I can't help worrying that I'll never shrink though. I mean, what if I don't shrink? What if I have to stay over 450 feet tall FOREVER? What if we never get to go home? What if…What if…What if. I don't know why I just can't start thinkin' everything'll go right for a change. I know I've got *some* right to worry, but still….

* * * * * *

We're at the play now. It's based on the history of Nordiaho. From the "birth" of Nordiaho through the civilization of it, all the way up to acting out the prophesy and the current Royal Family. Jameson has black hair that is about to his chin (boys in Nordiaho seem to copy the longer hairstyles that boys had out West in the 1860's and then the "rebels" had again in the 1960's). He has *black* eyes and is tall (he's maybe 6' 1", but it's really hard for *me* to tell). He played a ClanaTupek, himself, and the talking wolf who delivered the Prophesy. Apparently, he can shape-shift (according to Nathan anyway). Virgil played himself, an angel, and, ironically, he played Peyton during the "fulfillment of the Prophesy." If you ask me, Jameson should have played Peyton, because, even though both younger brothers are much shorter than Peyton, Peyton and Jameson both have black hair while Virgil has *red* hair.

Somehow, they also convinced Peyton to act in the play as well. Who did he play? Me. He wore stilts! Ha! I wonder whose idea that was….

* * * * * *

Katie's Narration:

I cannot wait until the battle! Hopefully, after it all is over and we've won, John will shrink. If you're wondering why I said, "once we win," not "if we win," I'll tell you why.

The SCLs don't have a John. It's that simple. With John, we might not even have to fight half of the battle. Some of the men might just freak out and run away. That would be a nice change.

The play was great by the way. We laughed like crazy. I was most surprised when Peyton came out as John. For two reasons: one, I was surprised that Peyton decided to do any acting in the first place, and two, he did such a dead-on impression of John that we all laughed. I heard/felt John leave the courtyard, and then I heard him laughing over the earpiece. It was so loud I had to take my earpiece out, and I saw the others doing the same. Even Peyton stopped his performance long enough to take his out, turn it off, and shove it into his pocket hastily. It was hilarious.

When we were back in the other ballroom, Peyton, Virgil, and Jameson came in. Jameson jumped when he saw John, but he didn't say anything. I did notice that he stuck next to Peyton after he saw John though.

"So, what'd ya think?" Jameson asked.

"Jameson, it's...'So what did you think'?" Peyton corrected him quietly.

"Oh please," Jameson groaned. "Like you can correct about grammar, gangsta, but, if it doth please ye, your Royal Highness," Jameson teased in a lilting accent, "What didst ye think of our theatre play, my dear fine friends?"

Peyton groaned and rolled his eyes at Jameson's antics and we all laughed.

"It was great," Tim said.

"It was very, very funny," John grinned down at us.

Jameson stared up at him. Then, when John stared right back at him, Jameson cleared his throat awkwardly. "Um, I have to go. Nice meetin' y'all." He bowed then he left the room.

"Peyton, if you don't mind my asking, why were you in the play? You don't really strike me as an actor. You seem more of a…uh… a swordsman and a gunfighter than an actor," Tim said.

Peyton laughed. "Surprise you though it may, I do enjoy acting. Well, in some circumstances anyway. But, if it makes you feel any better, I prefer the roles of fighters and soldiers better than romantic swoons and heartthrobs, etc."

"Well knock me over with a feather and blow me away," Andrew teased. "Ol' tough boy ain't as tough as we done did think," he drawled.

Peyton rolled his eyes and slugged Andrew on the shoulder. In response, Andrew pounced on him, and the two of them started wrestling.

If you ask me, the odds here are kind of uneven. I mean, think about it. Peyton, at least 7' 4", strong, huge muscles, seasoned, hardened by his "alley living" versus Andrew, six feet tall, slight, not soft from court life, but definitely not anywhere near as experienced (is that the right word?) as Peyton. I mean, that doesn't seem fair at all.

Virgil and Nathan looked at each other, and Tim looked at them with a grin.

"Weeeeeelll?" Tim drawled.

With a war whoop the boys joined in the wrestling match.

We girls looked at each other. "Why should we let the boys have all the fun?" Sarah smirked.

We grinned, and then, with war whoops of our own, we jumped on in, laughing and hollering.

To my surprise, after a minute, Andrew squirmed out of the writhing ball of people. Peyton jumped out after him, but, before Peyton could catch Andrew, Andrew was off like a shot. He ran across the room, beating Peyton even though Andrew's legs are a lot shorter. He scaled up one of the columns in the blink of an eye and perched on the ledge at the top. Peyton stood at the bottom, laughing up at him, and Andrew, perched at the top, laughed down at him. And John, lying on his stomach with his chin propped in his hands, laughed down at all of us.

* * * * * *

John's Narration:

We, well, they, horsed around for a little while longer and then it was time for dinner. We ate (the food here is amazing), and then we watched a "filmet" (a movie) called "Jupiter's Avenged." It was kind of neat. It was a superhero movie, but it took place underwater on Jupiter. (Not our Jupiter in the Milky Way, but *their* Jupiter in the Grindian Galaxy) These kids lived underwater in this undersea civilization that was in turmoil, and some of them had superpowers, so they united and saved everyone from the evil dictators. So yeah, it was exciting. Nordiahoan movies are actually really, really cool. Especially since they're so much more high-tech and "believable" than some of ours.

We also picked a new team name, since there are eleven of us now. We're the Enhanced Eleven. It's kind of like a play on words; I like it.

Now we're going to bed. Since tomorrow's the battle n' all, we gotta be well rested up. G'night.

CHAPTER 13

The Final Battle, For Now

Today's the day! This is nerve-racking! Here's how it's going to go today: We'd received word that the entire SCL army had assembled at the SCL headquarters. Katie, Sarah, Tim, Peyton, Kit, Nathan, Virgil, Andrew, and Leilani are going to draw all the men out and lead them to an uninhabited plain. I will be waiting there, hiding in the exact center of the plain, shrunk (thanks to Peyton), and underground (thanks to Priti, who managed to convince a groundhog to let me borrow its powers so that I could tunnel under the ground).

When the others get there, they are going to back into a circle above my hiding place and allow the SCL troops to close in a circle around them. Then, using my superspeed, I'm going to burst out of the ground and speed out to the edge of the troops. Peyton is then going to grow me and I'm going to use my superspeed and run around the troops really fast, hemming them all in and preventing them from escaping. Then, Katie, Sarah, Tim, Kit, Priti, Andrew, and Leilani are going to hit the deck, and, while Katie places a force field around me to keep me from getting hit by it, Peyton, Virgil, and Nathan are going to use their shock wave to stun all the troops. Priti is then going to remove SCL's mind control off of any man who needs that, and then I stop running and "wrap" myself in a circle around any remaining truly-evil-cream-of-the-crop, and we fight! So here goes. Wish us luck!

We ate a hearty breakfast in the ballroom, after which Queen Cathy, King Charles, princesses Liliana and Katiana, and prince Jameson all came to wish us good luck. Jameson offered to be our home team, monitoring our vitals, our escape options, our openings for attack, and our communications. We agreed, then we set out.

Or, we tried to. Instead, Eleanor appeared in the

doorway. Thank goodness she appeared as a hologram again, not a real person. If she had appeared as a real person she probably would have died. Why? Because as I was crawling out the ballroom doors, I looked at the doorway and no one was there. But, when I looked again, there she was, staring up at me, arms folded, her hologram figure sticking up out of my hand. I let out a yell and fell over backwards, almost landing on the others. I sat up slowly, panting.

"Sorry!" I whispered.

She smiled slightly. "No, Jonathan, that was my fault. I'm not that good at holographic teleportation yet, but I have something for all of you." She raised her hands and a stack of boxes appeared in front of us with one of our names on each one. "Don't worry; they'll fit," she grinned. "Good luck today, all of you."

Excited, we opened our boxes. Priti opened hers first. When she saw what was inside, she started squealing. She pulled out the contents. Katie gasped when she saw what Priti had pulled out and quickly opened her box. We all followed suit.

Now, I know y'all may be thinking. 'For crying out loud dude! Just tell us what was in the boxes already!', or you may be thinking, 'Just tell us so we can hear about the battle already!', or you may not be thinking anything at all. But I'll tell you what was in the boxes. Inside our boxes were... supersuits! I know some of us already have some, but, unlike our matching black ones that we had started out with, these suits were each personalized. These supersuits gave each of us our own superhero symbol and colors, too.

Katie's suit was a deep cobalt blue with a white arrowhead on the right shoulder. Sarah's was the softest pink with two blue bars on each upper arm. Tim's was blue and white tie-dye with a black wave silhouette on his left shoulder. Priti's was a deep green camouflage with a bright red paw print on each shoulder. Kitaileeo's was white with beadwork all over it. Peyton's was bright, fiery red with a mark of a computer on one shoulder and a bolt of flame on the other. Virgil's was red and white tie-dye with a bolt of flame in front of a cloud on each shoulder. Nathan's was a stormy blue-gray with a lightning bolt, such a white that looking at it could almost blind you, on each shoulder. Leilani's was pale blue with a sun on each shoulder. Andrew's was really cool; it was a green camouflage that resembled a World War II soldier's uniform. On each shoulder, there was a circle, red outer rim, blue inner rim, with a white star in the center. Over that there was a black silhouette of what closely resembled a double-barreled rifle. And mine is gold and silver tie-dye with three rocket-like daggers racing behind a crescent moon on one shoulder and a pair of barbells on the other shoulder.

Eleanor grinned. "You can take them on and off the way Kitaileeo taught you. They're like the first suits that we gave the original five of you at the beginning, but these are all personalized for both your power and who you are. Headquarters decided you'd earned them. Oh! I almost forgot; they automatically adjust to your body's size and shape, so, John, in your case, when you shrink, it'll shrink to fit you. Speaking of John, I hear you've acquired some new powers!"

"I have?" I asked, confused.

She nodded her head, smiling, "Yes Jonathan. When you blew the power-stealing powder on Earl, you acquired his powers, remember? Try it out; see if you can fly or if you're multilingual."

I took my earpiece out so that the chip in it wouldn't

translate for me, "Kit, would you say something to me in TukaTapei please?"

She grinned. "Kyeno okone hepno cheko?" (Well, did it work?)

I smiled widely, "Ayellah, Ictha heponoke hepno kya!" (Yes, I think it did.)

Everyone grinned. "Now can you fly?" Tim asked, his grin broadening.

"I dunno. Let's find out," I smirked, and, all of a sudden flew up a little into the air and hovered there. Tim crowed like a rooster and leapt into the air while everyone else high fived each other. I carefully lowered myself to the ground, grinning fit to burst and laughing.

We "spun-changed" into our new supersuits and outfitted ourselves with weaponry. In the bottom of our boxes we had found sheathes, holsters, and a utility belt that all matched our supersuits, so we used those. Then, at long last, we were ready. Ready for the battle that would decide the fate of Nordiaho.

"Well, are you ready?" Tim bounced on his toes. He and Andrew couldn't hold still, as if they were barely able to control their excitement. "Let's go, let's go, let's GO!"

"Please! Hurry up you guys!" Andrew echoed. "I wanna do some major avenging, or whatever you call it."

We laughed.

I turned to Peyton and Sarah, who were standing together. "Sarah, would you do the favor of turning me invisible please?"

She nodded and then she did. With a sigh of relief, I then looked at Peyton. "Peyton, would you shrink me please?"

He grinned, and, all of a sudden, I went from being the size of the room lying on the floor, to lying on the floor in front of the others, normal size. I leapt to my feet, still invisible, invigorated from being my normal height once more. Then, at long last, we headed out the door.

* * * * * *

Katie's Narration:

The wind was still, and the sun rose high into a brassy sky. We were sweating slightly, both from the heat and the anticipation and anxiety of the mission.

When we parted ways, John headed to the field where we were to "rendezvous" (with enemy troops in hot pursuit if all went well), and the rest of us headed to the SCL headquarters.

When we made it to the headquarter's location we paused. None of us had really seen the building from the outside before. It was ugly. Very, very, VERY ugly. The building was huge, industrial, and made of black-ish gray metal. I don't know if you've ever before seen a building that's just dark and menacing, but this building oozed darkness, literally.

We all took a deep breath collectively, then we all stepped forward, marching towards the building with purpose.

We infiltrated the compound stealthily using Sarah's invisibility as a cloaking device. We crept closer and closer to our target, the building's main communications array control panel. We had found the location of this panel during previous raids on the headquarters. Of course, during these, we had never seen the outside of the building because we had used the secret door that we found behind the waterfall. That control room had a passage that led all the way to the heart of the headquarters! Once there, I pulled a computer chip out of a pocket on my utility belt. It contained a message we had forced Earl to record from his cell this morning. I slid it into a slot in the PA system computer monitor, slapped the alarm button on another console, and, with alarms blaring and the message playing throughout the buildings, we ran out and assembled outside. We could hear the message playing on a loop. "Troops, leaders, honorable persons of our noble and proud group, we are under attack! Those filthy dogs, the Defenders of Nordiaho, have invaded our headquarters! They are currently assembling by the bay doors of wing 65A. Though they have beaten us before, we now have an advantage. *All* of our men and *all* of our soldiers are here! So, troops, leaders, brothers, to ARMS!" A great roar rose from the men in the buildings, and then ALL THE MEN ON THE CAMPUS rushed out of the buildings and formed ranks in front of us.

Peyton, who has the loudest voice, let it rip. "Catch us if you can, morons!"

We turned and ran, racing on pure adrenaline for the clearing. "John, are you ready?" I asked over the headset.

"Yep. Bring 'em on. I prefer a straight fight to all this

sneakin' around," he responded, laughing.

I chuckled, "Good, 'cause we're bringin' 'em all right!"

We reached the field and backed into a circle in the middle as planned. They grouped around us, mocking us for our stupidity. We just grinned. As soon as they had all arrived, I whispered into my earpiece, "John, NOW!"

The ground exploded all of a sudden, and the men were trapped as John ran out, grew, and ran around them all. They let out a yell, then a fierce battle cry. While they were distracted by John, the rest of us, except for Peyton, Virgil, and Nathan of course, hit the deck, and I created a force field around John. Then, with fierce battle cries of their own, Virgil, Nathan, and Peyton created their shock wave, knocking all of the men to the ground. Priti called the animals, and she quickly borrowed the powers of a pegasus and leapt into action.

Within minutes Priti had removed the mind control from all the men under its influence, and John, despite the men's pleading, had picked them up and set them down outside of his "tornado fence". (They did not like that!) Finally we were left with about 100 men to fight, a smaller number than I had thought it would be. We assumed battle positions as they recovered from the shock wave and leapt to their feet. For a moment, they seemed rather dismayed when they realized that the rest of the troops were MIA, but they quickly recovered and formed ranks. John quietly wished us good luck, then backed away slightly so that he didn't accidentally cause any problems.

We surged forward with a roar, meeting the soldiers head on. The battle lines moved back and forth as we used both our powers and skills, and the various weapons we had brought with us, to win the day against these surprisingly talented men. Peyton, whom we discovered is an excellent sword fighter, was easily defending himself against seven men, his sword blade flashing in the air and the ring of clashing steel echoing across the plain. Tim was using bow and arrow and his expertise at marksmanship to his advantage. Priti and the animals were fighting side by side, valiantly darting in and out amongst the men with battle cries of their own — screeches, roars, howls, neighs, and more. Virgil and Nathan were fighting side by side as well, performing miraculous acrobatic feats and combining those with their flame and lightning to make a powerful force to be reckoned with. Sarah looked like she was having the time of her life. She was using her invisibility to cloak herself, and then she was using the bars as "leverage points" for gymnastic moves that she combined with martial arts techniques to create her own fighting style. Andrew was using "gatling gun mode" to distract the men. Unfortunately, their armor turned out to be just as bulletproof as ours was, so it only created a distraction. But the rest of us could use that to our advantage. Leilani was acting as our eyes in the sky and was making it hail down on the men from quite a height. Kit was like a force in herself, taking out men right and left. They never even saw her coming, literally. (Unfortunately, I can't tell you *what* her powers are, or I'd get myself into trouble. Sorry!) John was keeping an eye on everyone, although I could sense that he really wished he could be fighting alongside of us. As for myself, I was using my powers to their full extent — placing force fields around the others, keeping troopers at bay, fighting hard, and pulling my weight just like the others.

Man after man fell, and, surprisingly, we were winning. But then, as it always seems to happen, the tide turned on us. Unbeknownst to us, the men had sent a contingency battalion… underground. Apparently they had a few people who could harness the powers of animals as well. Suddenly we were attacked by at least 200 men, all of whom burst out of the ground with fearsome roars.

"Back up!" Peyton yelled. "Defensive positions!"

We backed up to each other, forming a circle, shifting into battle stances and quietly bolstering each other's spirits. Leilani lowered herself to the ground and joined us.

"Plan? Anyone?" Tim whispered. "There are ten of us and about 60 of the hundred left, plus around 200 fresh men. I don't think we can swing it on just one-on-however-many anymore."

"You're right." Peyton said, his voice low and tinged with anger. "The fresh men will cause a problem, and we're already worn from fighting for a while and all that running we did earlier." He flicked his glance up to the men, who were watching us, waiting. "We need to work as a team."

We all agreed with him, but we had no time to form a plan, for the men suddenly decided they couldn't wait anymore. Either their patience ran thin, they decided they didn't want us to have time to plan, or they received an order from somewhere else, but they attacked.

Peyton raised his sword. "Attack!"

At the same time though, Tim yelled. "Hold 'em off!"

Out of the corner of my eye I saw them glance at each other. I knew that they had clashed in the past, because of their personalities and their drive, but I really hoped it wouldn't happen on the battlefield. Because that would cause problems. Suddenly, Tim nodded, conceding to Peyton. I don't know if he was conceding to his prince, or if he was simply backing down, or if he realized that attacking might just be the better way to go, but he still conceded.

Peyton grinned, then he said quietly, so that only we would hear him through our comms. "Stay in the defensive ring, but let's go! Attack!"

At once, we lunged. But everyone lunged in a different direction, based on where they were in the circle. So, all of a sudden, we were separated, and we didn't have people covering our backs.

"A team guys!" I screamed in frustration. "Work. As. A. Team!"

Then Peyton grabbed me and yanked me to the right. I was about to shout at him, when he whirled and skewered an SCL who had been coming up behind me. He grinned down at me, then he turned and pressed against my back. At least he and I had each other covered. Seconds later Sarah dashed over and joined us.

"Tim! Priti! Kit! Virgil! Andrew! Leilani! Nathan! Get over here!!" Sarah yelled, surprising me.

After a moment they rushed over, and we formed our circle once again. "Guys," I whispered over the headset. "Use your powers. Work together. Use the tools Eleanor gave us. Stay strong! We have to win!" The others chorused their agreement, and we leapt into action, still staying in our formation. Tim and Priti activated their pianthio holo displayers, creating multiple images of us, which ran among the bad guys, confusing them.

Quietly, Peyton told us to split into pairs, and to

protect each other's backs and go in and wreak havoc. We split up, Priti with Tim; Virgil with Nathan; Andrew with Leilani; Kit grabbed Sarah, muttering something to me about protecting her, since she had less of a fighting-inclined power. And Peyton and I were the only ones left. He looked down at me, shrugged, and then turned and pressed against my back again. It was slightly reassuring to be honest, to know that someone I could trust was backing me up. "I've got your back." He whispered, covering his mouthpiece. I was surprised I heard him over the noise of battle, but I smiled back at him and he grinned. Then we charged.

We found ourselves fighting next to Tim and Priti. Peyton was slashing with a sword of fire, and I was sending waves of my power into the men. Priti was sending in groups of animals, including holographically created ones, on her pianthio holo displayer, and they were fighting better than most humans I've seen. She was also borrowing their powers and using them to the greatest extent she could. Tim was sending laser thin blasts of water at the men, with enough force to cut like a bullet. There were screams all around us, but I was trying to drown them out. These men were evil.

They had to die. And if I was squeamish about it, if any of us were, they might win.

I heard Sarah and Kit letting off war whoops, and Leilani and Andrew yelling at the tops of their lungs. I heard Peyton breathing hard behind me, and I heard him let out a fierce yell as his sword rang out over the noise of the battle. I heard Tim berating the men and Priti calling out to different animals. I heard the animals growling and roaring and screeching. I heard the anguished screams of injured men. I saw the men falling, and I saw my teammates fighting and helping each other out.

The problem that we were facing, however, was that these men, unlike the men we had fought before in previous battles, had powers. All of them did. And they had strong enough powers to combat ours. And they had the power of numbers. They still had about 230 men, most of whom were fresh, so to speak.

"Guys," I said over my headset. "We need to figure out a way to use our powers together to beat them. Together we are more powerful than we are alone. We need to work together and combine our strengths." I heard them respond, agreeing with me.

"So, what do we know?" Peyton asked. "We know that when Virgil, Nathan, and I combine our fire and lighting, it makes a shock wave. And we know that Sarah has a rare power, and Katie is telekinetic. Priti can harness the powers of animals, which can only be unlocked if you have power stars. Tim is more powerful than most when he manipulates water, and Andrew can—" he broke off. "That's it!" he shouted, excitedly. "Tim, Andrew, you and your partners come over here! Quick!" They came over, their faces a mix of confusion, excitement, and slight exhaustion. "Tim, you and I will create two tornado-type funnels, starting small at us, and getting larger towards the men. Andrew, you shoot bullets into the tornadoes and they'll be funneled up to the larger ends and shot out at the men. That way we can distribute lots of bullets at one time and take out many men at once. Got it?" Tim and Andrew nodded, and they rotated so that Andrew was in between Tim and Peyton and the three of them were facing the main group of men, with Priti, Leilani, and myself facing away, protecting their backs.

I heard them create the funnels, and in my peripheral vision I saw the funnels grow and extend over the men. Then Andrew started shooting. I heard screams, and I knew the bullets were finding their marks. I was relieved that it seemed to be working, because, to tell you the truth, I was exhausted. It had been a long day, and I had been fighting harder than I ever had before. So I was glad we had found something that could help us win. But then, over the men's screams, I heard Peyton groan. "A telekinetic soldier stopped all the bullets in midair. I think we took out about 25 men though." But suddenly, there was a yell. Louder than anyone's yell should ever be. I froze. Peyton swore. "He shot all the bullets into John, in the only exposed place of skin."

I sucked in a breath. "Oh no." His face and neck. I whirled towards John, and I felt Leilani readjusting to protect my back as well as Andrew's. There were small pricks of blood all over John's cheeks and all down his neck. There was also a cold light of fury in his eyes unlike anything I had ever seen. In our moment of distraction, the men swarmed us. It was almost something akin to a football pile, or a big group of stray dogs fighting over a piece of food. And guess who was on which end…Quickly, we were overpowered. Leilani got sliced on the arm, and she screamed. How they had a knife that was able to penetrate her armor I don't know, but they did. Apparently. Peyton was singled out, and attacked by about twenty men - too many for him to fend off at once. They shoved him, hard, and pushed against him, until he lost his balance. He fell backwards, and I, being surrounded on all sides with no way to move away from him, was taken to the ground as well. Someone who must have had superstrength or something placed his boot on Peyton's chest, pinning him to the earth, with me trapped beneath him. Can I just say, especially when he's being pressed down hard by a "strongman", he's *heavy*. I guess that comes from his height. And, er, brawn. Tim and Priti were pressed up against one another, and Priti screamed as the arrows in Tim's back quiver dug into her skull. There were just too many men! We couldn't fight that many, not all at once, surrounded as we were, and injured or pinned down as some of us were. Suddenly, when we were thinking it was all over, a shadow loomed over us. John's hands swept in among the men attacking us and plucked all of us out of the crowd. He moved all of us to one hand and wrapped it around us. Then, I felt him rear back, and he punched the ground. Peering out through a crack in his hand, I saw what happened. When his, well, actually it was just two fingers, hit the ground, a shock wave radiated out from them through the ground. He sped out of the way, and the men fell to the ground in groups as the ground rolled and shook beneath them. John moved to set us down so we could go back to the battle while the men were dazed.

"Wait!" Priti suddenly called. "John! Do it again! But do it hard enough to make a deep hole in the ground. Remember, just like we did in our very first battle? When they fell deep enough that they got transported to that uninhabited planet of darkness for evil men to live out their days? Try to do that again!"

"Okay." John said, and I could tell that he was smiling slightly. He did it again. But then I heard him groan.

"What is it?" I asked him.

"Well, it did work. But... some of the men recovered surprisingly quickly, and they ran out of the way. Most of the men, um, went down with the ship, but there are still a few left."

"How many?" Nathan asked. He and Virgil were

doing surprisingly well for being closed in John's hand for the first time.

"Mmm, looks like about thirty." John said.

Several of us breathed sighs of relief. Thirty was a lot less than we had feared. And, hopefully, that meant the battle should end soon. John set us down, lay down around the men (kind of like a giant donut, honestly. Ha.) now that there weren't too many for him to circle around, and we shifted into battle positions. We had been battling for some time, at least three hours, with the hardest adversaries we'd ever faced, and we were exhausted, but bolstered by the fact that we were close to winning. I felt like falling over, but I knew I had to keep going. We took a collective breath, then we charged.

Fighting through fatigue, we met the men head-on, clashing physically, with our powers, or with our weapons. I took out two men by manipulating their atoms, sort of, via telekinesis, something Kit had taught me. Then I leapt into a one-on-one battle with a telekinetic soldier. Back and forth we went, sending our powers in strong waves at each other, blocking each other and fighting each other's strength. I could feel my power draining, and I was reminded of the time when I stopped the mind ray over John and then fainted, having used my power more than I had strength for. I could only hope I could last longer than that now. The two of us hit a stalemate, and I could tell that Peyton, still covering my back, was getting tired of staying in one place. Suddenly, the man just disappeared. Peyton and I glanced at each other over our shoulders. That was…weird.

Then the soldier with an incredibly strong power who was fighting Tim also disappeared. I saw Tim and Priti exchange glances as well. Suddenly, the most powerful men of the bunch, all of whom had been fighting one or two of us, disappeared. I caught a flash of black hair appear near Nathan, and I saw him jump sky high. Then he collapsed to the ground in shock.

"Virgil! Keep him covered!" Peyton yelled. Virgil shifted, trying to cover all of the directions at once. He was visibly nervous, unsure if he could protect Nathan from an attack on every side. Seeing the bad position that he was in, the soldiers eagerly switched their attentions to the two of them, hoping to wipe out two of our own. Peyton hissed in a breath, about to move, but then Andrew and Leilani were there taking up positions so that, with Virgil, they made a sort of circle around Nathan.

Before we even had a chance to figure out what was wrong with Nathan though, a blue field dropped down around all of us. The animals fighting alongside Priti, and the bullets Andrew was shooting, vanished into thin air. Peyton and Virgil's flame, Nathan's lighting, and Tim's water dropped to the ground as though the elements had all suddenly died. Peyton bit off a curse word, managing to stop it halfway out of his lips, and I heard Andrew let out an annoyed yell as Leilani did *not* manage to stop a word from slipping through her lips.

"What is it?" I asked.

"Looks like they've got a power stealer," Peyton said, tense against me. "It's a very rare power that allows the owner to suck away the powers of everyone he's fighting. They usually aren't able to utilize the powers they steal, but it does work excellently in an army, because then the other men with powers can attack while the other people they're attacking are powerless."

I looked at Sarah, catching her eye, and I was glad to see the determined grin that stole across her face. "Well." I said. "It's a good thing that I've lived 18 years without powers then. They are gonna find out that we're not as powerless without powers as they would hope."

Sarah laughed. "Oh, far from it."

Calmly, I unsheathed the large knife strapped to my calf and popped one of the spools of micro-filament wire out of a compartment in my utility belt. I only had one knife this large, and I was going to need it, so I tied one end of the wire through the lanyard tube and around the butt end of the knife. This was going to be… interesting. Out of the corner of my eye, I saw Sarah taking her ion blaster and her rapid-fire pistol out of their two holsters and taking off the safeties.

"That knife won't make it through their armor." Peyton muttered.

"I know." I whispered. That wasn't my plan. "Sarah you ready?" I asked.

"Yep." She said. "Here we go."

With a yell, I shot out my knife, whipping it, on the wire, around the torso of one of the men. I twisted my wrist, catching the knife on a connecting plate's edge of his armor. Then, I yanked. It hooked on the armor, ripping off a part of it, just big enough for Sarah to shoot through. And she did, nailing her mark on the first shot.

Peyton let out a low whistle. "Okay I wasn't expecting that." he chuckled.

I grinned, yanking the knife back to me to repeat the process. "Never underestimate ranch girls."

John burst out laughing, causing the men to clamp their hands over their ears. Peyton nudged me hard with one shoulder, sending me into a spin, putting him in the direction of the men. He lunged forwards, using the men's current distraction as John was still laughing, and jabbed out with his no-longer-flaming sword. I was glad Peyton, Kit, Leilani, Virgil, Andrew, and Nathan had brought their own weapons, since they had missed the chance to get some from the great "hoard" in the cave storage room way at the beginning. We hadn't had a chance to go back there to outfit them, what with all the captivity and stuff with John's being a giant and all. Speaking of Nathan...

"Andrew! How's Nathan?" I shouted.

"He's pretty dazed. I wish I knew why." Andrew replied, shooting a glance over his shoulder at Nathan, who was still on the ground, his face ashen.

Suddenly, Nathan was on his feet. "We have to finish this!" he told us shakily, but quietly, over the headset. "If we don't win this battle soon my dad is gonna send Ben out here to finish it!"

Leilani and Andrew gasped. Peyton sucked in a huge breath, and I could feel him holding back anger. At least, I thought it was anger. "How do you know that?" Peyton asked.

Nathan reddened. "Ben... told me. When all the really powerful men disappeared... th-that was him. He was trying to help us, because he knew if we didn't wrap it up soon, he'd have to end it. I don't know how he managed to get to us without Dad's realizing, and I don't know how he got out of his room either, but I think we need to believe him. Dad probably had him out of his room and prepping, and he must have sped here or something. That's why I was so shaken. Because he stopped and talked to me. I think he was telling the truth though. I... I trust him."

I felt Peyton breathing hard and fast against my

back, almost panting, his muscles still tight with anger. "*Trust him?!* Nathan, he almost killed you!! And—" he broke off. I sensed there were things he wasn't willing to tell all of us.

"Peyton," Nathan said softly. "I know you were friends with him. That makes sense, because you both had your ages accelerated," I was shocked, twisting to stare at Peyton, meeting only his back. He thrust his sword into another man, catching him between the connections of his armor and dropping him, anger in every line of his body. "and you two were the only two—"

"Nathan!" Peyton bit out. I had heard him switch his headset frequency so that he was only talking to Nathan, but I couldn't help but hear it. "Watch it. You know why that can't get out," he added, so low I hardly caught it.

Nathan paled slightly. "I was just gonna say you two were the only Nordiahoans with gigantism." I felt Peyton relax marginally.

"You are?!" I asked, surprised. That didn't make any sense. I got the feeling that Nathan knew something about Peyton that the rest of us didn't. Something

Peyton *really* wanted to keep a secret. But I let it drop.

"Yes, they are." Nathan said. "*As I was saying,* I know you two were friends, and that makes sense. There's nothing wrong with that. I mean, for crying out loud, I'm his freaking *brother*! And I say we should trust him and get this battle over with before he gets sent by Dad to kill us all. You know we can't fight him."

"You're right. Fine. How long do we have?" Peyton conceded.

Nathan glanced at his watch. "Twenty minutes from now."

I winced. Twenty minutes, sixteen men. They had powers, we did not. "Well, the odds are not exactly stacked in our favor…"

Tim interrupted me. "Aw to heck with the odds. I'd rather face long odds than face more-than-probable death."

I saw hands dipping to holsters, boot jets activating, Athapanouan throwing whorls and nunchucks being pulled from their holster-type-things, and friends dropping into battle stances. "Let's finish this." I said, readying my knife and wire. With a resounding battle cry, we leapt into action. As one. Whipping around from behind each other, we formed one long line, weapons at the ready, facing the men, ten strong and ready to deal out the last we had in us.

The next ten minutes passed in a blur of motion, a cacophony of screams and battle cries, a myriad of flashing sword blades (Virgil and Peyton, two swords each), gleaming knives and throwing whorls (myself, Leilani, and Kit), bright blaster bolts (Andrew, Sarah, and Nathan), and whistling arrows (Tim, with special armor piercing arrows Peyton had helped him make the other day). We took out ten of the sixteen men, basically one for each of us. They had fought well, using their powers against our weapons, and I'm honestly kind of surprised we managed to take out all ten of them in only ten minutes with no powers. But hey, we did!

The last six men turned out to be Leaders. When they realized that they were without the protection of their men, they turned and fled. They were displaying great cowardice in battle, and it made me sad, not going to lie. These men led the armies, made the devious plans, and manufactured the evil schemes, and then, when faced with a fight, they ran. Of course, they fled, only to run right into John's chest. They tried to climb up his shirt, but he brushed them off with one hand. I knew that there were eight SCL "Generals". Earl was one of them; we had him locked away in the palace dungeon. Lord Johansson was the one that I did not see among the six in front of us. In my eyes that displays even more cowardice than running. Not even to come to the battle that you have all of your loyal men fighting in, for you. If you are well and able to come and you do not, that is just… despicable. Ugh. I could see a cold fury in Kit's eyes as well, and knew that she and I shared the same thoughts.

"Let's take them." She said, readying her knife. This time, instead of keeping our line, we charged straight into the knot of men. They tried to fight back, but we had the numbers, and we weren't afraid. We overpowered them quickly, and they fell. Then their bodies, and the bodies of all the other men we had slain, vanished. I didn't know where they went, and I didn't care, as long as they stayed dead.

We stood there for a moment, breathing hard, and cleaning and sheathing our weapons. And then it hit us. After a long, long day of planning, preparing, and fighting, we had finally won! We had defeated the SCLs and liberated Nordiaho!

CHAPTER 14

Freedom For N.!

The celebrations that followed that day were humongous, but let me tell you about my favorite part of it all first.

After we won, we had a small celebration of our own right there in that clearing. We cheered and whooped and hollered for all we were worth. It was during that celebration when Kit atom-bounded away both herself and John. About a minute later, Kit reappeared and led the rest of us over to a cluster of trees at the edge of the clearing. Out of the trees walked John, normal size. For good.

We all started cheering again, and, laughing, we all jumped on him and practically smothered him in a huge group hug. He managed to squirm out of it after a minute, beet red and laughing himself. We introduced him then to everyone who hadn't met him at his normal height. Kitaileeo, Leilani, Andrew, Nathan, Virgil, and Peyton. Peyton went last. Tall as John was, he still had to crane his neck up to look Peyton in the eyes.

"Whew!" John whistled. "Dang Peyton! You're taller than I thought! You'd probably be a stellar basketball player."

Peyton stared at John. "A stellar what?"

John looked up at him. "You know, basketball, the game where you, oh, you know what, never mind," he laughed. "It's good to meet all of you for real. And it's nice having someone my age taller than me for once in my life," he laughed again.

* * * * * *

Later, we were heading back to the palace, cutting through some beautiful forest, when I noticed John lean over and whisper something to Sarah. Then he came back and walked beside me. Sarah led the others farther ahead of us, and, just as we were passing a waterfall, John touched me softly on the arm and motioned for me to stop. I did.

He waited until the others had disappeared from sight and then he took a deep breath. "Katie, I just wanted to say…thank you, so much. These past few weeks have been really hard for me, and for you too, I'm sure, and you…you helped me a lot. So, thank you."

During this, he had taken both of my hands in his own, so, looking deep into his eyes, I gathered up my courage.

"John, can I…tell you something?" I asked timidly.

He grinned at me. "Sure."

I leaned forwards and whispered in his ear. After I was finished, he stared at me in complete shock for a moment and then his face broke out into a huge smile. "No way! You know, I feel the same way.…"

I grinned. "Really?"

He laughed. "Yep." He folded me into a hug, then he bent over a little and, for a few seconds, we kissed.

* * * * * * *

One day later we proudly ascended the steps of the throne room in our supersuits. At the top of the steps stood Queen Cathy, King Charles, Prince Jameson, and the Princesses Liliana and Katiana. The entire town's population and more from the surrounding country had packed into the throne room. We reached the top of the steps amidst a multitude of cheers and all dropped to one knee. King Charles stepped forward and cleared his throat. "Citizens, on this proud day of Mahero 21, year 2022, or, in Earth terms, May 21, year 2022, it is my honor to present to you the team that fulfilled the prophesy: Tim, Fire-Cay; Katie, Water-Cay; Priti, Fauna-Cay; Sarah, Flora-Cay; Kitaileeo, Wind-Cay; John, Earth-Cay; and Peyton, Blood-Cay. The elements united at last! Not to mention their brave helpers, Nathan, Andrew, Leilani, and Virgil. The eleven of them have delivered Nordiaho from the evil clutches of the vile SCLs. May the people of the universe always know that they have a team of true heroes as brave as these fine people to call on in their most desperate hour. I hereby present each of you with the Grindian medal, the highest honor on Nordiaho." With that he stepped forward and presented each of us with a medal. When he had finished, he beckoned us to rise and turn to face the people. The cheers were so loud that we couldn't even hear each other even though we were all standing so close.

Later, after the ceremony, we all gathered in the largest ball room. Sadly, it was time for us "Earthlings" to go.

John's Narration:

I'M ME AGAIN! WAAAA HOOOOO!!!

Katie gathered us around her and nodded at Tim. He cleared his throat. "Before Kitaileeo's grandfather had to leave he gave Katie and me each a package and told us to distribute the contents once the battles were all over. These items will allow us to talk to each other no matter how many galaxies apart we are. Also, in times of desperation, they can be used to teleport to the place of need." He handed each of us a pendant on a cord.

It was beautiful. The outermost piece formed a sort of "U". On the top part of it, on either side, were two large, oval beads that were glowing red. They were connected together at the bottom by a slender tube that was glowing blue. In the center of the "U" was a glowing green orb, with three white rays of light radiating out from it towards the "U". But here's the crazy thing. The green orb was just floating in the center of the "U", and the rays of light weren't touching the orb or the "U"! The cord, which sort of resembled a leather thong, wasn't touching anything either! It was above the green orb, but it was about half an inch away from it. I have no idea how it worked, but it was so cool! I got the feeling that this pendant was going to be a source of way too many questions I wouldn't know how to answer at school, but I didn't really care.

"He also told me to tell you this, John," Tim continued. "On Nordiaho, if someone goes through an extremely tough trial and if they make it through the trial with a good heart and attitude, they receive a power pertaining to that trial as a reward. So, you have earned yourself the power to shrink and grow. Congratulations!"

Everyone cheered and clapped. Then the three of us "Earthlings" stepped forward. We said our goodbyes, put on our new "necklaces," held hands in a circle, and disappeared.

We found ourselves in the pizza parlor sitting at the table. The odd thing was (And I could only figure it was because I had already been back and time had technically passed then) the table was cleared, the lights were off, and no-one was there. I glanced at my watch and was confirmed in my guess. It was eight o'clock at night; the parlor had closed an hour ago. So we snuck out of the parlor and tiptoed into our dorm rooms and almost instantly fell asleep. (You think jet lag is bad, try interspace portal travel lag! When we left Nordiaho, it had been three in the afternoon, which meant there was a time difference of about five hours. Also, just space travel via portal can be quite exhausting.) Over the next few days, we settled back into the routine of college life and were doing okay, but it was really hard keeping everything a secret. Also, sadly, we seemed to have lost our powers upon returning to Earth. Katie surprised me with a neat woven belt, blue, white, and green, made of really… interesting threads. It fit perfectly, and we had quite a laugh when she revealed that she had gotten the threads from my plaid shirt, when I was a giant, and that the belt had been one of the things that I kept seeing her working on. When I asked her what the other things were, she just smiled. Sarah told me later that she and Katie both also had belts, although Katie's matched mine, and Sarah's had been made from threads from my red, white, and blue shirt, since they had used all of the rest of the blue, white, and green threads for the quilt. I wonder where it wound up... I still couldn't believe that we no longer had powers. Sigh.

But then it happened.

Tuesday evening I was at the shooting range with Katie and Sarah. We were having a ton of fun when we heard a scream. A little girl, maybe four years old, was running in front of the line of fire. Three things happened at once: she stopped, a gun fired, and we heard "cease fire!" yelled. But the bullet that had been shot was the bullet from a gun aimed in her direction. She froze, in a panic. I however, though panicked, did *not* freeze. I ran toward her.

All of a sudden I felt a familiar surge of power, and, in the three seconds since I had first moved, I had reached her, grabbed her, run her all the way back to her frantic mother, dropped her off, and raced all the way back to stand next to Katie and Sarah. (BTW, it's a *huge* shooting range, and the girl and I were at opposite ends of it.)

I froze, my heart racing. Katie and Sarah gaped at me. '*Oh my word!*' I thought, staring at my hands and arms in shock. '*My powers are back!*'

EPILOGUE

This Spells T-R-O-U-B-L-E!

Nordiaho:

In a cold dark cellar, Lord Johansson frantically grabbed the very last tube of power-stealing-powder — the one he had managed to snatch during his escape — wrapped it inside the hastily-written emergency-SOS-help-us-whatever-you-want-to-call-it-letter, and ran over to his private portal. He threw the package into the portal and watched it beam away. He let out an evil chuckle. "They thought I was bad on Nordiaho? With that horrible army? Let's see what they think when I pay them a visit on Earth. With a better army, too. And when they learn of my secret weapons? The only thing they will be able to do is fail. They have no idea how many Aces I've got up my sleeves! After all, all *humans* lose their powers in their return to Earth, so taking Earth from them should be like taking candy from a baby!" He laughed maniacally as he imagined his triumph.

After all, they had no powers anymore... right?

Acknowledgments

First and foremost, I thank my family: Mom, for encouraging me every step of the way. Dad, for helping me through the tough times of that horrid curse called writer's block. Anya, my "Little Chica" for reading my book over and over and always wanting me to tell her more of where the book/series was going and for giving me great ideas for the characters and their powers. JoelDavid, for constantly being cheery and optimistic. Dad-Dad (my grandfather), for being my great champion and reading over the book with me through all the changes and helping me to revise it, and for helping me to get it published. Grandmom, for being my wonderful editor and taking the time to scrutinize every detail of my manuscript. You guys are amazing and I love you!

Thank you so much to my English teacher, Mrs. Pryor, who helped me with my writing and encouraged me more than anyone could ever imagine.

Thank you to all my great friends, whether at school, youth group, AHG, or church, who inspired me and helped me along in the writing journey. Y'all stayed by my side throughout the whole adventure, and y'all are awesome. I can't count the number of times you guys were there for me and encouraged me in my writing and enjoyed reading all my different manuscripts I was playing around with on the side. Thanks for being the best friends, and second family, that a girl could ever hope for!

Special thanks to Evelyn Kowalczyk! I've known you all my life, and I'm so glad to have you as a friend! Many, many thanks for designing my cover and applying your amazing artistic skills to the challenge and creating a wonderful work of art! You are a fantastic person, a truly skilled artist, and an awesome friend!

Many, many thanks to Polly Holyoke, author of the fantastic Neptune Project trilogy, for reading the first few chapters of *The Voyage to Nordiaho* and giving me comments on it! Your books are amazing!

And also thank you to Clifton Welsh and Scarlet Blare, two other authors that I love, who helped me with my book and motivated me and urged me to succeed! :) Good luck with your own books!

About The Author

Summer Ryland lives in the country, "deep in the heart of Texas". Her family has a small ranch near where John, the main character of the story, lives. Her favorite things to do are ride her horse, do archery, read, write, whittle, shoot, draw, and hang out with her awesome friends and family. Summer learned to read when she was three years old and has been an enthusiastic reader since. She is home schooled, and attends Grace Preparatory Academy for some of her classes. She began writing Journey to Nordiaho when she was twelve years old and finished the book at about the same time she finished her freshman year of high school. Now she's a sixteen year old junior, and proud to publish her first book. You can write her at:

summerryland03@gmail.com

or

Summer Ryland
301 Main Plaza, Suite #148
New Braunfels, Texas, 78130

Made in the USA
Las Vegas, NV
09 September 2022